THE SLEEPWALKING GAME

A PSYCHEDELIC COSMIC HORROR

ERIK I L HORVAT

Published in Australia by Sad Clown Books and Print

First published in Australia 2025
This edition published 2025
Copyright © Erik I L Horvat 2025
Cover design, typesetting: WorkingType (www.workingtype.com.au)

ISBN: 978-1-923439-73-3

ABOUT THE AUTHOR

This is the debut novel of Australian author Erik I L Horvat, which is inspired by a series of dreams and hallucinations he had in his early twenties. Erik has always been noted for his disturbed mind and peculiar habits, as well as a relentless creative energy that has allowed him to distil his morbid obsessions into vivid stories about nightmarish creatures and outlandish scenarios. Erik has spent his entire life living amongst farmland in rural Victoria, with his experiences growing up there greatly shaping his first work.

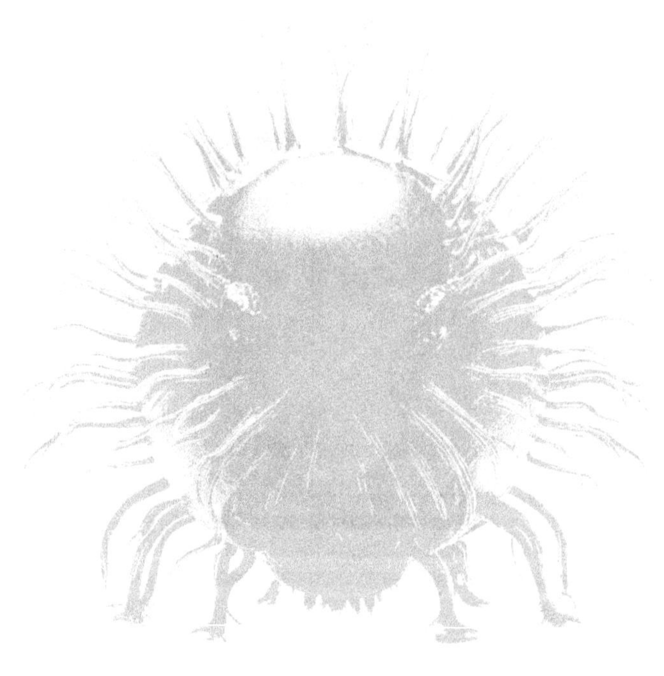

DISCLAIMER

Due to the extreme nature of the contents of this book, reader discretion is advised. It contains vivid depictions of violence, animal violence, sexual assault, blood, gore and overall insanity.

CHAPTER ONE

We both looked forward, stone-faced. There was nothing left to say. It had all already been yelled, screamed, sneered and murmured; not to mention punctuated by a series of long agonising silences and the sensation of the old man's hard-knuckled fists against my face. My only distraction from the excruciating tension was the painful throb of the twin bruises on my cheeks. But that wasn't much of a distraction.

The raging engine seemed to vibrate the whole car as we tore our way across the highway in the middle of nowhere. The landscape was dominated by colossal, towering mountains with snowcapped peaks that extended to the far distance. The old man made a hard right down a long dirt driveway that seemed to be much longer than any driveway ought to be. We had to stop two or three times to open and close the farm gates that blocked our way every couple of hundred metres. Eventually it led to a wide, dusty compound with several large aging wooden sheds and buildings orbiting one central two-storey farmhouse. It had dark-brown weather boards and old-fashioned window shutters painted a faded cerulean blue. An impressive verandah protruded from the front, with the height of the deck being a good four feet off the ground, and a simple flight of stairs that lay in the middle, leading down to the dirt. It looked to me like a long, jagged tongue spilling out of an enormous yawning mouth.

Sitting on the steps was a tall gangly man with scruffy blonde hair and a short bushy beard. He was wearing a filthy denim jacket, matching jeans and a brown broad-brimmed hat with a small, ragged hole in the top of it. The way he reclined on the stairs almost made it look like the house was spitting him out in disgust, pushing him away with the tip of its enormous wooden tongue. When he saw us coming, he sprang to his feet, sucking down the full length of his freshly lit cigarette all in one go as his chest swelled up like a balloon. The delicate grey finger of ash that clung to the butt of his cigarette dangled for a moment, then fell and turned to a puff of dust before it even hit the ground.

'How ya doing?' He called to us, approaching the car with a wide, toothy grin.

'You must be Mr Casey.' My dad called back in a friendly tone; a tone reserved only for business with strangers.

'That I am, and you must be Sam Thomson. I'll tell ya, you called just at the right time. We need new workers here like you wouldn't believe. It's a good thing you bumped into Gorden at the general store, or you might have never known there was a job going here. And this must be the man himself?' He circled around to my side of the car and shot his hand in through the open window like a javelin.

'Hi Mr Casey, I'm Otis,' I said nervously, shaking his bony, callused hand.

'Oh please, just call me Casey. Everyone else does. Welcome to Spicer Farm.'

I opened the car door with a rusty creak and stepped out onto the dry dirt. The early morning sun cast a long, imposing shadow from the farmhouse that stretched all the way to where we were standing.

'I'd like to talk to Mr Spicer myself, if I could,' My dad said, stepping out of the car as well.

'I'm afraid he's indisposed, but Mrs Spicer handles the day-to-day around here, and she said she definitely wants to meet you both before you take off, Mr Thompson.'

The front door of the farmhouse swung open with a laboured groan and a tall woman with long orange hair and large dark sunglasses holding a tall glass in her right hand, stepped out onto the verandah with the graceful, yet commanding stride of a naval captain marching onto the deck of a ship to inspect his sailors.

'Is this the new boy?' she asked, taking a sip from her glass. Peering over the rim with a piercing gaze.

'Yes Ma'am!' Casey replied cheerfully. 'This is Mr Thomson and his boy Otis.' She put down her tall glass on the balustrade and descended the stairs. Her smooth pale skin looked strangely out of place next to the sun-scorched leathery faces of the two men that stood beside me. Unearthly, but undeniably beautiful; the sort of soft, gossamer skin that looked as though it had been spun deep inside some dark cave somewhere and had never seen sunlight before. Skin so thin and delicate you might accidently tear through it if you reached out and touched her with your filthy, calloused hands. I watched the little patterns of fruit and flowers on her sundress dance hypnotically in the morning breeze as she walked – as if in slow motion – down the stairs.

'You know how to work hard, boy?'

My eyes snapped back into focus. She had stopped two steps short of the ground. Towering over me like some kind of pale, agricultural goddess.

'Because if there's one thing we don't need around here, it's another time waster,' she said in a stern, no-nonsense tone. Before I could answer, my dad clapped both his hands on my shoulders – a level of physical contact I was not used to. It felt manufactured and calculated and made me wince and my skin crawl – and said in that fake friendly tone of his, 'Work hard? All he does is work hard. He's not very bright, academically speaking; that's why I kept him out of school. But he knows how to read, he's good with the tools, and follows instructions like a dog. He's the kind of kid who only has to be shown how to something once.'

Mrs Spicer placed both hands sceptically on her wide hips, inadvertently pulling her dress tightly around her small waist and accentuating her stunning hourglass figure. I could feel her gaze cutting through me. Dissecting me. As if she could somehow read my mind with those cold, scrutinising eyes.

Then her face softened, and she stepped down onto the dusty ground.

'Mrs Spicer, love,' she said, extending a slender hand. I hastily rubbed my sweaty palm against my pants before shaking it.

'Hi, I'm Otis, just like Mr Casey said. I just want to thank you for this opportunity to work on your farm.' My words sounded rehearsed and mechanical to me. I wondered if she had noticed, or perhaps Mr Casey, or if this particular sharp stab of embarrassment was just for me to feel . Manifesting itself as a dull, nagging ache in between the small bones in the back of my neck.

'Come with me Otis. Let me show you how we do things around here.' She began to walk with that confident I'm-in-charge stride of hers. The rest of us quickly following suit. She walked just a little bit ahead of everyone else, speaking aloud without looking back, as if she were laying out details of the farm to a secretary. 'You couldn't have come at a better time. We have a very large holding of sheep, and cattle, but we have recently purchased new livestock and we've got all hands on deck preparing for their arrival. The entire property is bordered on all sides by protected forest, so if any livestock gets out then we'll be hard pressed to find them again. We lost three hundred head of cattle in '73 when a thunderstorm blew over a bunch of trees and ripped down part of the border fence. They ran right into the forest. You would not believe the hell we got from the Forest Department for that one: all sorts of fines for destruction of protected wilderness and all that crap. So, we're constantly checking for fallen trees and doing fence maintenance. That's a lot of what you'll be doing. Do you know how to use a chainsaw? It doesn't matter, we'll teach you.' She spoke fast and to the point. Everything about her exuded total organisation and control. 'We have fourteen workers. Fifteen now that you're here. And we have you all lodging in that building there.' She gestured towards a long Bunkhouse that looked as though it had been stretched out like a piece of elastic. With four wooden tables lined up outside.

'Now, here are the rules.' She stopped suddenly, turning to face me. 'If you break any of them you will be sacked without a second chance, you got that?' She said, pointing a long, thin finger at me.

'Yes ma'am,' I said, trying to swallow my nervousness.

'No bringing in outsiders onto the farm without first arranging it with me. And only me. No one is to lay a finger on my daughter Kelly, and no worker here is allowed into the main house under any circumstances.'

I cast a suspicious eye towards the large, looming farmhouse. Its windows were just a little too dark to see anything inside and half of them had their curtains drawn shut. Mrs Spicer snapped her fingers in my face and I was snapped back to attention.

'And that barn over there is completely off limits to everyone who works here.' She pointed to a structure that stood alone in an empty field, strangely isolated from all the other buildings. An old barn with boarded up doors and no windows – or at least none that I could see – covered in raw, rotting weatherboards. The wood turned to a pale, curdled grey by the cruel hand of time. Looking at it gave me an icy feeling down the length of my spine.

'Mr Spicer finds himself incapable of leaving the house these days, so he runs things from his desk and relies on me to oversee things out here. Casey will be responsible for your training and getting you settled in. If you have any other questions you can ask him. Now if you'll excuse me, Mr Spicer is almost done drawing up the plan for the new fences and I have to get them to Vincent before the day gets away from us.' And with that, she turned on her heels and briskly walked back towards the farmhouse without so much as a 'goodbye' or a 'it was nice to meet you'.

'Well, I think we can take it from here Mr Thompson,' Casey said, shooting me a reassuring wink. His seemingly kind and cheery nature made me feel a little bit better about the new situation I found myself in. But mostly I still felt rotten on the inside. As if my intestines were filled with writhing magots. My dad looked at me with his pale blue eyes. Sizing me up. Trying to decide whether or not it was even worth leaving me here, or if I'd just be back on his doorstep within a week. Perhaps with an angry Mrs Spicer twisting my ear and telling him that I fucked everything up.

'Don't do anything to fuck this up,' he hissed through his teeth. I instinctively looked down at my feet, desperately trying to avoid his gaze. Then he leaned in closer, a stale morning beer on his breath, and said, 'If you let any animals out, or do anything else to piss off Mr and Mrs Spicer, you'll be picking your teeth out of the dirt. You understand?'

I nodded my head, still looking at my feet. The bruised, torn-open skin on my cheekbones still burned from where he had punched me just days earlier.

'Yeah ...' I quietly choked out. He stared me down for another moment with lingering, scolding eyes. Without another word, he climbed back into the ute and drove away; a huge plume of dust trailing behind him.

'Come on, I'll show you where you'll be sleeping.' Casey scooped up my duffle bag and we set off towards the bunkhouse. I looked over my shoulder and took in the dusty atmosphere of the farm.

'Do you have much experience with animal husbandry? Someone as young as you, I wouldn't expect too much. What are you? Nineteen? Twenty?' he asked.

'Twenty,' I said, still looking around at the crooked buildings and wide-open fields. 'I once helped my dad slaughter a pig. I don't know if he told you anything about that,' I said quietly.

'No, he didn't mention it. Personally, I don't like to work with pigs ... they've got human eyes. Have you ever noticed that? It wigs me out. And they're really smart too. They *know* when you're about to kill them. You can try to trick them anyway you like, but when you look that pig in the eye, knife in hand, you tell me you don't see a human being pleading for their life.' He wrinkled up his nose at the thought. I slowly ran a finger over the jagged bite mark imbedded in my skin. The brown hoop-shaped scab that ran across my palm and along the back of my hand.

I'm probably lucky that pig didn't bite off some of my fingers as well, I thought.

'I've never really thought about it like that before,' I said.

'That's not to say I'm against animals eating other animals. That's just the way the world works, despite what those hippies will tell you. Circle of life and all that ...' he said as he opened the door to the bunkhouse. 'Now, there's twelve small rooms plus a kitchen and a bunch of tables outside. A couple of the higher-ranking guys around here have their own standalone cabins. If you see what looks like a bunch of tiny little sheds, that's what that is.' We walked down a narrow hallway with six doors lining it on either side. 'Here we go,' he said cheerfully as he swung open one of the doors. Inside was a room smaller than a prison cell. A naked mattress and pillow lay on top of a thin metal bedframe. A small crate with the words 'RAT TRAPS' stencilled across it in black paint served as the bedside table, with a candle in a jar and a box of matches on top of it. The room was so small that the tiny bed took up almost half the floor space, with nowhere to hang my clothes.

'Now I know it's not much ...' he said, tossing my bag onto the bed. 'But you've got your own room. I once worked at a place where they had twenty guys all packed into one big room on bunkbeds. The fucking snoring was unbelievable.'

I cast my eyes up towards the rich tapestry of cobwebs that dominated every corner of the ceiling.

'I'll give you a minute to settle in. If you want a broom to clean out those spiderwebs there's one in the kitchen. And there's a cupboard with sheets and pillows and stuff at the end of the hall.' He then turned and disappeared down the hallway, leaving me alone for the first time in this strange new place.

I sat down on the edge of the bed. A harsh and unexpected wave of dread and anguish suddenly washed over me. Up until now I had been cold, detached, and numb on the inside. I had watched the events of the last few days unfold as if they had been happening to somebody else. But I now found myself confronted with the fact that I had been at centre of it all along. The emotions I should have felt now bleeding into the front of my mind. Tears began to well up in my eyes, but I choked back the urge to cry.

'Crying is for pussies,' I scolded myself, quickly wiping my eyes with the back of my hand. I yanked my bag off the bed and it hit the floor with a dull thud. Then I very gently flopped onto the mattress, hoping it wouldn't just collapse and fall to the floor under my weight. The hollow carcass of a dead spider dangled directly above my face. Its lifeless body suspended by the dusty webs it spun so long ago. I now found myself sharply aware of where I was and what had happened; overcome with the exact kind of lucidity I had instinctively denied myself these last few days. The dam wall had burst, and I was now drowning in all the pent-up emotions I had been holding back. How I wished I could have stomached that 'Circle of life' Casey had talked about.

CHAPTER TWO

My dad was a mechanic. He had a garage on the edge of town that also doubled as a small service station. Five days a week I ran the bowsers and served the customers while he worked on the cars. The small brick building seemed to bleed grease and collect metallic car parts like a house collects dust. Out the back was an ancient weather-beaten Airstream caravan propped up by bricks and odd pieces of wood; its deflated tires fused to the ground. That's where Dad and his emaciated girlfriend Nicole lived. As for me, once the garage closed for the evening, I went to sleep right there on the oily floor, usually sandwiched between two car bodies. And in the morning, I'd just fold up my portable stretcher-bed and slide it back in between two steel work benches.

My mum had died giving birth to me – an event that seemed to have robbed him of any paternal feelings he might have had for me. Or perhaps it would have always been that way, even if my mother had survived. Sometimes, in the dead of night, he would stumble into the garage in a drunken stupor, jam his finger in my chest, and tell me how he never wanted a kid. During the day he was quiet, but I could see it in his steely gaze, his brooding demeaner and his determination to one day drink, or perhaps work, himself to death: whichever one came first.

In the overgrown backyard, enclosed by a shitty chicken wire fence, we had six pigs that someone had given Dad in exchange for a timing chain replacement. They were filthy creatures with dirty crumpled faces and fat bodies caked in mud. The pigpen was always a grotesque writhing mass of squeaking, squealing, and snorting. The town we lived in had less than a thousand people, and we were right on the edge, so I don't think the noises they made really bothered anyone. But they did keep me awake at night sometimes, with an occasional screech that pierced the silence when you least expected it.

*　*　*

It was a Sunday morning, so early it was still dark outside, when the door to the garage screeched open and banged against the wall. My eyelids flickered, but remained closed. Then I felt a heavy booted foot gently nudge me in the ribs.

'Do you feel like bacon for breakfast, boy?' I opened my eyes to see my dad looming over me in his brown, grease-encrusted coveralls. His voice was low and gravelly, with the kind of bass masculine crackle that could only come from a lifetime of chain-smoking cheap cigarettes.

'What time is it?' I asked, my heavy eyelids slowly closing again.

'It's time to get up,' he grunted, pushing the frame of my bed with his foot, and tipping it sideways. I had to throw my hands out onto the cold concrete floor so I wouldn't tumble out.

'I need your help outside,' he said, walking back towards the open door. He turned his head, his eyes catching the moonlight; two white, piercing pinpricks of light gleaming out of his darkened face. 'It's time to harvest the meat.'

I wrenched myself out of bed, a tangled mess of dark brown hair sweeping into my eyes. I sat there for a moment with my eyes closed, feeling the sensation of slowly falling backwards. Back into the warm welcoming embrace of unconsciousness. I forced one burning eye open, and then the other. The ancient clock-radio on the work bench read ten past four. It felt like I was the only person awake in the entire world.

Outside, my dad had setup a small row of powerful floodlights on a metal stand that bathed the entire yard in the glow of an unearthly white light. A steel rod had been jammed into the twisted branches of a tree, and several of what looked like thick steel clothes hangers with pairs of savage hooks on the ends hung there, like some kind of nightmarish empty closet. The outdoor tub we used for bathing was filled to the brim with scolding hot water, the steam spewing out into the cold night air. The pigs squirmed in their pen like a swarm of maggots in a carcass, casting long malformed shadows across the exterior wall of the garage.

'You and I are going to slaughter these pigs,' the old man said, sharpening a long carving knife. 'Bacon, and sausages and porkchops ...' He hummed to himself as the blade whizzed back and forth across the sharpening steel.

'Slaughter them?' I asked, my brain still half asleep. He didn't seem to hear me.

'Okay, when I open that gate, you're gonna grab the first one you see and drag it out.' He rubbed the blade against his thumb to test its sharpness. I looked into the pen. The pigs snorted and squealed and slammed against each other; disturbed by the almost painful brightness of the floodlights that were pointed directly at them. I gave my dad a troubled look.

'How am I supposed to grab it exactly? Is there a particular way? Or ...'

He placed a greasy, gnarled hand on the latch of the gate and looked at me with those white pinhole eyes, shining inside their darkened black sockets. The deep creases of his leathery white face carved into bottomless black chasms by the floodlights.

'Just grab the dirty little fucker by the hind legs and pull 'im out,' he snarled. The gate was cracked open and I squeezed my way in. The watery mud had mixed with the pig shit to make a slippery brown slurry. With each step I took, my foot sunk almost up to the ankle in the shit-coloured ooze. A grotesquely fat pig regarded me with suspicious, beady little eyes. Eyes with pupils that constricted as it launched forward, suddenly scrambling away from me. I threw myself at it, my fingertips lightly grazing its rump before I landed headlong in the ooze. I staggered to my feet and threw myself at another, tackling it around the midsection like a rugby player. We both went sideways into the slosh; a mass of grappling limbs and flailing trotters, coated head-to-toe in the slick wet mud. From somewhere outside the pen I could hear my dad shouting, 'Get 'im boy! Get 'im!' But his voice was almost drowned out by the screaming animals that frantically darted around the tiny pen. I finally gained some footing and managed to drag it out by its hind legs. The gate slamming shut with a click.

The old man grabbed one of its front legs with one hand, and with the other, plunged the knife strait into the pig's throat. A crimson jet of hot, stinking blood coated his arm from wrist to elbow. The pig convulsed so violently its feet slipped from my hands and flailed against the ground in an eerie sideways running motion. Dad leaped on top of the creature, and, straddling its belly, slashed harder and deeper into its thick swine flesh. Blood painted his face and chest in another violent spray. Mayhem ensued inside the pig pen as the other pigs tried to scramble up the fence or bore underneath it in a frantic attempt to escape; knowing one of them would be next.

The pig lay still, with blood bubbling out of its neck and pooling on the ground in a swirling, bright red puddle. Its lifeless glassy eyes staring into the nothingness as its feet continued to twitch and quiver. Dad staggered to his feet, the knife still dangling loosely in his fingers. We stood there for a moment, in silence, soaking in the scene that lay before us. He was glazed with blood, and I was coated head-to-toe in mud and pig shit. A thin trickle of blood began to drip from the slaughtered pig's snout, leaking out of its nostrils and landing in the puddle with a sickening *drip drip* sound. I felt a hot spike of vomit shoot up the back of my throat and into my mouth. I dropped to my knees and threw up a puddle of watery yellow sick.

'Oh, man up, you girl!' he spat with a mixture of disgust and embarrassment.

I tried to wipe my mouth but just ended up rubbing wet dirt across my teeth. At least I hoped it was wet dirt.

Dad grabbed one of the clothes hanger things and ripped into the pig's ankles with it – one hook in each leg. The sound of the pig's flesh being pierced was somehow crunchy, as if the hook was being pushed through a bag full of gravel. I tried to run my fingers through my filthy hair, but it had become fused to my skull.

'When you're done growing a pair, come here and help me lift this,' he grunted, yanking on the hooks to make sure they stayed in. He had peeled off the top layer of his coveralls and had tied the sleeves around his waist. The blood had soaked through to his white undershirt; painting his chest with a wet galaxy of dull red splotches and tiny flecks.

'We've got to get this hog up on the rack.' He pointed his chin towards the steel bar in the tree. We grabbed a hold of the dead pig and tried to heave it off the ground. The muscles in my dad's wiry arms tightened, and the tendons in his neck stood out like hideous cords of brittle sinew, spittle rolling down his chin. The awkward limp shape and the weight of its bulk was immense, but between us we managed to lift it.

The pig's head lolled loosely against my shoulder. Every time I adjusted my grip its jaw bounced up and down, making its teeth clack together. A nauseating feeling swirling in the pit of my guts every time I heard that hideous *chomp chomp* sound next to my ear. I squeezed my shoulder blades together as I felt the slack mouth drool a mixture of blood and spit down the back of my shirt. Could I also feel its lifeless tongue? Draped, damp and warm, down the side of my neck?

'Alright, up! Up! Up!' Dad gasped, the weight of the pig beginning to squeeze the air out of his lungs. He shoved as hard as he could with one arm and hooked the animal's feet onto the metal rod in the tree with the other. I could breathe again, and both my hands went straight to the gooey mess on the back of my neck. He wiped the drool off his chin with the meat of his palm, and – almost as an afterthought – snorted and spat a fat glob of mucus onto the muddy ground.

'Well, that was a shit fight,' he said, carving into the pig's throat again with the knife. Another slosh of blood poured out of its jugular and into a large white bucket that sat beneath it.

'Let's just shoot the next one. I didn't want to wake the neighbours with gunshots this early on a Sunday morning, but if we do it this way then it's gonna take all day.'

The pigs crowded together in the corner of the pen, as far away from the gate as they could get; the fence straining and bulging against their combined weight. I'll never forget the look of utter terror in their twisted pig faces. The way their dark, wet little eyes seemed to beg for mercy. The way they seemed to look straight at me. I turned away, a cold sweat breaking out across my forehead and making the mud on my face run down into my eyes. I scrunched them shut and pushed my palms into my eye sockets. The sound of the pigs screaming and wailing was almost unbearable.

Right at that moment I just wanted to cease to exist. Anything would be better than this, even not existing. And as I floated there in the darkness, with my hands over my eyes, I tried to picture what it would be like.

Then a loud *crack fizzle* brought me back into my body as my dad torched the end of his cigarette. He dragged on it hard, a dull orange halo of light illuminating his face. The bright red blood came up so far on his neck that it actually covered his chin, stopping just short of his thin bottom lip.

'Fucking hell, look at this mess!' Nicole's voice came from behind us. She stood in the doorway of the Airstream, wrapped in a worn-out sky blue dressing gown that was way too big for her. She craned her neck, looking at the gruesome carcass that swung from the metal rod, its mangled throat still drizzling blood into the bucket.

'It was really hard to catch,' I said, half apologetically. Her eyes widened when she saw that I looked like a swamp monster from an old horror movie. Then she turned back to my dad, still holding the knife loosely in his hand, smoking the cigarette with the other.

'Why didn't you just shoot the poor thing? It would have been a lot quicker and a lot more humane.'

'Because I didn't want to wake the neighbours. I already told you,' he hissed with that frustrated, short-tempered tone that was never too far away, especially if Nicole was in the firing line. He took another long drag on his cigarette before holding it out so she could have a puff. She leant forward to suck on the end of his smouldering cancer stick, then suddenly whipped her head back in disgust.

'Ew, no! You got blood on it!' She squealed, scrunching her face up and covering her mouth with her hand. He took it back and had another puff. I could see from the light of the Airstream doorway how the cigarette's white paper had been stained all over with bright red fingerprints. She put her arms around him and grabbed his arse with both hands, being careful not to touch his blood splattered chest and arms with her nice clean dressing gown.

'Ew, ew, ew,' she winced, retrieving a pack of smokes from one of his back pockets and a box of matches from the other. She loaded a fresh, clean cigarette into her mouth and lit it.

'You really should be shooting them,' she said, blowing out a jet of thick grey smoke.

'Do you want to do this? Maybe I can go inside and go back to sleep, and you can kill the rest of these fucking animals?' he snapped. There was a silence, followed by 'Oh, you're real fucking quiet now, aren't you?' He held out his arms like the crucified Jesus, tilting his head to the side in a ghoulish go-fuck-yourself expression. Her eyes slowly turned towards the dangling hog; blood still dripping from its face and neck.

'No ...' she said in a small voice.

'I'm ... I'm going to go wash my face in the sink,' I said quietly, trying not to look anyone in the eye as I squeezed past Nicole.

A huge pot of frothing water was boiling on the stove; the flames turned all the way up and licking the sides of the pot. I carefully removed the dirty plates and coffee mugs from the tiny stainless steel sink, being careful to make as little noise as possible. As I rubbed the spaces between my fingers under the tap, I looked up into the small mirror that hung above the sink and was confronted with the image of my own blank, emotionless eyes. My flesh felt cold and tight against my skull. The mud had already begun to dry and harden on my face, making it feel as though my skin were shrinking.

'Are you okay?' Nicole asked, gently closing the door behind her. Her long, thin fingers lingering on the doorknob for just a little too long before sliding off.

'Yeah,' I said, not looking up.

'I can't stand to see animals suffering like that ...' she said, looking sideways out of one of the tiny Airstream windows. I scrubbed my fingers a little harder and a little faster. I could still hear the muffled sound of the pigs wailing and moaning outside, but to me it was deafening.

'But I'm sure your dad would want you to know that that's just a part of life ... being able to do things like that,' she went on, half-looking outside, half-looking at her own faint reflection in the darkened glass. Good old Nicole, my ever-reliable translator for my dad's obscure life lessons.

'Really, I'm fine!' I shot back at her, before viciously scrubbing my face with both hands. Poor Nicole, she tried so hard to be nice to me. Sometimes a little too nice. My dad was a cold, hard, complex man who had never shown me so much as a shred of love or affection, and I had resigned myself to the fact that I would never fully understand him. In the three years they had been together, at least Nicole tried to be my friend, in a way. But we both knew that our relationship had become more complex than that. At least she never gave me any of that 'You know I'll never replace your *real mother*' crap. And, for that, I was abundantly thankful. Besides, a *real* mother would never do the things Nicole has done.

'I'm sorry ... I just didn't know we were doing this today. I just ... I don't know ... I just wasn't ready for it, that's all,' I said, looking back into the tiny mirror. My face was now clean, except for two rings of dirt around my eyes, and a few bits of grit in the crevasses of my nose and under my jaw.

'That's okay,' she said, dropping her dressing gown to reveal the cropped grey singlet and lacy white underwear she had on underneath. She was so skinny that you could actually *see* the slight up and down undulation of her ribs through the tight fabric of her singlet. Her underwear hugged the slight curves of her hips and the sharp jagged ridges of her pelvis, before slanting down again and pulling tight over the space between her legs.

I always tried not to let my eyes drift below her waist when she walked around like this, which was almost every day as soon as she got home from her job as a waitress. Shamelessly showcasing the many skimpy items of clothing in her beloved lingerie collection, which consisted almost entirely of sheer, racy underwear, no bras. And indulging in her evening marijuana habit.

She had almost no breasts to speak of. Just a pair of hard pointy nipples that poked through her top. It's the sort of thing you stop noticing after a while. She would sometimes triumphantly declare that she had never worn a bra before in her entire life. A true product of her time: a bra-burning hippy of the 1960s. Her free love ideals and rampant LSD use might have cooled off but even now, in 1976, she continued to go braless. But honestly, I didn't see why she would ever need one in the first place. She had the body of a twelve-year-old boy, complete with narrow hips, narrow shoulders, and a crop of dark hair that was buzzed almost down to her scalp.

She had shaved all her hair off one day with a pair of electric clippers after an argument with my dad, and had kept it impossibly short ever since. Inspired, she had told me, by the time the Mexican artist Frida Kahlo cut all her hair off after she divorced her husband Diego Rivera, to show that she wasn't defined by a man. She had thick black hair before that that spilled down her shoulders with impressive volume. But for almost a year now she had been sporting a bristly black buzz cut, that she wouldn't let get any longer than a few centimetres before she shaved it again.

She seemed to be one of those part-time feminists, with one foot in and one foot out. Most of the time she'd be quiet on the subject but whenever she would have a fight with my dad it would be quickly accompanied by a monologue about how she, 'Doesn't need a man' and that 'Men are ruining the planet'. And perhaps some kind of gesture of rebellion, like the aforementioned shaving of her head, or maybe the all-too-common declaration of, 'I'm never letting you fuck me again!'

I always secretly rolled my eyes whenever I over-heard her shouting this. Because I knew, without a shadow of a doubt, that when I came outside to brush my teeth later that night at the little garden tap behind the garage, I would hear the distinctive sound of squeaking furniture coming from the Airstream. Proving time and time again that her fangs had no venom in them.

Her only redeeming feminine quality was her face. Although she had hollow, sunken eyes and tight, jagged cheekbones, she had full pouty lips that gave her a vibrant, sexy quality, despite everything else. And long, curved eyelashes that any woman alive would kill to have.

I turned my head and became briefly focused on the cigarette that clung loosely to her ample bottom lip. It dangled there as if it were laying in the folds of a plush velvet pillow.

'Come here, let me get this shit out of your hair,' she said, gently pushing my head down into the sink and combing through my matted locks with her petite, willowy hands. I let myself relax as her long nails scraped pleasantly across my scalp, feeling the cruelty of the morning briefly melt away underneath the warm water.

'If you girls are done washing each other's hair, we've got work to do outside,' dad said, lurching into the trailer. 'Not that *you* have any hair,' he grumbled under his breath. I batted Nicole's hands away and quickly squeezed the water out of my hair. He had a cold look in his eyes, with dark red blood smeared down his chin just underneath his mouth.

'You're in my way, boy,' he said in a low voice. I shuffled to the side, drying my head with the small tea towel that hung beside the cupboards. He bent over the sink and scrubbed his bristly chin with his dirty fingernails.

'The blood's almost drained. Next we'll scald the hair off and gut it.' He snatched the tea towel off me and went to dry his face with it. My heart froze when he paused, looking down at the filthy mud-streaked rag.

'I want you to pay attention now. I don't teach you much, but this is a skill worth learning,' he said, tossing the tea towel aside and drying his face with the bottom of his blood-spotted undershirt instead.

We stepped back out into the cold night air. The grizzly scene was right where we left it. The slaughtered pig hanging lifelessly from the meat hooks. Its terrified fellow pigs huddled in the corner of their squalid mud pit. The large puddle of putrefying blood left behind already beginning to soak into the dirt.

'Alright, we need to dip the pig,' dad said as he tipped the pot of boiling water into the bathtub; some of it spilling over the edges as a huge plume of hot white vapour billowed into the air and disappeared into the darkness that hung above us.

'Dip the pig?'

'Here,' he grunted. He put down the pot and got ready to lift the pig again. I wrapped my arms around the carcass and locked my fingers on the other side, bracing myself for its staggering weight as Dad lifted it off the steel rod.

'Careful! Careful! Careful!' He barked as we manoeuvred it into the scolding hot water. Its rear end rested on the lip of the tub for a moment, causing it to start to tip.

'Fuck!' Dad let go of his end of the pig and threw himself onto the other side of the bathtub to stop it from tipping over. My body strained against the full weight of the animal as its limbs and head swung limply around me. My eyes bulged and spit dribbled down my chin as I shoved with all my strength. It twisted, then sloshed into the water, making a sharp hissing sound.

'Good ... that's real good ...' he panted.

'Why are we putting it in the bathtub?' I asked, straight away feeling stupid for asking.

'Because we need to scold the skin so we can scrape all the hair off,' he replied. For a second, he actually seemed pleased that I was asking questions. He didn't smile but something about his face made me think he would like to.

'Alright, onto the table,' he said, grabbing the hooks with both hands. The stainless steel outdoor workbench that rested against the back wall of the garage had been cleared of all tools and clutter. We hoisted the animal onto it. The carcass slammed onto the cold metal surface with a dull, wet thud. Dad went straight to work, scraping off the hair with a long, curved knife as huge plumes of steam and vapor rolled off its sickly pinkish-grey skin. It looked large and eerie in the powerful floodlights, as if it were the pig's ghost leaving its mangled corpse. Dad shaved off the damp hair like a barber trying to break the record for the world's fastest shave, scraping it all off with such speed and intensity that I half expected him to cut one of his fingers off in the process.

I dropped down onto one knee, trying to catch my breath, barely able to hear my dad's stilted words over the sound of the scraping.

'You want to keep the skin, because that's where all the flavour is,' he said.

I looked up and found myself face to face with the butchered swine. Its lifeless glassy eyes stared straight through me and made my blood run cold. The fleshy skin looked pale and washed-out in the floodlights. Dark, congealed blood oozed from its nose and mouth in thick clotted clumps.

'Come on, we have to turn it over!' dad snapped at me, already shoving it as hard as he could. We rolled it over onto its other side and he continued to frantically shave its skin as steam rolled off its body.

'Are you going to do the head as well?' I asked, not breaking eye contact with those two wet, black, pupils.

'No, we'll cut that off,' he said, not looking up. The hair piled up on one side of the table like a furry tumbleweed. I watched it grow in size before it unceremoniously blew off the edge of the bench and disappeared into the long black shadow cast by my father. Then he planted the knife in the pig's neck before standing up straight and giving his back a loud, stiff crack. I tensely waited to see what we were going to do next.

'Now, this is the tricky part,' he said, pointing a leathery, bloodstained index finger at me. 'You watch closely now. This is where you'll learn those skills I talked about.' He ran his hand along the belly of the pig towards the hind legs. 'First, you want to cut around the arsehole and genitals, like this. Not too deep though, you don't want to cut open the guts when you do it. Just enough to detach them from the outside of the body.'

I watched as the blade glided around the two orifices with a sickening, pealing sound.

'Now hand me one of those zip-ties.' He held out a hand. I searched the table and found a plastic bag full of zip-ties hanging from a nail on the back of the bench. He took one and tied off the arse end of the intestines.

'So shit doesn't come out,' he explained. 'Then you want to pinch the skin right here and cut all the way back to the arsehole. Be *very* careful not to cut open the guts, because if you do then you'll ruin the whole thing.' He pinched the skin between his thumb and forefinger and slid the knife in just under the base of the ribcage. Then he began jerking the blade downwards, like a man trying to open a suitcase with a busted zip. A dark red gash opened up along the smooth abdomen, in between two rows of hard pink nipples that made me think of Nicole for some reason. And with all the grace of a wartime surgeon, he plunged his hands in and pried open the stomach cavity. The skin parted like two fleshy curtains to reveal the glistening mass of wet gore within. From here it looked like it was still alive. Still pulsating. Still pushing fluids and squeezing bile through its gelatinous organs. You could see the heat rising out of it, and I gagged as the stench filled my nostrils.

'You want to scoop out the guts like this.' He grabbed my

wrist and forced my hand into the gory nightmare. The organs were slick and rubbery and warm. Everything seemed to just slide out of the way with a passive squelch as he pushed my hand deeper and deeper inside. He grabbed my other hand and pushed it into the viscera as well, almost up to the elbow. I fought back the vomit rising in my throat; the smell beginning to make my eyes water.

'Now slowly pull it all out,' he said, his eyes sinking so far back into his skull that not even the powerful floodlights could reach them. All he had now was a pair of shadowy black sockets that looked at me with anticipation and macabre encouragement. The light reflected off his teeth though, shining vicious and white; encased in a pair of thin, papery lips. I scrunched up my nose and scooped out the heavy, twitching intestines. My forearms and hands painted up to the elbows with slimy bodily fluids; some of it blood, some of it something else. I dumped the pile of gore onto the table next to the hog with a splat.

'No, no! In here!' he spat, raking the bleeding mass of entrails off the side of the table into a white plastic bucket. 'Now we have to cut open the rib cage. To do that you need to hack through the layer of cartilage that holds it all together.' He slowly slashed his way through it with a sawing motion. Each thrust of the knife making a nauseating bone-breaking sound that made my stomach turn. But what I saw next truly mortified me.

When the last piece of cartilage was sawn in half, and the last strand of sinew had been severed, he wasted no time at all wrenching open the pig's chest with a revolting crunch. If the sawing motion were some kind of sex, then this was undoubtably the climax. Two lungs, a heart, and an enormous liver glistened in the white glow of the floodlights.

'You always want to save the liver,' he explained, delicately lifting it out of the pig's body with a kind of gentleness I had never seen before. He held it like a father holds a newborn baby.

The way he might have held me once. I was caught off-guard by this strange thought and quickly shook it out of my head and focused on the fact that my dad was holding a slimy pig liver in his blood-streaked hands.

'See this? That's the gall bladder.' He pointed to a little sickly green sack that clung to the side of the liver. 'If that thing breaks then it'll taint the whole liver. You have to carefully cut it off, like this.' He took one of the smaller knives and gently scraped it off; taking care not to pierce the thin translucent membrane that held in the rancid, green fluid.

'A lot of these can be eaten,' he said, carving out and scooping up all sorts of rubbery organs and bloody offal. Placing them carefully into a separate bucket. I looked back down at the head, at the way its pale, bloodless skin had been stretched tight by death. How its jaw rested askew, upside down on top of its upper teeth. *Smash!* A meat cleaver slammed down through the pig's neck. Tendons snapped, bones crunched, flesh was sliced in half. The head rolled off the table and fell to the ground with a dull thud. It landed face up, its mouth hanging open in a silent, ghastly scream that only I could hear. The smattering of dark clotted blood around its mouth and nose looked wet and glossy in the bright light. And its eyes… those dead, black eyes staring up at me, accusing me, blaming me.

The old man torched the end of another cigarette.

'Fetch me that hose,' he said, letting the smoke waft slowly out of his nostrils. We hung the headless slab of meat back up on the rod and he hosed it down, washing out the last of the blood and entrails from its hollow stomach cavity.

'I'm gonna get the gun. We'll shoot the next one right between the eyes,' he said, pressing his index finger against his forehead and leaving behind a small red fingerprint between his eyebrows. He took one last big drag on his cigarette before flicking it into the overflowing bucket of blood. It extinguished with a fizzle.

As soon as I heard the garage door close behind him I started to hyperventilate. It was like there wasn't enough *air* in the air. I blindly reached out, trying to grab something for support. My hand landed on the dead pig, but it swung out of the way as I tried to lean on it. I fell to my knees, knocking over the bucket of blood and spilling it all over myself. I went down onto all fours and vomited into the pool of gore that washed around my knees. The yellow and red swirling together and mixing into a revolting orange-brown colour. My hands began to sink into the wet dirt, making me slowly slide down onto my elbows. My ears were ringing. All I could hear was the inhuman screaming that filled my head.

I jerked myself off the ground and staggered towards the pigpen. The poor creatures had seen everything and they knew that one of them was next. They looked at me with human eyes; pleading eyes. The bottom of the gate ploughed through the slosh as I forced it open.

'Get out of here,' I whispered. 'Go on, quickly, run.'

But they just pressed themselves harder into the corner, trying to be as far away from me as possible. There was something about their faces. Something that made me snap. I ran towards them in a crazed frenzy.

'Just fuck off, get out of here! Do you want to die?!' I whisper-screamed, trying to push one of the pigs in the direction of the gate. Panic gripped me and I kicked the swine in the ribs as hard as I could. It howled with pain and bolted right out of the pen. I balled up my fist and punched another one right in its ugly rumpled snout. The hog squealed and bit my hand, its hard, wet teeth slicing through my flesh like a butcher's knife. I whacked it in the nose even harder with my other hand; a splash of blood spilling out of its nostrils. It slammed me to the ground with its heaving bulk and made for the gate.

Then mayhem ensued. All the pigs suddenly ran out of the pen at once and disappeared into the night, stomping on my arms and legs with their trotters as they ran over me. Two wet crimson slices glistened in the torn meat of my hand. I got to my feet and trudged out of the mud, leaning on the gate, trying to catch my breath. My head was spinning. I could feel the adrenaline pulsing through my thin, shaking body. It felt like electricity in my nerves, and steel in my muscles. But the adrenaline rush quickly disappeared and, for the first time since I woke up that morning, the night was still, and eerily quiet.

'What the fuck is this?!'

My dad's voice tore through the silence like a thunderclap. He frantically scanned the scene with a look of utter disbelief in his eyes; disbelief mixed with white-hot rage. He marched towards me, rifle in hand. 'What the fucking shit?!' he screamed, throwing the gun to the ground, his eyes burning with a kind of crazed fury I had never seen before. Before I could say anything, he punched me right in the stomach. I felt more vomit shoot up my throat and spill out of my mouth. He grabbed a fist full of my hair and struck me right in the side of the face. I hit the ground like a sack of shit. He knelt down on top of me, and I felt his fist ruthlessly smash into one side of my head, then the other; the skin on my cheekbones tearing open with the third and fourth blow.

'What are you doing?! Sam, stop it!' Nicole screamed grabbing a hold of his arm. He threw her off and hurled her into the mud as if she weighed nothing at all.

'This little piece of shit can make his own fucking way! You hear that you little cunt?! You can get the fuck out of my house!' He yelled, standing over my limp body, pointing down at me with a wrathful finger, like the God of the Old Testament. I choked; a mixture of blood and watery vomit running down either side of my split and bleeding face.

CHAPTER THREE

I held the heavy star picket in place; its steel tip resting lightly in the dirt as Casey got the fence post banger over it. It was a sort of iron tube, with one end capped-off and a pair of handles on either side. It worked kind of like an inside-out sledgehammer, slamming the post into the dirt. Although Casey towered over me by at least a foot, he still had to hold it high above his head so it would go on properly. On his signal I let go and he drove the post down into the ground, smashing it again and again until it was deep enough to stand up on its own.

'So, what's the deal with Mr Spicer?' I asked, picking up the next star picket. I tried to sound as casual as I could, but on the inside I was burning with curiosity.

'What do you mean?' He panted, hoisting up the fence post banger again with all his might; his sinewy biceps bulging under the weight.

'How come he never comes outside? The way Mrs Spicer talked about it made it sound ... I don't know ... kind of weird. Like, is he a shut-in or something?' I asked, letting go before he smashed the next post into the ground. 'I'm just curious,' I said, looking sideways at the Farmhouse, which cast a long foreboding shadow towards us in the late afternoon light.

'Look, if you want to work here, you've got to keep your head down. Curiosity is only going to get you into trouble. Especially if you get curious about the wrong things. You might have noticed that the Spicer Family likes to have a certain amount of privacy,' he said, wiping a line of sweat from his forehead. Then he leaned in a little closer, scanning around us with a sideways glance to see if anyone was watching. We were completely alone for at least two hundred metres in every direction. The perfect time to tell a secret.

'I'll tell you,' he said quietly. 'But don't go around asking people about this. It's a sort of unspoken agreement we have around here. Everyone knows, but our employers don't like us talking about it.' He had my attention. If there was something being kept from me then I had to know what it was.

'Mr Spicer, or Old Spice as we used to call him, had a massive stroke about a year ago. Before then he was out here running the whole show, day in, day out. And that pretty wife of his was definitely not the force of nature you met this morning. She wasn't even allowed to speak to any of us, let alone order us around like she does now.' He looked at the Farmhouse thoughtfully for a moment before banging in the next post.

'Back then she always had bruises on her wrists, sometimes on her face. It was the kind of thing you had to pretend not to notice if you wanted to keep your job. Or at least pretend you were okay with it. He was a big man, Old Spice: big beard, wide shoulders. And he liked to keep his woman in her place. He'd sometimes tell the men that if you let a mouthy bitch like her say and do whatever she wants, then she'll end up walking all over you.' He paused for a moment, and I wondered who he pitied more, the Mrs Spicer of the past or the Mr Spicer of the present. 'Apparently, he can't even talk now, his mouth just hangs open like a dog's mouth. He can't stand up, or walk, or hardly move his arms. He depends on that woman for everything now. He's completely at her mercy, and she knows it. She wears the pants around here now, kid. And I say good fucking on her.' He looked over at the Farmhouse again, deep creases forming across his forehead, brooding a little over the story he had just told.

I thought about my own dad losing his temper. The way his sunken eyes seemed to burn with an inconceivable rage. The way his teeth seemed to twist in their gums as he grinded his jaws. I wondered how the tables might have turned if he was suddenly paralysed and left completely at my mercy. The tattered pulp of my cheekbones began to throb slightly. The parts that had split open had been discreetly sewn back together with sewing thread, which Nicole had boiled in a pot of water first to sterilise it, and I could feel a dull sting every time the wind blew against my face. I ran a finger along one of the wounds.

'Your dad hit you, huh?' Casey asked bluntly.

'Huh?' I coughed out, the question had caught me off-guard.

'What? If you walk around here with your face torn open like that, I'm going to guess that's why. Am I wrong?' he said. I scrunched up my nose and looked over at the Farmhouse, then into the field, anywhere to avoid eye contact.

'Yeah … sure … he hit me.' I rubbed my nose with the back of my hand, trying to think of something else to say. 'That's why I'm here … he wanted to get rid of me. He's always hated my guts since the day I was born,' I said, startled by my own honesty.

We walked silently up to the next post. The sound of the fence post banger seemed even louder than before.

'I don't think your old man really hates your guts,' Casey said, looking at me with warm, thoughtful eyes. The sideways sunlight illuminated his golden hair and beard in a way that was both comforting and unearthly.

'What do you mean?' I said, unable to bring myself to make eye contact with him for more than a couple of seconds.

'Look at your face. Smacked around the cheeks. He could have caved in your nose or broken your jaw, that's how you really hit someone if you hate their guts.'

I paused for a moment and thought about it. It didn't make much sense to me, but something about the way he said it somehow made me feel a little better.

'Besides, he cared enough to get you this job, didn't he? He could have just turned you out on the road, but instead he made sure you had somewhere to go.'

I curled my toes inside my shoes. This conversation was getting far too intimate far too quickly. Besides, if Casey actually got to know my dad then he would know that this was no act of compassion, subconscious or otherwise. I had already figured out that he wanted to send me here so I would be surrounded by the death and suffering of animals. Because to him I'm just a little pussy that can't stomach it and maybe this place would toughen me up.

'What exactly happened to Mr Spicer when he had his stroke?' I asked, trying to change the subject. 'Did you see it? Was it out here somewhere?' I said, pointing my chin towards the vast expanse of empty fields that surrounded us. Casey looked into the middle distance, trying to remember the details.

'No ... no, he was in his kitchen apparently. Fine one minute, then the next he was face down in his bowl of cornflakes. She said one of his eyes had turned completely black, as if it were all pupil, but the other eye stayed the same,' he said, making a round 'okay' shape with his thumb and forefinger and holding it up to his eye to emphasise how bizarre this part of the story was.

'She?' I asked.

'Mrs Spicer of course. They were sitting there at the breakfast table, and he just collapsed. Nobody's seen him since. He hasn't left that house in over a year. You won't catch him looking out of a window or sitting on the verandah either. Between you and me, Mrs Spicer once told me – shortly after it happened – that he's such a proud man that he can't stand to let anyone see him like that. A shell of what he used to be. So, he has effectively removed himself from society all together. So, everyone would remember him how he was, instead of what he has become. I guess he's holding onto that one last shred of dignity.' He looked thoughtfully at the Farmhouse again, and I knew he was thinking the same thing I was.

I bet Mrs Spicer snapped and murdered him in his sleep. Maybe he did have a stroke, maybe he didn't. But either way his rotting corpse is probably festering away underneath the floorboards as we speak. This thought sent a shiver down my spine. But I didn't dare tell Casey about my suspicions. *Maybe I'm reading too much into it. The story wasn't impossible after all,* I thought to myself as we banged in the last star picket. The sun dipped low over the horizon. The unfinished fence casting a set of long needle-like shadows across the field. We walked back towards the compound, taking turns carrying the heavy iron fence post banger.

'Hi Casey!' called a girl from the Farmhouse verandah. A skinny teenager wearing an ankle-length skirt and long pigtail braids that snaked down either side of her narrow shoulders and ended at her stomach. She looked more like a porcelain doll rather than a human being with smooth, pale skin, with not so much as a scratch or blemish on it. She quickly descended the stairs and met us on the dusty ground.

'Hi Kelly!' Casey said cheerfully.

'Have you met Otis yet? He's our new man on the land,' he said, gesturing towards me with both hands like a showman introducing an acrobat. I held out my hand to shake hers, but she didn't move a muscle.

'Hi, I'm Otis,' I said awkwardly, dropping my hand back down to my side.

'It's a pleasure to meet you,' she said flatly, eyeing-off my hand as if I were holding a weapon.

'Otis, this is Kelly Spicer, daughter to the equally lovely Mrs Spicer, whom you met this morning,' Casey cut in. She looked down at her feet and smiled, grinding the dust beneath her heel.

There was a sort of aloof sadness about her. Maybe it was the dark rings under her eyes, or perhaps it was just the fact that she didn't want to shake my hand. But there was something about her, something that gave me the inescapable feeling that there was something terribly wrong with this place and she knew it.

'We better go or we're gonna miss dinner. Once that food's gone, it's gone!' Casey said, spinning around towards the Bunkhouse with an exaggerated twirl. Kelly giggled, holding onto one of her pigtails with both hands and biting her lip.

'Yeah, me too ...' she said, grinning as he shambled away with his long, goofy body.

'Enjoy!' he said, waving his hand in the air without looking back.

'It was real nice meeting you,' she said, her eyes still lingering on Casey as he walked away.

'Yeah, I'll ... I'll ... see you around,' I said, stumbling over my words a little. As she began to turn to go back up the stairs, her smile dropped, and a doleful numb-on-the-inside expression washed over her face.

Something is definitely not quite right, I thought. But that was quickly followed by another string of thoughts. *Oh, come off it, that could be anything: social isolation, sad about her crippled dad, pining after Casey, the list is endless*. And with that, I turned on my heels and chased after Casey at a full sprint.

'Hey everyone! This is Otis!' Casey announced as we stepped through the door. A crowded room full of unwashed, burly men regarded us with a mixture of disinterest and bemusement. Each one was wearing a pair of dirt-encrusted jeans and a matching denim jacket, accompanied by the powerful smell of masculine sweat and just a hint of animal shit. As we pushed our way through the tight space, I noticed that everyone was lining up to get a bowlful of whatever it was that was bubbling away in the enormous pot on top of the stove. Casey handed me a bowl and we both stood in line, waiting our turn.

'So, you're Otis?' A deep voice came from behind me; the immense bass vibrating the tiny bones inside my ears. I turned to see a massive man standing behind me. He stood as tall as Casey, but he had huge bulging muscles and a gut to match. The deep, sunken scar that ran from the top of his right eye all the way round to the back of his shaved head told me that he was not someone to be fucked with.

'I'm Vincent. I'm the leading hand here.' He held out a plate-sized hand that engulfed mine completely as I shook it.

'So, you're the boss then?' I said, marvelling at the sheer size of his hand. He let out a deep, booming laugh.

'Yeah, that's right, I'm the boss. I've got Casey here mentoring you, but at the end of the day, I call the shots.' He scooped himself a ladle of soup, then another. 'If you work hard and keep your nose out of where it doesn't belong, then you'll fit in just fine here,' he said with a friendly, yet authoritative smile, looking me up and down before walking out of the kitchen. We filled our bowls and sat down at one of the wooden benches outside.

'So ... What's the deal with Kelly then?' I asked in between mouthfuls of soup.

'What do you mean?' Casey said, discreetly scanning the table to see if anyone was listening. Everyone else was engrossed in one conversation or another, paying no attention to us.

'I think she has a little crush on you ...' I said, smiling coyly into my bowl of soup. His cheeks took on a slightly reddish hue as he anxiously looked around the table again.

'I don't know what you're talking about,' he said, looking down at his soup. For the first time since I had arrived, he wasn't bursting out of his own skin with rambunctious energy.

'So ... you're not in charge here? For some reason I thought you were like ... the head guy,' I said, quickly trying to change the subject.

'No, I'm just good at training new people. I've been here longer than Vincent though, so people usually come to me if there's a problem that management doesn't need to know about,' he said, looking a bit more relaxed.

I could see in the embarrassed look in his eyes that he was well aware that Kelly liked him. But he had told me earlier today that he had just turned thirty, and Kelly looked like she barely made fifteen. Besides, everyone knows what happens when you fool around with the boss's daughter. Best case scenario, you get your arse sacked. Worst case scenario, you get your testicles blown off by the old man's shotgun. But I guess in this instance it might be *Mrs* Spicer pulling the trigger.

Tale as old as time, I thought to myself as I watched the last slither of sun sink below the distant mountain tops, leaving us with only the fast-fading blue twilight of the late evening.

CHAPTER FOUR

woke up in the middle of the night, my bladder bursting. I got to my feet and staggered into the dark hallway, holding out my hand in front of me like a vampire in an old movie. I couldn't see anything in the darkness and the unfamiliar hallway seemed to go on and on without end. Every time I thought I was nearly at the door, more empty space seemed to materialise before me. A small wave of relief washed over me when my fingertips finally met the cold, hard surface of the back door. I twisted the stubborn doorknob and stumbled outside, wrenched my penis out of my underwear, and released a powerful stream of urine onto the dry, dusty ground.

I quietly moaned, overcome with relief as I squinted through my sleepy eyelids at the silent, eerie landscape. The moonlight gave everything a strange silver lining. Sheep looked like little grey clouds in a shadowy field. Buildings had been reduced to nothing more than ominous black silhouettes that climbed upwards into an even blacker sky. And all the fence posts had become needle-like teeth that jutted out of the ground all around me.

I stumbled a little, stepping forward and planting my bare foot straight into my own puddle of urine. I groaned, stepping back only to find more wet ground behind me. I twisted my bottom lip downwards in frustration, closing my tired eyes for a moment before forcing them open again. I turned around and saw that I had actually walked at least a hundred metres away from the Bunkhouse, when I thought I had been standing just behind the back door.

What a pain in the arse, I thought as I started walking back. The ground had turned into a murky slosh, and each step I took I sank ankle deep into the cold wet mud. I could feel it in between my naked toes, and what felt like small creatures and slimy things slithering around my feet. *Must have been a lot of piss,* I was trying to stay sleepy enough to go back to bed, while also trying to stay awake enough so I wouldn't slip over and fall face first into the mud.

'I need your help, boy ...' A familiar voice came from behind me. I slowly turned my head, my eyes as wide as dinner plates, straining to see through the darkness. My dad stood there, dressed in his greasy brown coveralls. His eyes were just two sunken black sockets; his pupils, two thin pinpricks of moonlight.

'To do what?' I asked in a hushed whisper, suddenly wide awake. He turned and began to walk in the opposite direction.

'Bacon ... and sausages... and pork chops.' He hummed to himself in a faint sing-songy voice. His words becoming distant as he slowly disappeared into the darkness. The familiar surroundings of the farm had melted away, and all that remained was this strange muddy ground, stretching into an endless black nothingness in every direction.

I hastily chased after him, trying to keep my balance as my feet skidded across the slosh. The moonlight reflected off the watery surface of the mud, making parts of it look silver and glossy. I caught up to him. He was standing still, gazing into the darkness that lay before us. He wrinkled his brow, carving deep creases into the leathery skin on his forehead. But at the same time his bony face seemed completely devoid of expression. I stood at his side and strained my eyes to try and make out what he was looking at. A slither of something white was moving towards us. A vertical shape that wavered slightly like a mirage. I looked even harder. It was a person, a person walking out of the nothingness. My eyes widened as I realised who it was.

Nicole strode towards us through the mud, completely naked, confidently swaying her hips from side to side as she walked. I marvelled at her naked body: thin, slender limbs, a pronounced ribcage, a stomach so flat it was almost concaved and hipbones that jutted out so sharply you might accidentally cut yourself if you reached out and touched them.

Her sharp, pointy face wore a glazed expression, as if she were in a trance. She walked right past us as if we weren't even there. I turned around and saw that a stainless steel table had materialised behind us. Its shiny chrome surface standing out in stark contrast against the formless empty nightscape. She sprawled herself out on top of it, the mud falling away from her feet as she climbed up onto the table, leaving them smooth and perfectly clean.

My dad – also seemingly in a trance – walked over to her and pinched the skin at the base of her ribcage. He slowly turned his pale, skull-like head towards me, looking at me with his deep, pinprick eyes. His face gaunt and quietly angry. Those two glowing white dots burning deep within their shaded black sockets, furious with activity, like a raging storm concealed by the shadows of his face.

I was suddenly aware of the weight of a long, curved knife in my hand and looked down to see the razor-sharp steel glinting in the moonlight.

Why am I here? Why am I here with a knife in my hand and Nicole strung out naked on the butcher's block? I thought suddenly, cold beads of perspiration beginning to gather across my forehead.

She stretched herself out like a cat stretching in the afternoon sun. She looked as though she were on some kind of wonderful drug. Her full, pouty lips parted slightly, her eyes rolling back into her skull, her eyebrows knitted together with anticipation. I felt as though I were trapped inside someone else's body, helplessly watching from behind their eyes as they slid the knife under her pinched skin, her flesh giving satisfying resistance to the blade. But no, that was *my* hand holding the knife. She let out a breathy gasp and arched her back, pushing the knife deeper into her own body. I began dragging the razor-sharp blade down her stomach, slicing through her thin, delicate skin with ease. Blood cascaded down either side of her smooth, bony body and streamed off the sides of the table.

I gently pulled open her abdomen to reveal the shiny, twitching gore inside. The mass of pale, coiled intestines quivered as she ran her slender fingers through her short, sweaty hair. Her small rubbery organs slithered around my hands as I plunged them deep into her guts. It was warm; so terribly, terribly warm. And a chill ran down my spine as I tried to scoop out the bloody horror that lay within. She slid her sylphlike hands almost sensually down her chest and pushed them into her own gaping stomach cavity, helping me to scoop out the twitching mass of bloody entrails. She bit her ample bottom lip as it all tumbled off the side of the table and onto the muddy, blood-soaked ground, disappearing beneath the surface of the shin-deep ooze.

I gagged on the rank stench of her exposed guts as salty tears rolled down my cheeks. I doubled over as a hot spike of vomit shot up my throat and spilled over my tongue. My head was spinning. Vomit drizzled through my clenched teeth, and I could feel what felt like her small intestine brushing up against my ankle. And I realised, with a terror that pierced me deep within my chest, that I had been slowly sinking this entire time. I was now up to my knees in the mud; even the table had been sinking at the same rate I had been. And my dad was nowhere to be seen.

A special kind of helpless panic gripped me, and all I could think to do was stagger to my feet and carve into her ribcage with the knife, hoping that cutting out her heart would satisfy whatever dark cosmic deity had trapped me here – the author of the nightmarish scene I saw before me. I hacked her ribs apart like a butcher carving into an animal. Then I climbed up onto the table, straddled her gaping, empty stomach cavity, and pried apart her ribcage with a sickening *crack*. She convulsed, moaning loudly as if she had just reached some kind of twisted, masochistic orgasm; blood painting me from my thighs to my chin. Then she became still, her head lolling back as blood began to drizzle out of her mouth and nose, her eyes staring blankly into the nothingness.

I exploded awake. I sat up and grasped the sides of my small bed with twisted, white knuckles. My forehead coated with a greasy film of ice-cold sweat. It was just a nightmare. Just a goddamn fucking nightmare. I groped around at my surroundings to make sure I was actually awake, and I was really inside my tiny room in the Bunkhouse.

'Holy shit,' I whispered to myself. My room was pitch black, and my skin felt tight, too tight, and my jaw ached. Probably from clenching my teeth while I was asleep. 'Holy fuck,' I sighed under my breath, pushing my palms into my aching eye sockets. Now I really did need to piss.

I got to my feet and shuffled down the dark hallway, running my fingers along the wall so I knew where I was going. My hand silently bumping up and down over the closed doors that lined the narrow corridor. I turned the stubborn knob and opened the back door as slowly as I could, trying to silence the screech of its rusty hinges.

The cool night air caressed my naked chest as I scooped my

penis out of my underpants. I curled my toes in the soft, dry dirt, the sensation reassuring me that I was indeed awake, and the nightmare was nothing more than just that, a nightmare. I breathed in the crisp fresh air, listening to the exquisite sound of my own stream of urine meeting the dry powdery soil. I let my head roll back, puffing out my cheeks before letting out a sigh of relief. I soaked in my surroundings. The farm at night looked exactly like it did in my dream, down to the last bone-chilling detail. I let my cock flop back into my shorts with a tremendous sense of accomplishment, as if my quest to drag myself out of bed to take a piss outside was some kind of herculean task that I had somehow managed to complete against all odds.

I peered across the fields, widening my eyes as wide as they would go, straining to see through the darkness. The forbidden barn stood alone and foreboding in the tall grass. Its crumbling walls tightly concealing whatever mysteries lay within. An ominous hulking black shape that seemed to be both completely invisible and inconsequential, but at the same time somehow at the centre of something sinister. As I looked, I got the strange, unsettling feeling that it was somehow the source of my nightmare.

I slowly turned to go back inside, my eyes lingering on the mysterious building. Looking at the farm at night made my dream feel far too real. It was time to retreat back to the safety of my sarcophagus. Then the air suddenly turned ice cold, and I watched as a jet of frozen breath escaped my lips and all the muscles in my body seized-up with fear. I gritted my teeth and couldn't un-grit them. My jaw was locked in place. Spit dribbled over the rim of my trembling bottom lip and down my chin like a rabid animal. I was about to wrench open the door and leap back inside when a shadowy figure appeared in the corner of my eye. She exited the farmhouse, wrapped in a brown herringbone coat that was way too big for her and extended all the way down to her ankles. She began to walk in the direction of the Forbidden Barn, stopping now and then to search the compound with sharp, suspicious eyes, her arms loosely folded around her stomach.

It was Mrs Spicer. I hadn't seen her since I arrived almost two weeks ago. Without her sunglasses her face seemed somehow thin and withered. Her eyes were dark and hollow, and her cheeks looked concaved and sickly in the top-down lighting of the moon.

I crouched down on the ground in a half-hearted attempt to hide, hoping that the long dark shadow cast by the Bunkhouse would conceal me. She clutched her stomach and puffed out her cheeks, her meticulously sculpted eyebrows knitted together in an expression of pain and worry. She quickly walked into the field; her powerful, confident stride reduced to an urgent, panicky stagger. She careened her way through the tall grass and struggled for a moment to unlock a small door on the side of the barn, before disappearing inside.

I suddenly got the inescapable feeling that I was being watched. Slowly, I turned my head, my eyes bulging from their sockets, straining to peer through the darkness. The old Farmhouse loomed towards me out of the void. It felt like each one of those black windows concealed a thousand dark, twitching eyes, all staring directly at me. Thinking, watching, waiting. My heart slammed against my ribcage. I crawled backwards, back inside and closed the door behind me. The all-consuming tenebrosity of the hallway hugging my body as I rested my forehead against the cool wood of the closed door.

CHAPTER FIVE

sat at one of the crowded outdoor tables, tearing into my serving of mass-cooked eggs on toast for breakfast. I stared blankly at the Forbidden Barn. My wide, unblinking eyes must have made me look slightly unhinged as I wolfed down my food without even looking at it. Then I felt the unmistakable presence of a tall, lanky man sitting down beside to me.

'You're not going to believe this dream I had last night,' I said, looking down at my massacred food for the first time.

'What?' An unfamiliar voice answered. I turned my head to see Martin, one of the farmhands I didn't know very well, sitting beside me.

'Oh, um ...' I stuttered, my mind hitting a mental block. 'Where's Casey?' I finally choked out. He squinched up his weird-shaped face and cocked his head towards the Farmhouse.

'There's a new guy. He's gone to meet him,' he said.

'Oh.' I continued staring at the barn. It was no less mysterious during the day then it was at night. I could feel a burning curiosity eating its way into my brain. Starting just behind the eyes and boring its way backwards into my skull until it finally quelled, becoming a hot little itch in the back of my head.

'Who's the new guy?' I finally asked, turning my head. But Martin was already gone, and my plate was empty. How long had I been sitting there, staring?

'Hey everyone, this is Luther!' Casey's voice rang out over the breakfast chatter. Beside him stood a gnarled, gangly man with long scraggy hair and a bushy unkept beard. He grinned at everyone and nodded, his scabby lips stretching back to reveal several missing teeth. The ones that were still there were a curdled yellow, resting loosely inside his blackened gums. If I had to guess his age, I'd say he was about fifty. But he was in such godawful shape that he could have been around forty and just looked fifty. He looked like he had swum through an ocean of dirty heroin needles to get here .

'I've been working farmland for over twenty years, so don't you all worry about me being another clueless prick,' he called out in a friendly, but gravelly voice. His larynx probably withered away to a rotten pulp by decades of chain-smoking. He seemed to have a sunny disposition, but something about him just didn't seem quite right to me. I could feel it in the tight unease at the base of my spine and the way his face made my jaw seized-up and lock shut.

I grimaced at him, knowing I was safely hidden amongst a sea of new faces. I watched as he talked with Casey. I couldn't tell what they were saying, but something about that mouth, and his vile papery skin made my blood run cold.

I turned my head away, looking for something that might distract me. I looked towards the Farmhouse and felt my eyes widen as I saw Mrs Spicer standing at the bottom of the Farmhouse stairs, engrossed in a discussion with Vincent. They took turns pointing at a clipboard, then pointing out into the fields. She was wearing a pair of high-waisted denim jeans that hugged her curvaceous hips. And a pair of black, low-cut high-heeled boots that did nothing to bring her even close to Vincent's eyeline as he towered over her. But the strangest thing was her face: she looked radiant and beautiful. Not a single crease under her eye or imperfection in her skin. She was definitely not the same ghoulishly skeletal woman I had seen last night, and I began to wonder if I had dreamed that part as well. I observed her glowing skin and the slight blush on her pale cheeks from the cool morning breeze. I scrunched my eyes shut and shook my head a little. Either I didn't see her at all last night, or her true features had been obscured by the moonlight.

'Alright everyone, listen up!' Vincent's voice tore through the chatter like a sledgehammer. And like a pack of trained dogs, every single man immediately fell silent and stood to attention.

'We've got new cattle coming in today. I've got Group A unloading, Group B branding and Group C moving them into the field. I'm going to need group C to move the sheep into the adjacent field as quickly as possible, because apparently this prick decided he needed to deliver them a day earlier than we agreed, so we're underprepared. And be careful, we've got new

lambs popping out of those ewes every five seconds! Now go!'
He threw his pointed finger out towards the driveway like an
iron ball shooting out of a cannon.

Everyone jumped to their feet and ran to their posts like
ants running around on the ground before a storm; half of
them taking the time to frisbee their dirty plates into the
kitchen sink as they scrambled to get ready. I was part of Group
B, heading towards the Shearing Shed which also – as I would
find out – doubled as a branding station. This building was a
large one storey shed, clad in vertical wooden boards with a
broken gable roof. I caught up to Casey who was also part of
Group B.

'What's the deal with the new guy?' I panted.

'I don't know. Just some drifter looking for a job.'

'I don't like him. Something about that guy gives me the
creeps.'

'It's the teeth, isn't it?' He grinned, rubbing his index finger
over his own pearly whites.

'It's all of him,' I said, unamused by how laid-back and
carefree Casey was being. I had the strangest feeling that I
had seen this guy before.

A colossal truck rolled down the driveway, its cage-like
trailer packed to the top with cattle. The horn announced its
arrival with a deafening blast. The overwhelming stench of
cow shit trailing behind it like the invisible tail of a commit.
The truck rolled to a stop and a small man in a red cap and
blue coveralls descended the seven-foot drop from the driver's
seat. The sight of this tiny man climbing down from the cabin

of this huge truck, then standing next to Vincent as they both passed the pen back and forth to sign the paperwork was almost comical.

I gagged on the stench as I peered into the enormous steel rectangle that contained dozens of glassy-eyed bovine faces, swarming with noisy black flies that crawled in and out of their wide, hairy nostrils. The cattle were unloaded by five other farm hands and prodded single file into the cattle yard beside the shed; a series of twisting and turning metal walls that would feed them into the building one by one. Three iron rods rested with their tips inside a small fire, burning inside an old oil drum with the top cut off.

'Have you ever branded a cow before?' Casey asked, pulling out one of the rods to reveal a glowing yellow tip in the shape of a stylish 'S F'.

'No, I haven't,' I replied, hypnotised by the white-hot glow of the branding rod. The first cow had been squeezed into the cattle crush: a steel cage that hugged the cow's body on all sides, rendering it completely immobilised. Only the cow's head poked out of the front, looking around with its huge wet eyes, assessing the situation with a disturbing lack of concern.

'You want to use a rolling motion, like this,' he said, opening a small hatch on the side of the crush, exposing the animal's rump. He pressed the iron on the creature's skin with the scolding hot end, rolling it from top to bottom just like he said. The cow's eyes shot wide open, its pupils constricting into two tiny black dots. I winced. I'd never heard a cow scream before, but it sounded eerily human. Its huge yellow teeth gnashed together as a jet of hot white smoke hissed from the cow's scorched flesh and its panicked legs slammed against the tight steel walls of the crush.

'Ha ha, yeah!' Luther howled with excitement. I jumped, not realising he was in the shed with us. Two guys walked over to uncage the cow, and I hurried to help them. The beast staggered out of the crush, stretching and flexing the leg that had been branded. It seemed to have instantly forgotten all about the searing pain it had just suffered and walked off complacently into the second cattle yard leading into the field.

Off to greener pastures, I thought to myself.

'You've got to let me go next, boss!' Luther said, enthusiastically walking over to the fire pit to pick up another freshly heated branding iron. As he walked past me, we made eye contact. And for a split second his eyes widened ever so slightly, and I knew in that instant that he recognised me too. Then, as he curved his hand tightly around the base of the iron rod, I saw it. The thumb on his left hand had been sliced clean off. All that remained was a jagged scar that ran down the side of his hand where his thumb used to be. My blood turned to ice in my veins, and my skin began to crawl as I took a step back, then another. The interior of the shed seemed to recede away from me, and I could taste my own heartbeat in my mouth. He speared the next cow in the side with the branding iron.

'That's nice ... That's real nice...' he said in an almost sexual tone as the smell of burning flesh filled his nostrils.

CHAPTER SIX

lay awake in bed, with the sheets pooled around my body, staring up into the darkness. My tiny bedroom was pitch black, but I could still feel how close the walls were. My mind – which had become a constant buzzing swarm of thoughts, fears, and suspicions – had been temporarily silenced by my late night onanism. And in the empty abyss of my mind; in the black desert of thoughts; formed the image of Mrs Spicer. The Mrs Spicer I had seen this morning, not the one I saw last night. Her body slowly materialising out of the darkness. Each layer of detail bleeding through and adding to the last, like watercolours soaking into a piece of paper. Her pale, gossamer skin taking shape inside the shadows; dissolving from black into a thin, translucent grey, then finally into a soft, creamy-white. Her colourful sundress – the one she had been wearing the day we met – stretched tightly over her Junoesque body.

I drank in the image, savouring every detail, every colour, every exquisite flavour. But slowly, my thoughts drifted away from her, and instead turned to one of my more precious memories.

*   *   *

I sat on the hard wooden church pew, its uncomfortable shape digging into both my back and legs at the same time, examining what looked like fingernail marks on the little shelf in front of me. Every pew had a little ledge on the back of the one in front of it, so you had somewhere to put your bible, or hymnbook, or whatever. The dark varnish had been scratched away to reveal the lightly coloured raw wood underneath.

No doubt the work of a bored child ... or perhaps an anxious adult. The priest's voice droned on in the distance as I scanned the floor and walls for something to entertain myself. Just another Sunday morning church service, with the seconds crawling past like hours. My dad sat next to me, the only time of the week you would catch him with his hair combed and his face washed. He looked very unnatural to me, as if he were wearing a disguise. In the same way people sometimes dye their hair or grow a beard when they are hiding from the police. Or perhaps like a wild animal that had been cleaned up, shaved and put into a freshly ironed shirt and was now posing as a human being. His hollow cheeks were already becoming dark and scratchy, only a couple of hours after his weekly shave.

He was one of those part-time Christians who was only in the game because he was inherently afraid of death. He didn't give much of a shit about Jesus during the rest of the week, but his strategy seemed to be that if he put in the miles with his church attendance then maybe he would have enough points to get into Heaven.

He glared intently at the pulpit, silently scratching his index finger against the seat of the pew, craving his hourly cigarette. His hands, which were usually blackened with grease and oil, were clean and untarnished except for the little lines of black grit trapped underneath his cuticles; survivors of his long morning session with the nailbrush.

I looked at the walls, several stained glass windows lining both sides of the church, bearing the likenesses of different saints and martyrs no one ever talked about. A four-foot-tall porcelain statue of the Virgin Mary with the baby Jesus in her arms stood to the left of the alter, held halfway up the wall on a little wooden platform. A similar statue of the adult Jesus stood on the right. I looked up at Jesus. He stared down at me with his lifeless painted-on blue eyes. His paperwhite skin and robes made him look like some kind of terrifying, vengeful ghost. A ghost that would only appear here, once a week, to remind me that the rest of the time he was silently watching my every move, listening to my every thought and spying on my most private moments. And if I did the tiniest thing to displease him, and did not beg for his forgiveness, then he would personally see to it that I burn in Hell for all eternity. I always imagined removing just one of those tiny little pieces of wood from the bottom of the platform, just to see that huge, heavy statue fall from its high place on the wall and shatter against the hardwood floor. But then I'd look up at his blank, emotionless face, a face that said, 'Just try it, and see what happens'. Then I'd shake the thought from my mind as if my immortal soul depended on it.

Of course, I hadn't believed in any of that stuff since my early teens – too many plot holes, I guess – but goddamn, that would be some scary shit if it all turned out to be real. Jesus held out his rigid porcelain hands to reveal two bloody holes in his palms. Words like *impaled* and *skewered* bounced around inside my head as I inspected their perfectly circular shape. Whoever made this statue made the nail holes too smooth and clean. If a man really had been suspended by nails in his hands then they would be way more mangled and gory than that.

We all rose to receive communion. My insides tightened as we all shuffled down the aisle in two neat little lines, dreading the awkward three seconds of intense eye contact with Father Marcus as he gave me 'the body of Christ'. His stone-cold eyes always seemed to look straight through me. His insidious gaze slicing through my retinas, cutting through the soft jelly of my eyeballs and burning a hole all the way through to the back of my head. He placed the wafer in my cupped hands and I quickly put in in my mouth, turning away from him as I took my seat again.

While you were waiting for everyone else to finish receiving communion you were supposed to silently kneel and pray. I never did pray though. At least not properly. I didn't feel the presence of an all-powerful god anywhere behind my eyelids. Instead, I felt the profound and undeniable lack of one, accompanied by the vast empty space an omnipresent being would leave behind if he should suddenly cease to exist. I knelt with my elbows resting on the back of the pew in front of me, peering through my intertwined fingers while I pretended to pray. I liked to watch other people slowly make their way back to their seats. Imagine going to the same place, week after week, with the same group of people and being more familiar with the backs of their heads than their actual faces. But there was one face in particular I was getting to know very well. I watched her as she slowly walked past me in the line of people returning to their seats. Her short-sleeve shirt buttoned up all the way to the top, with the collar neatly folded down. Her concealed breasts stretching the buttons apart ever-so-slightly, revealing a tiny slither of the cream-coloured skin underneath. Her modest church clothes not quite accommodating the curves of her feminine body. Her dark-brown plaid skirt came down just past her knees. But I knew outside of church she was a half-way-up-the-thigh girl for sure. Or at least she'd like to be. Her mousy brown hair was cut into a short, messy bob with a tangled fringe that caressed the tops of her eyes as she walked, her head lowered. A ghost of a smile crept across my face as I watched her through my fingers. Her eyes met mine in a fleeting sideways glance, and that same muted smile found its way onto the corners of her soft pink lips as well. My heart fluttered, my body suddenly feeling lighter than air. She walked past my pew, and I turned my head as far as I could without rousing suspicion, my eyes turning to the side as far as they would go just so I could watch her for a few more seconds.

I caught a glimpse of her smooth, hairless calves as she walked away, suggesting two long, slender legs hiding just beneath her skirt. I turned back and continued pretending to pray, trying to cover my giddy smile with my clasped hands.

*   *   *

Everyone shuffled out of the church, their dull grey faces reflecting the dull grey sky that hung above us: an expanse of dirty overcast white, with a smattering of dark grey rumpled clouds. It looked like some kind of enormous cosmic ashtray, as if the world rested atop a giant upside-down cigarette butt, about to be stubbed out by God himself.

I weaved my way through the crowd: old ladies in their felt coats, old men in their tweed blazers, mothers in cotton dresses and fathers in their freshly ironed shirts, trying not to make eye contact with anyone so I wouldn't have to talk to them. Dad leaned against the side of the stone church steps, making love to a freshly lit cigarette. He didn't care what I did with my free time, so long as I was back before dark and ready to run the bowsers again first thing on Monday morning. But this was the weekend and I intended to enjoy it fully. And for the last few weeks that meant a recuring no-strings-attached make-out session with Loreta Biggs – the girl in the long skirt and buttoned-down shirt – in the woods after church.

I slipped around the back of the rectangular bluestone building, making sure I was out of sight of the small crowd of churchgoers still mulling around before making off towards the tree line. A small clearing had been carved out of the wilderness to have the church built way-back-when, and this provided the perfect cover to easily slip away and vanish after the service without anyone noticing.

I was leaping out of my skin with excitement. I could feel my pulse thudding away in every inch of my body. The tall, twisted trees rose up in front of me, shrouding the mysterious forest floor in shadows. Damp grey and brown leaves covered every inch of the ground and the dark humus felt soft and spongy underneath my feet as I walked deeper and deeper into the woods. The air tasted crisp and fresh, nourishing the inside of my lungs in a way the stale indoor church air never could. After walking for ten or so minutes and climbing over rotten logs and navigating around blackberry bushes, I scrambled over a steep embankment and slid down the other side.

This was our spot: the undulating landscape formed a large bowl-shaped dip that concealed us on all sides. This was a place where mushrooms dominated the forest floor and the ancient spirits of a forgotten people still silently stalked the forest: remnants of a oneness with nature inconceivable to those who had been civilised to death and believed that that statue of Jesus really did watch their every move, judge their every action, and could hear their every thought. I came here to experience a return to nature, to escape the prison of social convention, if only for an hour or two.

I descended into the bowl, peering through the twisted trees covered in slippery green moss. Lory was nowhere to be seen. She always arrived first and would be waiting for me right here on top of this log. A cold breeze rustled through the canopy, as if to punctuate my sudden feeling of unease. A huge fallen tree rested atop the soggy ground, its roots torn out of the forest floor and sticking upwards, fingering the air with its hard, thin tendrils.

'Lory?' I whispered. No answer. 'Loreta?' I whispered a little louder.

'Bahhh!' she shouted, shooting out a hand from underneath the log and grabbing my ankle. I jumped, my muscles seizing up as I darted away.

'Fucking hell!' I yelped. Her pretty face suddenly popped up from behind the log.

'Oh, come on. You would have done it to me!' she laughed. I reached down and combed through her tangled mess of brown hair with my fingers, raking out the handful of wet leaves that clung to the side of her head. She had on one of those plastic yellow raincoats, which shielded her nice clean church clothes from the mud and grit that seemed to ooze from the trees around us.

'I was watching you before,' I grinned.

'I know … I was watching you watch me,' she said, biting her lip and grabbing me by the collar with both hands. She lunged forward and planted her lips on mine. 'I've been waiting for this all week.' She bit my bottom lip and whispered through her teeth. As she spoke, I noticed another little yellow leaf ensnared on the top of her head. But before I could pull it out she pulled away from me, peeling off her yellow raincoat and draping it over the damp mossy log. She sat down on top of it and patted the spot beside her, biting her lip again and looking at me with large, hungry eyes.

Her lips were soft. I curled my fingers around the plastic fabric of the raincoat as she greedily hugged my bottom lip, cupping my face with both hands. I pulled back, my eyes still closed.

'When are you going to be my girlfriend?' I asked in between kisses.

'I told you. My parents won't let me have a boyfriend,' she said, aggressively pecking me in between each word.

'You're eighteen, you should be able to do whatever you want,' I retorted.

'Not if you want to keep living under my roof!' she said in a deep, masculine voice, mimicking her father. 'Besides, could you imagine? Mum, dad, I want you to meet my new boyfriend, the white trash rat from the petrol station who didn't go to school.'

'Ouch,' I said, attacking the space underneath her jaw, fighting the urge to give her a big purple hickey. Hickies weren't allowed with Loreta.

'Besides, this is way more fun don't you think? I feel so naughty,' she said, redirecting me back towards her lips. I slid my hand up under her skirt, gently squeezing her warm, soft thigh. She moved her hand onto my lap, her fingers curling around the throbbing mass in my pants; gently flicking the end of my zip with the tip of her finger. She pulled back, her eyes still closed, her lips still parted. And after a tense pause that felt like it would never end, she finally asked,

'Can I suck your dick?' In a slow, breathy whisper, as if working up the courage to ask the question had almost overwhelmed her and she came close to not even being able to speak the words.

My heart was racing. She had often pawed at my crotch through my pants, commenting on how big and hard my penis felt, with that girly, breathy voice of hers; but this was different. I tried to answer, but the question had knocked all the air out of my lungs, and my skin suddenly felt hot and sweaty.

'Y-yeah … I'd like that …' I choked out in a pathetically nervous tone.

My heart was slamming against my ribcage as she pulled out the raincoat from underneath me and laid it out on the muddy ground so she would have something to kneel on. I leaned back on the log as she unbuckled my belt, her cheeks turning bright red as she drew in a long, slow breath between her teeth, followed by a nervous, shaky exhale.

This is it, she must have thought as she curled her fingers around the waist of my pants. She yanked them down.

*   *   *

'I'm all wet…' She bit her lip, the deep red blush on her cheeks growing even brighter. My heart was still racing. All my senses felt as though they had been turned up all the way, with that almost surreal sense of clarity that immediately follows an orgasm. I could hear birds chirping in the tops of trees kilometres away. I could smell the rotten log I was sitting on, and the dirt and mud by our feet. The forest seemed greener and more dense; the landscape stretching away from us. And the thin, translucent rays of hot sunshine filtering down through the trees seemed brighter and more fiery than they did before.

'Can I touch it?' I asked. She looked at me confused for a moment. Then I cocked my eyes down towards the hand that was between her legs and suddenly she understood. I had never seen a real vagina in the flesh before, let alone touched one, and the prospect of seeing hers right at that very moment filled me with an excitement I had never known before. She bit her lip harder, squeezing her thighs together as she nodded with shy eagerness.

'Just don't put your fingers inside me, okay?' she said.

'Why not?'

'Because I said so,' she said, half playfully, half sternly as she leaned back against the log. She pulled up her skirt and I slowly slid my hand up between her soft, hairless thighs.

CHAPTER SEVEN

rolled my tongue around the inside of my mouth; sliding it wetly over the inner walls of my cheeks and behind my gums. Things had escalated and I ended up giving her head as well right there on the rotten log. The bewitching taste of her vagina still clung to my tastebuds; only a ghost of what it was twenty minutes ago, but the lingering flavour was no less fascinating. I was as high as a kite. My mind consumed by a pleasant, filmy haze that made it difficult to think. All the while the perfect image of her pussy lay clear and opaque in the black darkness just behind my eyelids whenever I chose to close them.

I reached the edge of the forest where the tree line met the deserted highway and drifted down the road towards home. The forest was a rich tapestry of razor-sharp greens that continued to tower over me on either side of the road. And the sky was now filled with huge looming storm clouds bruised purple with impending rain that almost seemed to swirl around the exact spot I was walking along. The unmistakable howl of a car tearing through the otherwise silent air snapped me back into my body. I felt my pupils constrict as I turned my head to see where the vehicle was coming from. A rusty white ute with a slightly crumpled bumper flew down the highway towards me. I casually stepped off the side of the road, my ankles disappearing into the long grass that lined it on either side, giving the car plenty of room to pass me by. But as it got closer it slowed to a crawl, its worn-out brakes crunching as it pulled up beside me. A friendly-looking man smiled at me through the open passenger side window, a hint of playful concern on his slightly sunburned face.

'Hey, you want a lift?' He called to me through the open window in a gravelly voice.

'Sure, why not?' I smiled back. The passenger side door opened with a rusty crunch and I climbed in. 'I'm just going a few minutes that way. I'm Otis. What's your name?' I asked as we tore off down the road.

'Oh, if anyone asks, you can just say I'm a friend.' He grinned, still looking forward. His cryptic answer baffled me, but sometimes you just meet people with a strange sense of humour, so I didn't think anything of it.

'You live far from here, Oat?' he asked, adjusting the rearview mirror so he could see my face without turning his head.

'Yeah ... just a couple of minutes down the road,' I said again, awkwardly pointing in the direction we were headed. 'Are you from around here?' I asked, scanning the filthy interior of the car; my eyes zeroing in on the porn magazine laying blatantly on top of the coffee-stained dashboard.

'I'm from the other side of the mountains, Kilsnide originally, but I like to move around a lot. What do they call it? Wanderlust?' he said, the reflection of his eyes in the rear-view mirror looking at me with a strange calculating thoughtfulness. He scratched at the week-old stubble on his chin, which matched the weeks' worth of growth of hair on his recently shaved head.

'You like girls huh?' He laughed, noticing me eyeing-off the girly mag. He snatched it up and tossed it onto my lap. 'Go ahead, have a look. You know you want too,' he chuckled, winking at me through the reflection in the mirror. There was a topless blonde woman on the cover, squeezing her large breasts together and pinching her nipples.

'There, that'll get your dick nice and hard,' he said under his breath, his eyes looking at me more intensely than before. I looked down at the woman winking at me with one crystal blue eye and blowing me a caked-on red lipsticked kiss. The name of the magazine was *Depraved*. This appeared to be their February issue.

'You got yourself a girl, Oat?' he asked. There was something in his voice he was trying to restrain; an excitement he was trying to hide, with little success.

'Yeah ... sort of,' I said looking out the window, beginning to wish I had just walked home instead of accepting this ride.

'Yeah, I love girls. Fat girls, skinny girls, those lonely housewives with them big ol' titties. They'll do anything for a thrill while their kids are at school and their husbands are away at their nine-to-fives. I used to be a milkman. You know how easy it is to get a bored, pill-head housewife with big tits to suck you off when you turn up with that milk in the morning? By the time I would get to the end of my rout I'd have nothing left in my balls.' He laughed hard, clearly remembering it fondly. 'And don't get me started on those tight little virgin schoolgirls! They've got pussies so small you can barely squeeze your prick into 'em. But believe me, you can if you try hard enough!' He slapped the steering wheel as he spoke, grinning from ear to ear. That's when I noticed a couple of his yellowing teeth were missing, making his smile seem more creepy and threatening than it did before.

'You're probably too young to understand right now, but when you get older, you owe it to yourself to try some of that *tight* jailbait pussy. The younger the better,' he said, squeezing his thumb and forefinger into a small circle as he emphasised the word 'tight'.

'What flavour is your girl?' he asked, nudging me in the ribs with his elbow.

'Flavour?'

'Yeah, is she some slutty little piece of arse you nail behind the schoolyard?' he asked, excitedly nudging me again even harder than before.

'I ... I don't go to school,' I said, now *really* wishing I hadn't gotten into the car with this freak. He looked over and saw that I hadn't yet explored the contents of the porn magazine.

'Go on have a peek inside, those sluts will blow your mind,' he said, aggressively tapping the cover. The hard sensation of his index finger pressed through the stack of pages, straight into my penis. I squirmed uncomfortably in my seat, looking down at the glossy picture of the topless woman.

'You can just drop me off here, my house is just around the corner,' I said, discreetly fumbling at my seatbelt.

'I like you Oat ...' he said, beginning to slow the car down while blindly groping under his seat for something. 'You should come round to my place sometime ... I've got some porno tapes I think you'd enjoy. We could watch them together, maybe smoke a little grass...'

He made a hard right down a dirt road, the unexpected swerve slamming me back against my seat. The car ground to a halt – just out of view of the highway – with a small cloud of dust rising from the back tyres. He turned to me with a revolver in his hand and a vicious, depraved gleam in his eyes; his cracked and peeling lips stretched tightly over his manky gums. His grin was repulsive. The little red tears in the soft tissues of his lips pulled apart slightly to reveal the blood-red flesh underneath.

'Well, I tried to get you nice and hard, didn't I? Tried to turn you on by showin' you girly mags and talkin' about pussy. But it looks like we're gonna have to do this the hard way,' he sneered, pointing the gun at me. A spike of panic pierced my heart and pinned my lungs shut. He reached over and grabbed at my crotch. I pushed myself hard up against the seat, trying to flinch away as he squeezed my penis and testicles together.

'You're just gonna have to close your eyes and think of that slutty little bitch of yours,' he said, cocking the hammer of the gun to drive his point home. I squeezed my eyes shut, desperately searching the darkness for God, for Loreta's pussy, for anything. But all I could find in that space behind my eyelids was a stark, bleak emptiness. I rolled my tongue around the inside of my mouth, but all I could taste was fear. Tears rolled down my cheeks as I tried to say something – tried to think of something to say that might save me – but there was nothing. All that came out was a long shaky exhale as I gripped the grimy seat, white-knuckling two fistfuls of the coarse, dirty fabric. Rain began to pelt the outside of the car. And I watched with wide-eyed terror as he unzipped the fly of his jeans. His long dirty cock sliding out of its denim confines and slumping lazily onto his thigh; a bloated slug covered with thick roping veins. He gathered it up in his free hand and swung it around, slapping it against his thigh to try and get it to engorge a little more. It had been thoroughly marinaded in the human filth of his unwashed clothes; loathsome, repulsive, and smelling like a public urinal. I tried in vain to hold my breath, to keep the grotesque stench out of my nostrils, but I had to breathe the tainted air eventually.

'Why don't you start by jerking me off, nice and slow,' he said, grabbing my wrist so hard it felt like he was going to break it. His cock was warm and firm, and I could feel his pulse throbbing through the tangled mass of veins that lay just below his skin. I winced as I began to slide my hand up and down his shaft, trying not to look directly at its putrid shape. He cupped the side of my face with his hand, I tried to pull away, but he pressed the barrel of the gun against my forehead.

'You've got a pretty little mouth,' he said, running his

thumb over my lips. 'Now, let's see that pretty little tongue of yours.' I squeezed my eyes shut and poked out my tongue. He slid his thumb into my mouth as heavy salty tears rolled down my cheeks. It tasted like engine grease and the tell-tail human mire of men of his particular seedy breed.

'Mmm, you've got a tongue like a little girl. Perfect for sucking a big fat cock like mine,' he leered, squeezing his words through his clenched teeth as trembling droplets of spit rolled down his bottom lip. I gagged as he pressed his thumb deeper into my throat, his fingernail scraping lightly against my uvular. He grabbed a hold of my hair with his other hand, the gun still resting loosely in his grip, but no longer pointing straight at my head.

I opened my eyes to see him sneering at me with smug satisfaction, forcing his filthy thumb deeper and deeper down into my helpless throat. My blood boiled and my head began to shake as if I were having a seizure. Adrenaline welled up inside my body and coursed through my veins with such ferocity that I thought my muscles might snap off my bones and tear out of my skin. I suddenly shrieked through the mouthful of dirty thumb; foamy spit spilling out around his hand as I glared at him with unrestrained fury. I bit down as hard as I could, my teeth slicing through hard bone and soft tendons. He screamed, a violent jet of blood spraying out of the stump of his severed thumb, painting both our faces and the ceiling of the car. His whole body seized-up as he looked down at the oozing, bloody crater on the side of his hand, his eyes bulging out of their sockets, his face twisted with pain. The severed thumb rolled loosely around the inside of my mouth; it tasted metallic, and a little bit salty. I spat it right into his face. It bounced off his forehead and landed somewhere on the floor.

I grabbed the wrist of his other hand and tried to wrestle the gun off him, slamming it repeatedly against the dashboard. In a stunned panic he fired all six rounds straight through the windshield of the car, sending a shower of jagged shards of broken glass raining down on both of us. I found myself temporarily deafened by the roar of the pistol; the sound of my attacker's screams replaced with a high-pitched ringing in my ears. His head lulled backwards as he tried to cover his mangled hand; blood still haemorrhaging out of the gaping stump. My heart slammed against my ribcage, my body still surging with adrenaline. The rain from outside poured in through the shattered windscreen with blinding ferocity, making it difficult to see. I screamed my best blood-curdling war cry straight into his ear and smashed my fist into his rotten yellow mouth.

I don't know how many times I punched him, but it was a lot. My mind was foggy. My vision reduced to nothing more than a pinprick of focused, white hot rage. I flung open the car door and spilled out onto the ground, bringing with me a shower of congealing blood and broken glass. I sprinted into the woods; running until my veins burned and my muscles refused to go on, falling to my knees on the muddy forest floor, gasping for air. The trees spun around me, my consciousness waning. My hearing slowly coming back to me as the sound of the pelting rain grew louder and louder. I looked down at my trembling hands to see what looked like a small bone sticking out from between two of my knuckles. I gently tweezed it out of my ragged flesh with two fingers, placing it into the palm of my blood-streaked hand. It was one of the man's rotten yellow teeth.

CHAPTER EIGHT

exploded awake, sitting up in bed as one solitary bead of cold sweat rolled down my forehead and into my eye. I pressed the palm of my hand into my eye socket, trying to stop the salty sting. I groped at the bed sheets around me, my racing heartbeat slowly returning to a normal pace. It had been a long time since I had had that recuring nightmare: getting raped in the mouth at gunpoint. Feeling that hard, revolting shape jammed down my throat. Although I tried as hard as I could to forget about what had happened on the highway two years ago, the memory had burrowed its way deep into my subconscious like a parasitic insect, where it had laid a clutch of sickly yellow eggs. And every night since an egg has hatched and an identical nightmare has crawled its way out the dark recesses of my mind and forced me to relive the experience in my dreams. Only in these nightmares I never got away. I never bit off his thumb and ran like hell. In these nightmares I stayed where I was and had my open mouth lowered down onto his crotch.

I ran my fingers through my sweaty hair, scanning the darkness with wide, disc-like eyes. Even if there was somebody there in the room with me, I wouldn't be able to see them; darkness clung to everything like a thick black tar. I gently rubbed my cheeks, the bruises and torn flesh had mostly healed now, but the muscles in my face ached from clenching my jaw while I slept. The wind howled outside, vibrating the tin roof and every loose wooden board that was exposed to the elements. Vibrating in a way that made me question the structural integrity of the building I was sleeping in. I pulled on yesterday's clothes and made my way outside, hoping that the cold night air might wash away the disturbing aftertaste of my nightmare. The mental flavour clung to the roof of my mouth as if I had actually been forced to do those horrible, revolting things.

I gently creaked open the back door, flinching as it groaned on its rusty hinges. A strong wind slapped me in the face with an unforgiving harshness that said, 'Yes you are awake, and yes it was all just a dream'. I inhaled deeply, feeling the icy sting forge its way up my nose and down into my lungs, watching the trees whip back and forth as if they were made of rubber. Some of the more ancient-looking sheds and buildings seemed to lean in the strong winds. Their supports probably eaten out by white ants decades ago, leaving their timbers hollow and papery. I gazed through the darkness; the grass in the fields rhythmically swaying back and forth, giving it the appearance of a vast black ocean with deep rolling waves. And across that dark, foreboding sea floated the Forbidden Barn; colossal and unmoving, despite the vicious gusts of wind that hammered against its time-worn walls.

I could feel that itch again. That red-hot itch of curiosity that burned in the back of my head, just beneath the skin where it was impossible to scratch. I curled my toes inside my shoes – trying to remember if I was wearing them or not – and began to walk towards it. A flock of sleepy sheep fled in terror as I straddled the rusty barbed wire fence. They were probably afraid that I had come to kill them, like a butcher in the night. I drifted, empty-headed, past the spot they had run from. My hair flailed wildly around my face as I pulled my denim jacket tighter around my body, the tall grass swaying around my legs as I trudged through the field. The spiky seed heads batting against my thighs, piercing through the thick denim, and lightly pricking my skin.

The barn loomed tall in the sky. Its old unpainted weatherboards heaved in the roaring wind. Its ancient grey bones barely visible in the dim moonlight; the ghost of a time long since passed. I was close enough to see the foundation. It stood atop a stone platform made of large, stacked rocks that were cemented together, sticking up almost a meter off the ground before the timbers started. With a dirt ramp covered in tall grass leading up to the main entrance. I approached the two huge barn doors, sealed shut by several wooden barricades bolted across them. I tugged at one, hoping in vain that there might be some way of getting them off without needing to pry them off with a crowbar. The heavy wooden frame of the barn shuddered in the wind, as if it were flinching away from my touch. I walked around to the smaller door on the long side of the building, the one I had seen Mrs Spicer unlock and disappear into the night before. It was a small rectangle with an enormous padlock hanging from a rusty sliding bolt.

'What are you hiding?' I quietly whispered as I reached out to touch the padlock.

I pulled my hand back hesitantly, a deep groan coming from somewhere deep within the barn; the sound of wooden beams twisting against each other as the wind howled and moaned. I suddenly felt as though something were watching me. That there was a single dull, grey, watery eye concealed somewhere in the darkness. Silently observing, judging, scrutinising me. I turned and quickly began walking back towards the compound. Keeping my head down and trying not to look back at the barn.

That same flock of sheep had come back to the fence-line by the compound, and once again took flight in terror as they saw me coming back. All except for one tiny slither of white, which remained pressed hard up against the barbed wire fence. I thought it was just some loose wool tangled up in the wire, but as I got closer I saw that it was standing on four thin legs. The shape of a small lamb materialised out of the darkness, becoming clearer and more defined the closer I got. It had gotten its head caught in the barbed wire's vicious talons and was trying in vain to pull itself free. It began to jerk and wrench even harder when it sensed my presence.

'Shhh, Shhh, it's okay ...' I whispered, reaching down as gently as I could, trying not to frighten the poor creature. 'I'll get you free.' I placed my hand on the underside of its chin and delicately unhooked the sharp barbs that had buried themselves underneath its skin. The lamb slid free of the fence, but as it pulled away, the skin on its face tore clean off. Leaving behind a dangling bloody mask, suspended from the wire's cruel teeth. The lamb convulsed wildly, still standing on its feet bleating and savagely gnashing its jaws in pain. I could see the raw, shiny muscles constrict and flex as its yellow, lidless eyes rolled back in their sockets. Its crooked teeth gleamed in the darkness, unobstructed by the lips it no longer had. In a panic I tried to grab a hold of its tiny body. But as my hands touched it its woolly skin peeled off its sides, exposing wet, angry, red ribs that glistened in the dim moonlight. Blood painted my arms up to the elbows. I seized the lamb by the neck and threw it to the ground, strangling the wretched creature with all my strength; desperately trying to put it out of its misery. The skin around its neck crumbled beneath my hands like wet tissue paper. It was like trying to hold onto a bunch of pipes wrapped in meat and slathered with slick oil. Slippery, so horribly, horribly slippery. I felt something give way and burst inside its throat, and the lamb stopped struggling; it's mouth ajar and twitching in a silent preternatural scream. Tears pooling around the rims of its raw, exposed eye sockets, reflecting what little moonlight there was in its lifeless, glassy stare. Heart beating its last beat; legs weakly kicking their last kick; and those eyes, those terrible, terrible eyes, taking their last haunting look at a world they barely knew.

Blood coated my arms, chest, and thighs. My fingers had

fused to the mangled pulp of the lamb's neck and made a sickening peeling sound as I pulled them away. The violent frenzy had churned the muddy ground into a gory pool of dull red sludge. The lamb lay in the wet dirt in a bloody, twisted mess; blank watery eyes staring up at me; its tattered skin strewn around us like red and white confetti.

CHAPTER NINE

My fingers still felt warm and slippery, even though there was no blood on them. I felt like my encounter with the lamb last night had changed something inside me. Somehow both my body and my thoughts seemed strangely alien to me. I felt disconnected, as if I were watching someone else's life through their eyes, and I was only along for the ride: a passenger, or perhaps even a stowaway secretly tucked away in the back of someone else's subconscious.

Luther shoved his way past the other hungry workers, trying to secure himself a seat at one of the overcrowded tables. I stared at him with unblinking, bloodshot eyes. An orange sunset stretched out behind me like a magnificent, dreamy backdrop. But I wasn't looking at that. My eyes were fixed on the rapist that sat only two tables away. I rolled my tongue around the inside of my mouth. I could almost taste his skin, almost feel his thumb pressed against the soft end of my throat. I couldn't decide if I wanted to dive over the table and strangle him to death – just like I strangled that lamb – or run for my life in the opposite direction, trying to get as far away from him as I possibly could. Casey sat down across from me with his evening bowl of soup, obscuring my view with his denim-clad, string-bean body.

'I know who he is,' I said, craning my chin, trying to get another look over his shoulder before looking back down at my bowl. I'd been waiting all day for a quiet moment to tell Casey my secret, and this was it.

'Who? The new guy?' He asked, turning his head to see who I was looking at.

'Yeah, it was a couple of years ago … I was hitchhiking. He picked me up, then pulled a gun on me …' I said, stirring the contents of my bowl. Casey slowly stood up, walked around to the other side of the table, and sat down next to me.

'Is he dangerous?' he whispered. A huge wave of relief washed over me as I realised he was taking this seriously and for a moment I dared to believe that everything might be okay.

'Yeah,' I whispered back. 'Like I said, I was hitchhiking, and he picked me up in his car. Turns out he was a fucking psycho. He pulled out a gun and tried to shoot me.' Reliving the experience had made it almost impossible to open my mouth properly and I had to force my words out through my clenched teeth. It was like I had developed some kind of mental block that was keeping my jaw clamped shut. Subconsciously protecting myself from people putting things in my mouth, I suppose.

'How do you know it's him?' Casey asked, cautiously eyeing him off. Luther sat at the other table and seemed to be telling some kind of dramatic story, waving his arms around as he talked, a big yellow grin on his face. Everyone seemed to be getting along with him. Everyone, that was, except for Patrick – a big man with a shaved head and a square jaw. Luther had sat down in the empty space right next to him, and as he flailed his arms around he jabbed Patrick in the ribs with his elbow more times than I could count. Patrick didn't seem to like that.

'I didn't recognise him at first because he didn't have a beard back then. But then I noticed that he's missing his left thumb. That's because I bit it off when he attacked me,' I said anxiously. I couldn't bring myself to tell Casey about how he made me jerk him off or how he was about to make me suck his dick. That was the sort of thing that only happened to girls. Pretty girls who find themselves all alone in strange places and have no way of defending themselves. Not to men. Not to a teenage boy walking home along the side of the road in broad daylight. It's unheard of. If it hadn't actually happened to me I would have thought it was impossible. My muscles seized-up and my jaw locked even tighter as I thought about it.

'Holy shit ...' Casey whispered, discreetly trying to sneak a look at Luther's hand. 'Look, I believe you. But, unless he causes any trouble here on the farm, we can't really get rid of him. The Spicers want anyone they can get right now, and I mean *anyone*. So as long as he behaves himself here, there's nothing we can really do to get rid of him,' he said, still watching the new farmhand suspiciously. 'I'll tell Vincent about it though.' I could see it in his eyes that he was searching for a way to help me.

'No, don't ... I don't want him to know that I know,' I said, looking up from my bowl. 'I don't think he's recognised me yet ...' I whispered through my teeth, hoping it might mask some of the desperation in my voice.

'Well, let's keep a close eye on him anyway.'

I dunked my empty bowl in the kitchen sink and scrubbed it with a bitter, feverish intensity. There had to be a way to get rid of this piece of shit. He only arrived here yesterday, and already I could feel my sanity beginning to slip. He didn't say anything, or look, or smile at me in any particular way. But there was something about the tiny wrinkle under his eye, the way the corner of his mouth would sometimes twitch upwards and the carefree way he carried himself around the place, completely unburdened by the misery he has caused. And not just for me, but also for God knows who else. How many other teenagers walking beside the road? How many women walking all alone down dark alleyways or little primary school kids who played a little too close to the schoolyard fence?

I stared blankly at the wall, scrubbing the same bowl over and over again, lost in the bleakness of my own thoughts. The soapy water felt dank and slimy between my fingers as I rubbed the tattered kitchen sponge in little circles. I could feel my sense of reality crumbling around me. Breaking down into a fine dust before blowing away in the harsh, unforgiving winds of uncertainty. Maybe I don't need to kill him. Maybe I just need to cut his dick off. Seeing that revolting appendage severed and bleeding on the ground might finally set me free. Maybe if I ground it into the dirt with the heel of my boot, squeezing out the last few drops of clotted cruor and mashing it into a pulp; maybe then it wouldn't haunt my dreams and rape my mouth while I slept.

The tin bowl bent in my hands, slipping out of my wet fingers, and snapping me back into my body. Startled, I fished around in the sink, feeling for the warped piece of thin pressed tin I had just bent in half. I jammed my thumbs into it and folded it back into shape as best I could.

There was too much on my mind. It felt like I was being buried alive under the crushing weight of my own frequent and vivid nightmares, the disturbing, violent deaths of animals, and now the man who attacked me two years ago sleeps just a few doors down the hall, forcing me to now sleep sitting upright with my eyes open, and my bed jammed against the door. It was all suffocating me. There wasn't even a coffin. Just a hole in the ground I had been thrown into, with spadefuls of dirt heaped on top of my naked body, my lungs straining to breathe as the weight of the soil bore down on my ribs.

I went back outside and gazed at the last few thin rays of fading sunlight. The vast expanse of wilderness and mountains around me all said, 'Run! You could just run away now and this whole nightmare would end!' I could. I have certainly thought about it more than once. But where would I go? What would I do? And besides, I might be able to escape him physically, but I'll still see him every night when I close my eyes and try to sleep. And in the end that's where he's done the most damage. He may have only attacked me once, but he's done that a thousand times over in my dreams. I ran my fingers through my greasy hair. Gently at first, but my anguish quickly boiled over and I began to claw at my scalp with a vicious intensity.

'Ah, there you are.' An austere, female voice came from behind me. I turned to see Mrs Spicer standing there, feet apart, with her smooth, manicured hands resting on her wide, slightly tilted hips. She looked like a stern schoolteacher, about to lay down the law on a misbehaving schoolboy.

'I'd like to have a word with you Otis. Come with me,' she said, beckoning me with a long, slender finger. The tone of her voice was authoritative, but at the same time dismissive. As if somewhere behind those eyes she knew that the affairs of little boys were small potatoes compared to the trials and tribulations of her own life. But nonetheless she was in charge and it was her job to resolve them.

I followed her as she strode back towards the Farmhouse. Watching the pendulum-like movement of her impossibly long legs as they swung back and forth beneath her ankle-length cotton skirt. A cold feeling gripped me as I realised she had probably seen me trying to break into the Forbidden Barn last night. She mounted the stairs, the hard soles of her shoes making a sharp clacking sound against the wood, overshadowing my own softer footsteps. I had never set foot on the verandah of the Farmhouse before, and a queer feeling came over me as I did. Remembering how entering the Farmhouse was expressly forbidden.

We're still technically outside, I thought to myself, in an attempt to relieve the crawling sensation under my skin. A stylish set of wicker furniture lay in a comfortable arrangement around the spacious wooden deck.

'Have a seat,' she said, sitting cross-legged on an enormous armchair and lighting a pencil-thin cigarette. She cupped her hands around the flame to protect it from the evening breeze, closing her eyes thoughtfully as she took her first few puffs.

'Now, imagine my surprise last night,' she began, shaking out the match, 'when I came out here for a breath of fresh air, only to see one of my employees strangling the livestock under the cover of darkness with his bare hands.' She looked at me the same way she had the day I arrived, with that same scrutinising gaze, staring at me as if she might be able to read my thoughts, grey smoke wafting out of her nostrils.

'I thought I would give you a chance to explain yourself,' she continued, cocking her head to one side, and pointing at me with her cigarette hand. My mind raced, groping around in the emptiness for a half-believable fake explanation I could give her. But in the end the truth seemed more believable than anything I could makeup. Or at least a half truth.

'Well, I went outside last night … you know … to relieve myself. And I saw this lamb tangled up in the fence, so I went to untangle it, and … well, its skin just started peeling off. I can't explain it. It sounds crazy, but that's really what happened,' I said, my skin growing cold and tight.

'Really?' she said, raising a suspicious eyebrow.

'Yeah, and well I couldn't just leave it like that, so I had to put it down … you know … choke it out,' I continued, my skin tightening even more. She stared at me intently with two unblinking eyes. A long ribbon of smoke cascading out of the end of her cigarette and wafting around her face in a grey spidery haze.

'Was it just the one lamb?' she finally said, stubbing out the butt of her cigarette in a stylish glass ashtray on the little table beside her.

'What do you mean?' I asked stupidly.

'Was it the only lamb with peeling skin? Or were there others? Has anyone else noticed this kind of thing happening, or been talking about it?'

'Oh, ah, no, I only saw the one,' I said, stumbling over my words.

'It's not unheard of. There's this rare medical condition that makes the skin fall off newborn animals sometimes. I don't remember what it's called, but it happened to a friend of mine in '68. Came out one morning to find two lambs skinned and writhing around on the ground in a bloody mess.' She sucked in a sharp breath through her teeth. 'You're not in trouble Otis, you did the right thing, putting it out of its misery. But next time tell someone when something like this happens. This is not the sort of thing I should have to be worrying about right now,' she said, shooting a discreet sideways glance towards the Forbidden Barn. It was quick – just a flicker of the eyes – but I saw it, and I wondered if she knew about my secret nocturnal visit last night.

'Well, it looks like we have nothing else to discuss. Unless there is something else you want to tell me?' she asked.

Now was the opportunity to tell her about Luther. To tell her about what a violent pervert he is, and that he should be immediately run off the property. I opened my mouth, then closed it again, a single thought rearing its ugly head right at that crucial moment.

What if word gets out that I jerked him off? At gunpoint or not, I couldn't face that kind of humiliation, not on top of everything else I had already suffered. If Luther's seen packing his bags and hitting the road, people are going to be asking why, and somebody's bound to find out. Mrs Spicer's not the kind of woman to take anything at face value. She'll pry the whole story out of me, one gory detail at a time. I couldn't bear to suffer that kind of indignity. Not now. Not ever.

'Nope, nothing.'

'Then we're done here. Goodnight Otis,' she said, standing up and flattening her skirt over her thighs. 'If you see this sort of thing happen to any other animals, tell Vincent,' she said, opening the front door. 'Or Casey,' she added as an afterthought, flicking her hand dismissively in the air as she disappeared into the Farmhouse, leaving me alone in the hanging silence.

It had grown quite dark now. The last slither of fading twilight stretched paper-thin over the horizon. I descended the stairs and began to walk back towards the Bunkhouse. But halfway across the compound I paused, turning my head back towards the Farmhouse, rotating my eyes sideways as far as they would go so as not to rouse suspicion. A small, pale face looked down at me from one of the second storey windows. I turned all the way around and looked up. It was Kelly, wearing a pink nightdress with her long brown hair spilling freely down her shoulders. The impressive volume of which made the rest of her body look thin and tiny by comparison. Her eyes – which were more socket than eyeball – widened as she realised I had caught her spying on me. Her lips parted in a silent gasp as she quickly disappeared out of view.

I needed to know what they were hiding inside that Forbidden Barn. Every interaction I've had with that family seemed off and suspicious.

Maybe it's because the decaying corpse of Mr Spicer is sealed inside the barn. Maybe his maggot-infested carcass was tossed onto the floor and forgotten about. Or they could be hiding a magical flying fuck machine, powered by farts for all I know, I thought to myself as I creaked open the front door of the Bunkhouse and stepped into the small kitchen. Three or four guys were still mulling around, washing dishes, and drinking cups of tea out of chipped enamel mugs. Martin sat on a rickety chair in the corner, scratching behind one of his wingnut ears with a dirty fingernail.

'What's the missus want with you then?' he asked, scrunching up his twisted nose and taking a sip from his mug.

'She was asking about a dead lamb. She figured I had something to do with it,' I replied, a sudden wave of exhaustion washing over me after my tense encounter with Mrs Spicer; my eyelids becoming heavy and drooping.

'Did you?' he asked bluntly, taking another sip from his tea.

'Yeah, I went to take a piss last night and saw it was tangled up in the fence. I tried to pull it out, but it was so cut up I ended up having to put it out of its misery,' I said in a dry, matter-of-fact tone. I didn't have the energy to explain the whole 'skin falling off' thing again.

'Uh ... and here I was thinking that was a fox's handywork. But a fox that doesn't eat what it kills?' he said, wrinkling up his nose again and shaking his head.

'You got me. I'm the fox,' I said, holding up my hands like a criminal that has just been caught by the police.

'We all thought you were getting chewed-out by Old Spice,' he said, looking down at his mug with one cocked eyebrow, swirling his tea. My eyes snapped wide open, the heavy, tired feeling dropping away and immediately being replaced with burning curiosity.

'Chewed-out by Mr Spicer?' I said, puzzled. 'I thought he never comes out of the house, and nobody ever sees him.' A lightning bolt shot up my spine and into the back of my head.

'Oh no, people still see him alright. It doesn't happen very often, but if you do something – and I mean if you royally fuck up – then he's gonna call you up to that house there and personally chew you out. And from what I understand, it's a pretty terrifying experience. Guys come out of that Farmhouse white as a ghost. And they won't tell you what he said to 'im either, or what happened.' Martin downed the rest of his tea and tossed the cup into the sink. 'You best behave yourself, boy,' he said, giving me a sly wink.

All heads whipped around as a loud crash came from the hallway. Two men tumbled into the kitchen: a blurry mass of flailing fists and savage, kicking legs. Everyone sprang to their feet, and I pressed myself against the wall, trying to stay out of the way of the fight.

'I'll fucking kill you, you fucking cunt!' one man screamed as he pounded the face of the other with his split and bloody knuckles. It was Patrick – the man Luther was elbowing in the ribs at the dinner table – and the man he was punching was none other than Luther himself.

'Get the fuck off me you crazy prick!' Luther howled, trying to shield his face with his arms.

'This! Is what! You fucking! Get!' Patrick yelled, his words punctuated by a series of savage punches, mashing his nose into a gory pulp. Two guys grabbed a hold of Patrick and yanked him off Luther, who then curled up on the floor like a burned-out cigarette.

'You crazy fuck.' He coughed out his words with a mixture of blood and spit. Seeing his caved-in nose and blood-streaked jaw brought a hint of satisfaction to my tormented mind. He staggered to his feet, long strands of blood and drool dangling from his slack, toothless mouth.

Luther lunged at Patrick, shrieking, and tackling him around the midsection. The other two guys were knocked aside, one of them landing on a wooden chair and smashing it apart, sending broken pieces of it sliding across the floor. Luther snatched up one of the busted chair legs and started laying into Patrick with it, like a cop bludgeoning a criminal with a baton.

'Stop, you fuckheads!' Martin shouted as everyone dived in to grab one of their limbs, restraining the two men and bringing the fight to an abrupt end. 'Now I don't know what you two are fighting about, but it ends now, you got that?' he said, knitting his bushy grey eyebrows together, casting a dark shadow over his wrinkled old eyes.

'This piece of shit started it!' Patrick spat, pointing at Luther.

'I don't care. If you think it's worth losing your job over, then go on ahead and keep fighting. Otherwise, I suggest you two use your words and work it out like men, and maybe that way the boss doesn't need to know about this little misunderstanding you two had tonight,' Martin said, pointing a gnarled old finger at the two men to emphasise his point. They both shrugged off the hands of their captors, glaring at each other with dark, brooding eyes. Patrick snorted hot air out of his nostrils and held out his hand.

'Not a word?' he said through his teeth, begrudgingly accepting the gravity of the situation.

'Not a word,' Luther said, hesitantly reaching out and shaking it.

'Now, let's all go to bed and forget this foolishness. We've all got a long day of work tomorrow,' Martin said. Everyone began to clear off, but I stood silently in the corner, watching Luther bent over the sink, dabbing his crumpled nose with a damp cloth.

The opportunity to make him disappear – no questions asked – had come and gone in the blink of an eye. I couldn't tell anyone about the fight now because everyone had already agreed to keep it quiet. If I said something, then everyone would know that somebody dobbed.

I walked down the hallway with everyone else. A couple of

people were poking their heads out of their rooms and asking what all the noise was about. The witnesses saying things like 'Just a friendly argument' and 'Ah, some people just don't know how to use their inside voice'. I closed my bedroom door behind me and rested my forehead against its cold, hard wood.

'This place is a fucking circus,' I whispered to myself, my words fading away unheard into the darkness. I peeled off my clothes and flopped onto my tiny bed, my jaw clenching from the stress and my eyes burning from the fatigue. I felt my body begin to melt into the mattress as I finally gave myself permission to give into the exhaustion. Watching the familiar dance of static behind my eyelids.

I wonder if this is what dying feels like, I thought to myself as I slowly slipped away into a deep, black unconsciousness.

mashed the meat of my palm into one of my aching eye-sockets as I slowly forced my other eye open. The room was dark and hollow, with a single blade of moonlight slicing through a part in the curtains. I scrunched my eyes shut, trying to force sleep back upon myself, but it was no use. I sat up in bed, my spine drooping forwards as I let the insomnia have its way with my body. I staggered to my feet and padded barefoot out of my room and down the hallway, reluctantly playing the sleepwalking game.

I felt compelled to be outside. The air inside my room was choked and stuffy, and I felt like I'd never get back to sleep unless I got at least one breath of fresh night air. The shadows were so thick it was as if they were painted on. And I smiled to myself – my eyes half closed – as I imagined a team of workmen with cans of black paint, coating every surface of the hall with big paintbrushes.

I reached the back door and threw it open. Outside an endless field of waist-high grass swayed back and forth in the ghostly light of the full moon. I curled my naked toes in the dry, powdery dirt, feeling its satisfying softness. I turned to close the door behind me, but when I looked back the entire Bunkhouse had vanished. All that was left behind was a vast expanse of grassy field that stretched out endlessly in every direction.

Where am I? I wondered as I walked aimlessly through the field. That's when I noticed the curious way the grass seemed to grow at an astonishing rate – suddenly appearing out of the bare earth and reaching the height of my waist before turning grey and withering away again, making way for the next wave of tall grass to grow back again the instant the previous one had completely composted back into the soil. An entire life cycle completed and repeated every few seconds. This made the whole landscape rhythmically pulse and ripple under the moonlight in the most bizarre way.

'Far out …' I whispered to myself as the grass engulfed my lower half again. I craned my chin upwards, examining the dark grey clouds that raced across the black sky. I could make out the faint shapes of human faces in their dense vapour. Some were blank and expressionless, others had their jaws twisted open in a silent ghastly scream.

I began to walk quickly in the direction they were headed, tracking their movement across the sky with wide, unblinking eyes. I found the vertically swaying grass more disorientating now rather than interesting, and I fell over more than once trying to keep my eyes on the sky. The clouds were now going too fast to follow, and I tripped over again as I tried to break into a run, slamming my face straight into the dirt. Grass grew up and around me as I tried to get up, consuming my entire body for a moment before I got to my feet. There was dirt caked in between my teeth and I scrubbed at it with a fingernail as I looked back up at the sky. But all the clouds had evaporated into the vast expanse of black nothingness that hung above me, leaving me once again aimless and lost. Only the moon remained, casting a dull white light that partially illuminated the shadowy landscape. I stared hard in the direction the clouds had gone, but there was nothing. Nothing except ... a fence?

It was very far away, and I had to squint to make sure I wasn't imagining it, but yes it was definitely there. A barbed wire fence stretched out in the distance, being covered and uncovered by the grass in a disorientating game of peekaboo. The fence posts stuck out of the dirt like thick, twisted fingers, with several lines of cruel, unforgiving wire stretched tightly between each one. I began to walk towards it, a sudden pang of anxiety piercing my chest. Then another, and another. Each one more sharp than the last. I suddenly became desperate to find a way out of this strange place.

As I got a little closer, I noticed a pale shape slumped against the base of the fence. It was hard to make out between the rhythmic sprouting of the grass, but it almost looked like a person. I broke into a slow run, then a sprint. My bare feet sinking into the loose soil as they padded against it, slowing me down. The mysterious slumped shape became more and more human the closer I got.

'Hello?!' I called out. 'Are you alright?!'

As I got closer, I could see it was a young girl. Her smooth, thin arms were splayed out against the fence like the crucified Jesus. A hideous mass of barbed wire wrapped tightly around each wrist, forcing her to hang limply from the fence with her knees resting on the ground. There was a metre or two of bare earth on either side of the fence where the grass didn't grow, and when I reached it I collapsed onto my hands and knees, gasping for air. I could feel thick beads of sweat rolling down my naked chest and stomach, the soles of my feet painted black by my run through the field.

Her hands hung lifelessly from their confines, her thin fingers curling slightly as she sensed my presence. The wire's wicked barbs had carved into the flesh around her wrists, letting two long, thin streams of blood run down her arms and into her deep, hairless armpits like some kind of perverse stigmata. I grabbed a hold of the thick volume of long brown hair that covered her face – so long that it almost rested in the dirt in front of her – and gently rolled her head back.

'Kelly?' I whispered in a shaky voice.

Kelly looked up at me with vacant, glazed eyes that didn't seem to see me. Her pink nightdress was filthy from the waist down, and her legs were coated in dirt and mud as if she had been dragged there. I tried to untangle one of her wrists, but I could hardly see what I was doing in the darkness and sliced open one of my fingertips on one of the tiny bloodthirsty blades.

'Fuck!' I spat, putting my shredded finger in my mouth. I grabbed a hold of one of her wrists at the base of the tangle, trying to yank it free. But to my horror, the skin underneath her hand rolled off the flesh like a blanket rolling off a bed. She threw her head back, trying to scream, but no sound came out of her mouth. Every breath I tried to take snagged in my throat; my own heartbeat pounding inside my head. I twisted her hand back and forth, trying to wrench it free from the wire. Tears pooled under her eyes and flowed down her face in two glassy streams. I felt naked and vulnerable as I knelt there in the dirt, wearing only my underpants, yanking, and pulling at the bloody pulp that was now her wrist. Her hand slipped free of its restraint, degloving her palm and fingers in the process, leaving her skin hanging inside-out – raw and bloody – from the coiled wire. The greasy flesh of her exposed nerves and sinew twitched and spasmed, the angry, bloody mess glistening in the moonlight, sickly and wet.

'Oh God ...' I moaned under my breath as her skinless hand flopped onto her muddy lap. I set about trying to untangle the other one, her skin coming apart as I yanked and twisted it. It slid free of the wire as she slumped forward, her hand turning inside-out, and her head flopping limply against my shoulder. I put my hands on either side of her ribs and tried to pull her upright, but that was a mistake. I could feel the loose, detached skin peeling off her sides and sliding around underneath her nightdress. Dark red blots began to grow and multiply as they bled through the girly pink fabric. She reached out, trying to grab a hold of me with her oozing, disfigured hands, leaving behind dark bloody handprints on my chest and arms. Her breath was quick and shallow. I scrunched up my face, trying to hold back the tears as I looked around desperately for someone to help us. But we were completely alone in the darkness. I tried to hold her up by her thin, narrow shoulders, but her delicate skin crumbled beneath my fingers. She slumped onto the muddy ground in front of me, leaving me with only two red handfuls of human flesh. I bent down over her, my hands shaking violently, my chin trembling.

'What do I do? I don't know what to do,' I sobbed. Several long sweaty strands of hair clung to her face. I hovered my trembling hand over it. I wanted to brush the hair aside, but I didn't dare touch her.

'You need to tell me how to help you,' I cried, finally brushing one of the matted locks to the side of her face – the one that was covering her eye. My fingertip ripped apart her forehead like wet tissue paper, exposing the glistening white bone underneath. She convulsed slightly, her face twisted with pain, but her eyes were still somehow glazed and vacant. Her mouth still didn't make a sound, even though it hung open in a ghastly expression of pure horror. She batted weakly at my face, as if trying to fight me off, her raw bloody fingers leaving thick gory streaks across my chin and neck.

'I don't know what to do!' I choked out, grabbing her by the neck and shaking her tiny body back and forth, her hair whipping around her face as the back of her skull thudded against the wet dirt. The skin around her throat quickly deteriorated and fell apart, exposing a slippery windpipe and the tort, rubbery muscles that lay beneath. I could feel the blood surging through her raw, tangled veins as I tightened my grip around her neck.

'I can't help you. I ... I can't ...' I squeezed my words out through my clenched teeth as large salty tears rolled out of my eyes and dripped down onto her face. I tightened my grip even more, squeezing her fragile little neck with all my strength, a long strand of drool escaping my trembling lips and pooling onto her cheek. She grabbed feebly at my wrists, helplessly trying to free herself from my savage stranglehold, but it was no use.

She looked straight through me as her slippery, skinless hands slid up my forearms, coating them in her bright red blood. I hunched over her and put the full weight of my body into throttling her. Her grip loosened, before she finally let go and let her arms fall limply to the ground.

'I can't ... I can't help you ... I can't ... I can't ...' I cried, more spit escaping my clenched teeth. Her eyes bulged from their sockets, her face turning a grotesque shade of bruised red. Blood and spit mixed together in the corners of her mouth, forming a foamy diluted pink liquid that trickled down either side of her face. With a trembling hand I tried to wipe away the horrible foam: my delicate shaky touch tearing away the skin on her cheeks.

She didn't flinch. She didn't move. She was dead.

I slowly released my grip on her crushed throat, congealed strands of blood clinging to my fingers as I pulled my hands away, growing long and thin before snapping off one by one. Her neck lay in a ghoulish twisted mess, wrenched into a horrific, almost zigzagging shape. The skin shredded off. The veins and sinew crushed and mangled. The small bones along the back of her neck pulled apart and horribly misshapen. The ground around us had become a large, shallow puddle of blood with Kelly's body laying half submerged in it. The lower half of my legs disappearing into the muddy red slosh as I knelt on top of her. I stumbled backwards, shrieking into the vast, all-consuming nothingness, until my lungs ached and my throat burned.

CHAPTER ELEVEN

My nightmares and my waking hours were beginning to run together in a seamless blur. Like the changing of one reel of film to another in a movie theatre, impossible to tell when exactly one stops and the next one begins. I could no longer remember when I went to sleep, or when exactly I woke up, if I had even woken up at all.

I stared out of my window at the sunrise that was just beginning to pierce the horizon, slowly focusing on my own reflection in the dusty glass. My eyes sat inside two grey, fleshy pockets. Two dark, hollow craters underneath the bony ridge of my perpetually furrowed brow. Two seedy bloodshot balls of deflated jelly that sat unnaturally sunken in their swollen eyelids. My face looked thin and gaunt; a combination of constant work and no sleep withering away my body. I poked at one of my dark, fatty eye bags, pulling the skin down with a long, bony finger to inspect the dull white of my eye. I pulled my finger away and looked through my reflection again, shifting my gaze towards the Farmhouse that lay just beyond my window.

Is this still a dream? I curled my fingers against the palms of my hands – feeling the grainy sensation of skin dragging across skin – and decided it probably wasn't.

I tugged on my clothes and marched outside, the icy morning air stinging my face. I got to the foot of the verandah stairs and looked up. The Farmhouse stood tall and foreboding in the morning stillness. I was almost certain that the gory spectacle I had seen last night was nothing more than just a nightmare – a product of the demented dream factory that was working overtime inside my head – but I still had to make sure. My hands clenched anxiously into two tight fists as I craned my chin upwards, trying to see past the verandah and perhaps into a window. But all the curtains were drawn, and the house was quiet. I quickly walked around the side, taking several large steps back so I could see in through the second storey windows. But they were all dark and empty.

'Damn it, doesn't anybody get up in the morning anymore?' I whispered to myself in frustration. A sharp stab of surprise shot through me as I heard a door open and close behind the house. I slowly rounded the corner. The morning sun was now bright enough to see everything clear as day.

A few large white sheets billowed in the wind; suspended from a set of long wire clothes lines that were behind the Farmhouse. A heaped basket containing more freshly washed white sheets stood at the feet of someone. She stood behind one of the sheets, only her small fingers visible above the white square that covered her. I watched as she stepped aside and bent over to pick up another sheet. Kelly looked up and gasped when she saw me watching her, shooting straight up and throwing her hands over her mouth to silence the high-pitched yelp that escaped her lips.

'Sorry, I just ... um ...' I stuttered as she looked at me with large, wary eyes. Her skin was completely intact and she was very much alive. I turned and quickly began to walk away; embarrassed that my nightmares had become so bad that they were starting to make me lose my grip on reality.

Some of the other workers had already begun to gather at the outside tables for breakfast, swilling bitter black coffee out of chipped enamel mugs. I quickly walked past them with my head down, trying not to look conspicuous. The small kitchen was alive with yawning unshaven faces and dirty undershirts. The smashed pieces of broken chair had been cleaned up and thrown away – the tiny room put right again after last night's brawl. I poured a cup of coffee and hurried back outside, planting myself in an empty seat and raking my rigid fingers through my greasy hair.

I stared down at the black liquid that rippled inside my enamel mug. I didn't want to drink it; I knew if I did, I would be in for a vicious, throbbing headache. So, I just sat there, content enough to hold it in my hands and try to look normal. I drew in a sharp, laboured breath as I looked up across the tables. The mug suddenly slipped from my fingers and fell to the ground, the coffee seeping into the dry, thirsty dirt. The world suddenly seemed to spin around me. *Am I seeing things?*

How much have I dreamed and how much has actually happened? Luther and Patrick sat together at the next table, chatting away, and laughing as if nothing had ever happened. But it had to have happened. The chair they had broken had vanished, their knuckles were bruised and split, Luther's nose was completely flattened, and they had three black eyes between the two of them – all evidence of the previous evening.

I scooped my mug off the ground and clutched it tight with both hands, telling myself there must be a reasonable explanation for all of this. I stood up and moved to the table behind them, sitting with my back to them so I could listen to what they were saying without making it look like I was eavesdropping.

'I'm telling you she doesn't care where she gets it. She'll suck your dick right there on the spot if you catch her alone. She's practically gagging for it,' Patrick said, half whispering.

'I'm not surprised, the second little girls turn what? Fourteen? Fifteen? They just become needy little sluts. I bet her tiny little pussy is just soaking wet all day long,' Luther sneered, chuckling under his breath. 'And have you seen the way she walks around here with that tight little body? She knows what she's doing. What she needs is to be held down and have that tight little arsehole of hers stretched out. That'll teach her for being such a fucking little tease.' Luther forced his words through his rotten teeth with an aggressive hiss. Clearly he had been thinking about doing exactly that since the moment he laid eyes on … *Wait, were they talking about Kelly?*

'But that's what I'm telling you, she's no tease. She always puts out for the guys around here,' Patrick continued in a sly whisper. 'Only the other night she choked down my cock behind the Hayshed. You should have seen the tears running down her pretty little face. I throat-fucked the gag reflex right out of her. Now she can deepthroat like you wouldn't believe. We're talking so deep you can almost feel the tip of your prick inside her stomach,' Patrick said. I could almost hear the depraved grin in his voice. 'But she likes to play hard to get. You've got to be bold. You've got to be aggressive. She'll pretend like she's not interested, maybe even put up a little fight, but it's all for show. If you hold her down, pull up her skirt and put two fingers in her tight little pussy, it turns her on like turning on a light switch,' Patrick said with a satisfied chuckle. 'But you can't tell anyone about this. If her folks find out it's game over for all of us. And don't talk to any of the other guys about it either, you never know when a good thing like this can be ruined by a rat.' There was a pause in their conversation, as if they were looking around to see if anyone was listening. I looked down at my empty mug, one side of it was covered in a thin layer of dirt mixed with coffee. I was incensed. I gritted my teeth and balled up my hands into two tight fists. But at the same time, I wondered why Patrick was egging Luther on like this. He was clearly lying about Kelly's promiscuity, I could feel it in my bones. It was like trying to put together the pieces of a puzzle that didn't quite fit, no matter what arrangement you put them in.

'Well, I've got half a mind to try my luck tonight,' Luther said in a greasy tone, gathering up his empty plate and mug.

'I'd think you were a fucking queer if you didn't!' Patrick called after him as he walked away, chuckling to himself as he downed the rest of his coffee. 'Let's see what they do to you after that, you fucking cunt,' Patrick spat under his breath. Suddenly it all clicked – nothing will get you fired faster than messing around with the farmer's daughter.

Holy shit, that's cold, I thought to myself as I slowly turned my head to see Patrick rising from his seat.

I felt sick. Dread twisted inside my stomach. I wanted Luther to disappear so very badly, but I didn't want Kelly to experience the same hellish torment I had to endure every day because of it.

Could I stand idly by as someone else's humanity is taken from them? Their soul taken from them? Just to get mine back? Just so the nightmares would end, and I could finally sleep again at night? Could I even do that, after this? I went to take a sip from my dirt encrusted mug, forgetting that it was empty.

CHAPTER TWELVE

Two tractors forged their way back and forth across the field in neat horizontal lines – an atonal symphony of loud grinding, chomping and crunching sounds blaring from both of them. The first one trailed a wide, flat slasher behind it, cutting down and churning up the long dead grass with ease. The second tractor followed a few rows behind, trailing a huge bailing machine that devoured the freshly cut grass, compacting it into tight little rectangles that it left behind in its wake.

'So ... Martin was telling me that people still see Mr Spicer from time to time,' I said, lifting one of the heavy hay bales onto the back of a small flatbed truck, which crawled along at a snail's pace, following the path of the tractors.

'What are you talking about?' Casey panted, also throwing a hay bale onto the back of the flatbed.

'When I first got here you said nobody ever sees him, but last night Martin was saying people still do.'

'Well yeah, but only two people have seen him though. Just a couple of guys causing so much trouble that Old Spice had to sort them out himself,' Casey said, grabbing a hold of another bale and hoisting it up with his long, sinewy arms.

'What did they do that was so terrible exactly?' I asked.

'Well shortly after Mrs Spicer took over this one guy Peter wasn't having it. He made this whole song and dance about how he wasn't going to take orders from a woman and that he demanded to see the "real boss". He even forced his way into the Farmhouse to see him. But Old Man Spicer must have really let him have it, because he came out of there barely five minutes later as quiet and compliant as a Catholic schoolboy. He even developed this weird drooling problem afterwards. And sometimes he'd just zone out and stare into space, like this.' Casey pretended to be catatonic for a moment, going glaze-eyed and letting his mouth hang open.

'Who was the other guy?' I asked getting a firm grip on another hay bale.

'His name was Miles,' Casey said, scratching his hairy chin. 'He tried to burn down the old barn one night.'

I felt my ears prick up.

'Why would he want to do that?' I quickly asked, turning my head to look over at the mysterious Forbidden Barn that loomed in the distance – padlocked and barricaded shut.

'He kept having these weird nightmares apparently, about it coming to life and trying to eat him and all sorts of crazy shit like that. One night he just went completely insane, took off his shirt, lit it on fire and ran at the barn screaming about how he had to "Burn them before they hatch!" I don't know what he was talking about, but he managed to start a pretty decent grass fire on his way over there. The guys got a hold of him before he could actually light the building on fire though. But, holy shit, that's a night I'm not gonna forget any time soon,' Casey said, also looking over at the field containing the Forbidden Barn, squinting a little as he reimagined the night in question.

'Did he also come out all fucked up?' I asked.

'Of the fire?' Casey said, returning his gaze to me.

'No, after seeing Mr Spicer.'

'Yeah, he was pretty rattled but I reckon it was more from his mental breakdown than anything else. He got really quiet after that too, didn't say a word until he got killed in a tractor accident about a week later. Honestly, I'm not sure why they didn't just fire him. Poor bastard probably needed to be in a mental institution,' he said, drawing in a sharp breath at this last thought before scooping up another hay bale. I slowly turned my eyes back towards the Forbidden Barn. It stood there with an insidious aura. As if it were somehow alive and staring at me.

'So, what happened to Peter?' I asked.

'He just moved on one day. It happens. Guys come and go all the time in this line of work. Most of the guys here are just part-time drifters, looking to work long enough to get some cash together before moving on somewhere else. Sometimes people just disappear without saying anything at all. You go to check their room one morning when nobody can find them, and all their stuff is gone. They just up and leave without telling anyone,' he said, wiping a line of sweat off his forehead with the back of his hand.

'What do you think is in there?' I asked, pointing my chin towards the barn.

'In the old barn? I don't know, probably just some personal things they don't want us workers getting our greasy mitts on. I knew a guy once, he had a great big shed just like that one, stacked all the way to the top with old furniture. All sorts of wardrobes and leather couches and antique tables, all packed in so tightly you couldn't even step in through the front door.' I looked at him for a moment while I thought about it. He was the level-headed friend that had singlehandedly kept me from going completely insane since I had arrived at this place. I wanted to tell him that. I wanted to tell him about my nightmares, to express to him the true depth of my anguish and hope that he might tell me that everything was going to be okay. But I couldn't bring myself to be that vulnerable. Not to him, not to anyone, not now. But right here in this space and time he meant everything to me. He was the only good thing in a world where all I had was my suffering.

'I never would have thought of that,' I said, scrunching up my face, wondering what my dad would have to say about all these girly feelings sloshing around inside my head. 'Does Kelly hang around much? I mean, around the workers?' I asked, gritting my teeth over what the answer might be.

'Why do you ask?' Casey said, cocking a blonde eyebrow.

'No reason, just interested in the comings and goings of everyone on the farm,' I replied, which wasn't a complete lie.

'You'll see her walking around a bit and poking through

the buildings in her spare time, but Mrs Spicer doesn't like her getting too friendly with the workmen. I don't blame her. There's some real rough lids around here,' he said through his teeth as he looked around at all the other guys working in the field. I squinted over at the far side of the field where Luther was driving the slasher tractor; a big toothless grin on his face, probably in the middle of some kind of perverse, paedophilic daydream.

'Yeah … there is,' I said, a terrible feeling crawling up the back of my spine.

*   *   *

I dropped the last hay bale in place at the top of the stack. The Hay Shed was now filled to the top with a neat stack of rectangular bales that held together like the giant bricks in a fortress wall. The afternoon sun hung low in the sky, casting a golden sideways light that stretched across the whole landscape. The darkened mountains in the distance were eclipsed by a vibrant orange haze that seemed to almost crash over them like a tidal wave of light. The vast expanse of empty fields that encircled us swayed rhythmically in the light breeze that rolled across them, and a faint rustling sound could be heard from the trees that border the property: a black forest with dark shadows and a glowing golden canopy.

The Hay Shed had no walls, just a corrugated iron roof suspended atop several iron supports that stood about two storeys tall. I was the only one young and nimble enough to climb up the sheer vertical sides to get to the top, and still be able to make it back down again. I stood on top of the pile as the other guys tossed, pushed, and hoisted the bales up to me, making the enormous cube of hay grow taller and taller until I had to stoop over so my head wouldn't hit the corrugated iron ceiling. With the job done and the daylight beginning to quickly fade away, everyone was knocking off and heading back to the Bunkhouse to get some dinner.

'Are you good to get down Otis?' Casey called up to me.

'Yeah, I'll be fine, you guys go ahead! I'm gonna sit up here for a few more minutes and enjoy the view,' I called back. The golden rays of evening sunshine transformed everything it touched, and for the first time in a long time, I felt somewhat peaceful. Something about the indescribable beauty of it all made me feel as though everything was going to be okay.

'Okay, well just scream like a maniac if you get stuck up there!' Casey laughed, turning to follow the others back to the compound. I lay on my back, the view of an otherwise lovely sky obscured by the ceiling. But I didn't care, I loved the feeling of how high up off the ground I was. The stacked hay bales becoming an unexpected oasis from a nightmarish and unpredictable world.

'Well, look who's late to the party.' An annoyed voice crept up the side of the stack and into my ear.

'Well shit, I had trouble getting that piece of shit slasher off the back of the tractor. Fucking thing nearly cut my hand off!' Luther's voice hissed.

'Well, looks like you conveniently missed out on all the hard work.' The other voice grumbled.

'Why don't you go pull that stick out of your arse. I was just doing my job. I was gonna stay here for a while anyway to make sure you clowns did it right. Knowing you lot, this whole thing will probably fall down by tomorrow morning, and we'll have to stack it all over again,' Luther shot back.

'Whatever,' The other voice said, growing distant as he walked away. I flattened myself hard up against the hay. I couldn't move. The realisation that I was now left completely alone with Luther made my body freeze in place. The muscles in my limbs were so rigid I thought their fibres might snap under the tension. I curled my fingers into the hard straw bed I was lying on, white-knuckling two fistfuls of the stuff as I stared with wide, desperate eyes up at the darkened ceiling. A terrible silence hung in the air for a moment, before it was finally broken.

'I thought I might find you sneaking around out here. Come to climb on the haystack have we?' His creepy voice slithered through the air. My jaw clamped shut; but he wasn't talking to me.

'I'm allowed to. My mum said I can when there's no one working here.' A timid, girlish voice replied.

Oh god it's happening, it's actually happening! A terrible, helpless feeling swirled like poison in the pit of my guts.

'Only naughty little girls tell lies like that. Are you a naughty little girl?'

'I think someone's calling ...' she said quickly. I could hear her turning away.

'Where're you goin'? I thought you came here for a roll in the hay?' His voice darkening into a predatory growl.

'Ow, let go of me you fucking arsehole!' Kelly shrieked. I heard the dull thud of a struggle, followed by a muffled scream for help, certainly not loud enough for anyone except me to hear. My jaw tightened even more. I forced one shaking hand into the front pocket of my denim overalls; grasping the small knife I was using to cut baling twine. It was an old steak knife with the pointy tip snapped off, but the remaining blade had been made razor-sharp with a whetstone. With every inch of my body trembling, I dragged myself flatly across the surface of the hay and peered over the edge.

He had one hand clasped firmly over her mouth, holding her tiny body against his. She was trying as hard as she could to kick and punch him, but her small fists seemed to have no effect. His eyes gleamed in the failing light with a horrible glassy reflectiveness. He licked the fingers of his other hand with a perverse zeal; his long grainy tongue sliding flatly over the length of his palm and fingers like wet sandpaper.

'Please, don't!' I think I could hear her trying to say, her voice muffled by his hand which was still clamped tightly over the lower half of her face, the stump of his missing thumb resting just below her nose.

'Ho oh, playing hard to get are we?' He sneered. 'You wanna walk around here showing off that tight little body do you? I know what you really want you little fucking tease!' He spat through his handful of rotten yellow teeth as he forced his spit glazed fingers down between her thighs. She grabbed a hold of his wrist with both hands, desperately trying to pull his hand away as she continued to try to scream for help, tears streaming down either side of her face. But it was no use, he was going to get what he wanted.

Adrenaline welled up inside me and coursed through my veins. I shrieked the shriek of an unhinged, homicidal maniac as I slid down the side of the haystack, knife in hand, an avalanche of loose straw trailing behind me as I hit the ground. He looked up right as my booted foot made contact with the side of his head. He slammed to the ground like a sack full of shit. Kelly scrambled to her feet and ran for her life.

'Ah! What the fuck?!' Luther screamed, staggering to his feet, still holding the side of his head with his eyes scrunched shut. I screamed my lunatic war cry again and plunged the blade of the knife strait into the crotch of his pants. It made a sickening *pop* sound as it tore through the denim and berried itself deep beneath his skin. He howled with pain, his eyeballs popping out of his head, and thick strands of foamy drool oozing out of the corners of his trembling lips. Blood drizzled down the front of his pants like red piss. He grabbed a hold of my wrist with both hands, pulling the knife out of his bleeding genitals. He tried to wrestle it off me, but he was no match for my crazy adrenaline-fuelled strength. I kneed the butt of the knife and drove it straight back into his dick, slicing open that revolting worm and letting its insides spill out. Something small and rubbery slid down his trouser leg and rolled onto the ground next to his foot. He stared down in utter horror and disbelief at his own severed testicle, laying glistening and red in the dirt. I threw him against the haystack, kneeing him repeatedly in his mangled groin, feeling his shrivelled organs ooze and fall apart as I inflicted my savage violence upon them. His scream was so shrill and loud that it could have woken God himself up in Heaven. But it was too late for that now, God had been asleep for too long; forcing me to take matters into my own hands. He crumbled to the ground, slumped against the wall of hay, cupping his bleeding wounds with one trembling hand while trying to shield his head with the other, begging for mercy in words so slurred it was practically gibberish.

'This is what you fucking get!' I screamed, grinding his disembodied testicle into the dusty ground with the heel of my boot. I was in such a bloodthirsty frenzy that I hadn't noticed the small crowd of men in their undershirts gathering around us. A meaty hand clapped me on the shoulder and spun me around, and a fist the size of my head punched me right in the face. I dropped to my knees, the knife slipping out of my fingers, ears ringing, people frantically running around me in slow motion. Vincent yanked me up by the collar, my nose haemorrhaging blood, streaming down my mouth and chin. He held up his enormous fist and punched me again; this time sending me backwards into a deep, black unconsciousness.

CHAPTER THIRTEEN

The morning sunlight pierced my eyelids, coming through as a red blur. A lightning bolt of pain shot through my head as I tried to sit up, forcing me to flop back down again as my whole body screamed in agony. I curled my toes inside my shoes. I was still fully clothed, just crumpled up and dumped onto the bed. Tossed aside like a used-up tissue from the night before. I gently probed at my swollen eyes with the tip of my finger, the pain in my fustigated nose telling me that what happened last night definitely wasn't a dream. I could feel the caked-on blood clinging to my face, making the skin around my mouth and nostrils hard and tight. As I stretched my jaw, I noticed that someone was kind enough to stuff a fistful of toilet paper up my nose so I wouldn't bleed to death in the night. I picked at one of the exposed ends, pulling out a matted mess of blood-soaked tissue paper. I blew my nose straight into my cupped hands, excreting a gooey mixture of clotted blood and thick yellow snot.

'Oh god ...' I groaned, wiping the goo onto the sheets. I

rolled off the bed and crawled onto the floor on all fours like an animal, my forehead hanging low and pressed against the floorboards for extra support. I spat another glob of thick bloody mucus onto the floor before forcing my eyes open and staggering to my feet, knocking over the little bedside table in the process. A small piece of paper slid off the table and wafted to the floor beside my knee. It read, *When you wake up come and see me. Mrs S.*

I scrunched my eyes shut, squeezing the rotten canker behind my eyelids before opening them again. The small Bunkhouse kitchen was completely deserted. It was already late morning, and everyone was probably already up and hard at work somewhere outside. I eyed off the small pool of dry blood on top of the kitchen table and wondered if it was from me or someone else. I slowly raised a hand to my mangled face and ran a finger over the tight mask of crusty dry blood that coated my mouth, nose and jaw. I turned on the sink tap and dabbed at my nose with my damp fingers: tender but not broken. I wondered what kind of trouble I might be in. *Did they call the police? Surely, it's a crime to carve up another man's genitals. Did I kill him? Did he bleed to death after I cut his dick off? I've heard that's what usually happens when somebody gets their dick cut off. They just bleed to death on the spot.* I thought about making a run for it. *Just disappear like all the other drifters. Become a wanted fugitive, hopping from place to place, avoiding the law. Did Kelly say anything in my defence? I did save her after all.* The kitchen door swung open and slammed against the wall.

'There you are. I thought you'd be awake by now.' A bass

voice came from the doorway. I jumped, shooting my hand out and turning off the tap. Vincent stood there, tall and imposing in the harsh morning sunlight. He looked at me as if I were some kind of dangerous animal, the tightness in his muscular forearms telling me that he was ready for violence, if it came to that.

'Mrs Spicer wants to see you.' All thoughts of making a run for it suddenly fluttered out of my head, like a flock of birds escaping from a cage.

'Right now?' I stammered. He nodded, the sunlight pouring in from behind him deepening the long, sunken scar on his face. I awkwardly squeezed past him as he remained in the doorway, giving me very little room to get out as he looked down at me and grimaced. I walked quickly towards the Farmhouse. I could still feel his eyes looking at me. His hard, steely gaze boring into the back of my skull with an almost inhuman intensity.

Oh God, I am so fucked. The cold air ate through my skin as I mounted the verandah stairs, my insides twisting into a panicky knotted mess. The front door of the Farmhouse was closed and silent; concealing whatever surreptitious oddities the Spicer family didn't want the outside world to know about.

I knocked on the door, the sound echoing through the silent house as if it were a vast, empty cave. Then I heard the unmistakable *clack clack* of high-heeled shoes on a hardwood floor. I watched as the brass doorknob twisted and the large heavy door slowly swung open.

'Ah, hello Otis,' Mrs Spicer said, her face looking thin and hollow. Her eyes were like two dark pits. She was probably exhausted from all the commotion the night before.

Did I see her amongst the small crowd that had gathered around the Hay Shed? She wore a thick green turtleneck sweater that came up to the bottom of her chin, hugged the swell of her breasts and dangled loosely around her stomach.

'Have a seat,' she said, closing the door behind her and joining me on the verandah. 'First of all, Kelly told me what happened, and I just want to thank you for doing what you did,' she said, lowering herself down onto one of the large wicker armchairs. I let out a slow, shaky breath, not realising that I had been holding it since she opened the door.

'She did?' I said, slowly sitting down on one of the other armchairs.

'That piece of shit tried to have his way with my little girl,' she hissed, violently tapping the bottom of a pack of cigarettes until one popped out. She torched the end of it with a match and looked up at me with a sly look in her eyes.

'Just between you and me, I thought you might like to know that he lost his other testicle while I was sewing up his knife wounds.' She dragged hard on her cancer stick. The little orange flame blazing as the air rushed through it. 'It was just hanging on by a thread, it seemed easier to just cut it off with a pair of scissors rather than try and push it back in,' she said, smirking as she blew two grey tusks of smoke out of her nostrils.

'Makes sense to me,' I said, chuckling nervously as I dug my fingers into the armrests of the chair. 'Did anybody call the police?' I asked anxiously. Mrs Spicer sat back in her chair, her legs crossed, and her arms folded lightly over her stomach, curling her body into a loose ball of folded limbs. The cigarette dangling loosely between two of her pale slender fingers. Then her eyes cooled, turning cold and calculating.

'Look, the last thing we want around here is the authorities poking around and disrupting our productivity. If the cops come in, then they'll want to talk to everyone who was there, which was *everyone*. The next thing you know they find out that one of our farmhands has a warrant out on him for something or other. Then they find out that five or six of our guys are draft dodgers they've been looking for since '69 and they snatch them up too. And before you know it I've lost half my workforce. So no, no one called the police. We are perfectly capable of handling anything that happens on this property ourselves. I came down to the Bunkhouse and sewed up Luther's wounds myself, right there on the kitchen table. Not that he deserved my help, but we don't want anybody dying here now do we? Then I dragged him back here to the house so my husband could fire that gutter rat himself. You should have seen him sitting there, holding his bleeding, empty sack with both hands. He pissed himself too when my husband really started tearing into him. I hope it stung when the piss got into his knife wounds,' she scowled, taking another long drag on her cigarette before crushing it out in the glass ashtray. 'Besides, if we did call the cops then you'd be going to jail for attempted murder, and that's not what we want now is it?' Little puffs of smoke wafted out of her mouth as she spoke.

I shook my head. Words failed me.

Why is she protecting me?

Because you're a goddamn hero, that's why! a voice inside my head answered. 'Because you're a hero,' she said, looking at me intently with unblinking eyes, as if she had read my mind. 'You're *my* hero. You're *Kelly*'s hero,' she said, pointing up towards the second floor of the house. 'You should be proud that you castrated that piece of shit. I'm only sorry you didn't cut his dick off as well.'

I caught her stealing a quick glance at my crotch as she spoke. Or maybe she was looking at the huge patch of Luther's dry blood that was still streaked across my knee and thigh.

'And don't worry about him going to the cops either. He knows if you go down for the stabbing then he goes down for child rape. I don't think we'll be seeing him again,' she said.

'So, he's gone for good?' I asked, leaning forward in suspense. I felt as though a huge weight had been lifted off my chest, and I could breathe deeply again for the first time in God knows how long.

'Yep, we turned him out last night. He told us Patrick put him up to it but that doesn't change a thing,' she said, fishing out another cigarette. There was only one left in the box and she used her long, manicured nails to delicately tweeze it out of its cardboard prison.

'Did he get fired too?' I asked, deciding I should gleam as much information as I could before I was cut loose.

'Who? Patrick? Oh no. What he did was slimy without a doubt, but at this rate we can't afford to lose any more workers, especially not one as good as him. But that's not to say he didn't escape unscathed. My husband called him into his office as well and really put the fear of God into him.' She cupped her hands over the quivering end of her cigarette and torched it with a match.

'S ... so he's still here?' I asked. She looked at me like I was stupid.

'Yeah,' she said bluntly, shaking out the match, the cigarette dangling loosely between her lips. I suddenly had the burning desire to see Patrick for myself; to see if the stupefying effects of Mr Spicer's wrath was really everything they said it was. That burning desire quelled into that distinctive little itch inside the back of my head as I fought the urge to excuse myself.

'I need everyone I can get, since Casey, Mark and Quinton all decided to quit at the same time,' she said flatly. My eyes shot up to meet her gaze.

'Casey's leaving?' I said, unable to hide my hurt surprise.

'Yeah, he's been umming and ahhing about it for a while now. I guess last night's fiasco was the kick in the pants he was waiting for,' she said, looking down thoughtfully at the smouldering end of her cigarette, the smoke wafting around her face in a spidery grey haze.

'Well, I better let you get on with your day. Business as usual.' She dismissed me with a wave of her hand as she slowly rose from her chair. My ears seemed to be ringing. The pillars of the verandah, the furniture, the exterior wall of the Farmhouse all seemed to be growing distant as the news of Casey's leaving began to sink in. I got to my feet and shook her hand, not fully aware of where I was anymore. I slothed down the stairs and shuffled into the middle of the compound. The buildings seemed to slowly swirl around me as I wondered where exactly I was supposed to be right now. The inescapable feeling of isolation was intensified by the fact that I couldn't see another human being in any direction, the Farm was as dead as a ghost town. I became lightheaded and began to question whether or not *this* was also just another dream.

'There he is!' A voice jeered from somewhere. A bunch of men were returning to the Bunkhouse for their lunch. Some of them walking past me with indifference, others looking me up and down with a wary eye as they gave me a wide berth. Two or three of them came right up and punched me on the shoulder saying things like, 'Good on ya Otis,' and 'That creep had it coming.' Casey trailed towards the back of the pack.

'How'd you pull up?' he asked, with a look of good-natured concern on his face.

'Yeah, I'm fine. My nose isn't broken,' I said, poking at it with the tip of my finger to demonstrate its unbrokenness.

'I was the one that stuffed all those tissues up your nose.' He grinned, wiggling his finger in a manner suggestive of a nose stuffing.

'I hear you're leaving,' I said as we began to walk back towards the Bunkhouse.

'Yeah, well, I've been thinking about moving on for a while now. I got offered a job on my cousin's sheep and horse station in Bulleto, so I reckoned I'd take it, get some new scenery,' he said, sliding his long hands into his back pockets and kicking up the dust as he walked.

'It doesn't have anything to do with … with last night, does it?' I asked, my words getting caught in my throat as I tried to swallow my swelling emotions.

'What? No, no of course not,' he said like an adult trying to reassure a small child. 'I've seen a lot of crazy shit, okay. I was in Vietnam. It takes a lot more than an unhinged backwoods knife fight to scare me off. I'm just leaving because I'm leaving, and that's all there is to it.' He paused for a moment, as if thinking carefully about what he was going to say next. 'What you did last night took a lot of guts and if you're gonna make it in this world you're gonna need guts. I'm only sorry it had to come to that. That I couldn't do anything to help until it was too late.' This was a side of him I had never seen before. Behind this fun, goofy façade was a very serious man, hardened by the unexpected and horrifying things he had seen in his short life. And after weeks of telling me to keep my chin up and to consider that things might not be as bad as they seem, he had left me with this final thought: *Be on your guard and keep a weather eye. Because real monsters wear human skin and hide in plain sight. And you never know when one might rear its ugly head. Because when it does you need to be ready for it.*

At least I think that's what he was saying. Perhaps I'm overthinking it.

CHAPTER FOURTEEN

’s been two weeks since Casey left but it feels like a lot longer than that; my diluted sense of time slowly eroding the memory of his kind face. Every night I am plagued by nightmares and strange dreams, and every morning I explode awake, dripping with sweat and anguish. Every day I am met with the sight of Patrick drooling into his morning coffee. His previously bronzed skin had become a pale, bloodless white as if he were deathly ill. He hardly breathed a word to anyone. And if he did, it was only in short, barely intelligible sentences. But despite all this, he still somehow managed to perform his farm work with effortless efficiency. All the while gazing off into the middle distance, watching invisible objects float through the air with his now permanently vacant, washed-out stare.

I wanted to know what happened to him. I wanted to know who, or what, or where Mr Spicer really was. And I wanted to know what they were keeping locked up in that fucking barn. So many things just didn’t seem to make sense, and for some reason I was the only one who was noticing it. For everyone else it was just business as usual. How could these people not see that something was terribly, terribly wrong? There were too many questions, too many holes; and therein were planted the seeds of isolation and detachment that had grown like weeds between the growing cracks in my mind. My sense of reality and continuity slowly fading away into the background. I felt more and more like a stranger inside my own body. As if the Farm and all the people who lived there were all nothing more than figments of my own deluded imagination.

'Holy shit!' Martin yelled. I whipped around to see what was going on. I had been assigned to be his assistant while he tried to fix the faulty power take-off on one of the tractors. This had led the old man down a rabbit hole of trying to fix a thousand little problems all at once, taking me along for the ride. A small part of the engine had burst into flames, spraying a jet of hot orange sparks strait down onto the dirt floor of the machinery shed. He had the engine running and the spinning drive shaft was slowly eating through a bundle of thick wires that were resting haphazardly on top of it.

'Turn it off! Turn it off!' he shouted, struggling to get to his feet after being down on his elderly knees. I leaped up the side of the huge tractor tire and turned off the key. Martin sprayed the fire with a dusty old fire extinguisher and peered through the open hatch on the side of the tractor.

'Ah, shit...' he grumbled. 'Go get me some electrical tape,' he ordered, not looking up from the smouldering engine, pointing in the general direction of the workbench. I went through several small drawers in differing states of disorganisation until I found it. He fished around inside the tractor for the damaged wires, pulling them up to examine them. The friction had peeled off part of their rubber casings, exposing their shiny metallic insides. He taped them up with his wrinkled old hands, shaking with the kind of quivering tremor that only very old men seem to have when they try to do fine work.

'There, that's better,' he grumbled, scratching his chin with a set of oily black fingernails. He had started to grow a short, bristly beard since Casey left. It was only two weeks old, but it was as white as a ghost.

'Try it again,' he ordered, closing the hatch. I climbed into the driver's seat and turned the key. The engine roared back to life. No sparks, no flames.

'Alright, well it looks like we fixed the PTO at least,' he said, scratching the back of his head thoughtfully as he walked around the back of the tractor to inspect it.

Finally, I thought to myself as I scrunched my tired, swollen eyes shut, letting them rest for a moment in the cool, refreshing darkness behind my eyelids. I could hear a strange sound: a sort of dull buzzing sound. When I opened my eyes I found myself standing outside next to the Hay Shed, with the golden evening sunlight stretching out across the fields.

'Oh God, not again...' I moaned under my breath, pressing my palms into my sunken eye sockets. I started having these little microsleeps shortly after Casey left. I would just rest my eyes for a moment, but when I open them again I'd find myself somewhere else, with no idea how I got there. I was guessing that I was so exhausted all the time that I would just randomly fall asleep on the spot. And even more disturbing than that, I must have started sleepwalking, because I almost always woke up somewhere else. But it was the jarring, instant jump forward in time that scared me the most. It was like blinking. I would blink and loose a few minutes. Blink, and suddenly be somewhere else.

The rank smell of rotting blood filled my nostrils as I looked down at the dry brown splat streaked across the ground and up the side of the haystack.

Up to about crotch height, I noted to myself. A swarm of bloated black flies – slow and sluggish from the cooling weather – buzzed loudly as they investigated the crusty mess, clustering on top of a small walnut-shaped object that lay in the dirt. I didn't have to shoo away the flies to know what it was. The fetid odour of decomposing flesh was enough.

I turned my eyes back towards the golden sunset that dominated the evening sky. But its majestic calming stillness had no effect on me this time. I just stared at it, emotionless and catatonic.

I wanted to believe so badly that Luther was the reason I felt like this. That he was the reason I was being plagued by constant and debilitating nightmares. And if I could just find a way to get my justice, perhaps then I could return to that quiet state of mind I was fast forgetting. But even though I had destroyed him, that I had taken back my power, and he no longer lived inside my head and haunted my dreams, now that I had literally castrated the man, nothing had changed. I still had nightmares, granted they are no longer about him, but they are still nightmares none-the-less. I still exploded awake in the dead of night, clutching the sheets, and searching the darkness with wide, frightened eyes. Only now it wasn't him I was looking for. I could sense the presence of something else lurking in the deep black shadows in every corner of my bedroom. Something less than human. It was as if he were just a distraction, and I had been so preoccupied by my fear and hatred of him that I hadn't noticed something else – maybe even *someone* else – making a home for itself in the dark space just behind my eyelids. Eating and digesting tiny parts of my mind, like a worm burrowing into the soft flesh of a rotten apple.

'Hi ...' A quiet voice came from above me.

I looked up and saw Kelly's head popping out from the top of the haystack, her small fingers curled around the edge of the hay.

'Hello,' I managed to say, mentally slapping myself in the face to bring myself back to the moment.

'Do you want to come up?' she said in a hushed voice. I drew in a sharp breath, sucking the air in through my teeth before letting out a slow, drawn-out sigh.

'Sure,' I said. I dug my fingers into the side of the hay and began to climb up. I was almost at the top when she dangled a skinny arm over the edge, helping me to the summit. She pulled me on top of her body, her thin pointy bones digging into my hips and ribs as I shifted awkwardly to the side. We lay on our backs next to each other and stared blankly at the corrugated iron ceiling.

'Come back to the scene of the crime?' she said sardonically.

'Looks that way,' I said, still staring at the corrugated iron ceiling.

'I just … I just want to thank you … you know … for stopping him,' she said, propping herself up on her elbow. Her cold suspicious eyes had become warm and genuine and filled with shy gratitude. Large brown eyes with little flecks of green around the pupil.

'I had my own motives as well,' I said.

'What motives? What did he do to you?' she asked, furrowing her brow slightly.

Clearly it hadn't occurred to her that he might have been hungry for something other than fifteen-year-old girls now and then. Or maybe he was just an opportunist, taking what he could get, like a starving hyena. I shook this thought out of my head and drew in a deep breath.

'I've never told anyone this before … b … but … but he tried to rape me too,' I said with a shudder, that first "but" getting caught in my throat.

'What did you do?' she asked, her eyes looked wet and shiny in the twilight.

'I bit his thumb off.' I grinned with bittersweet satisfaction. 'I was a lot younger, he had a gun, it's a whole story I don't want to tell,' I said, rubbing my face with both hands, my slight smile fading away.

'I would have bit his dick off as well,' she grunted as she laid back down.

'I wasn't planning on letting him get that far.' I grinned

again, little tears pooling in the corners of my eyes. 'I should have killed him. I really should have killed him when I had the chance, but I didn't, I just ran away. And every day … for weeks after it had happened … I returned to that exact spot… with my dad's gun and a hunting knife the size of a fucking machete, ready to murder that fucker. Ready to finish him off. But he was gone. All that was left behind was a pile of broken glass covered in dry blood, and a pair of tyre tracks that led back to the highway. And I would stand there … every day … and think about how he was out there somewhere, still alive, still picking up teenagers by the side of the road… still…' I felt a single trembling tear roll down either side of my face as I looked up at the darkened ceiling. There was a long silence. I could almost hear her mind grinding away, trying to think of something to say as my face grew cold and emotionless again.

'Do you ever have nightmares about what happened?' I asked, finally breaking the silence.

'Every night,' she said quietly, folding her hands protectively over her crotch. 'I dream that I'm in a dark place with no clothes on and I can't see anything. Strange hands are touching me and trying to put their fingers inside me. I can't see who it is, but I know that they're *his* hands.' She folded her arms tightly over her slight frame. A subconscious attempt to cover as much of her body as possible; trying to physically protect herself from a monster that now lived inside her head, possibly forever.

We both stared silently into space. I turned onto my side and looked over at the compound. Men at their tables having dinner. Buildings cast long yawning shadows in the curious angle of the gloaming light. And beyond it all, past the Shearing Shed, past the Farmhouse and the Bunkhouse, over a fence and through a field, I could see the Forbidden Barn. Standing silently. Watching. Waiting. A hulking black silhouette with a thousand wet, seedy little eyes tightly clustered together all over its dark, shadowy surface. Invisible eyes that stared back at me with a cold, calculating malice. I quickly turned and looked back up at the ceiling.

'Do you know what's in that old barn?' I asked.

'I ... I don't know, I'm not allowed near it,' she said widening her eyes a little. She was not expecting this line of questioning, but at the same time I could hear it in her voice that she was relieved that someone else had noticed that something was amiss. She rolled onto her stomach and propped herself up on her elbows so she could see the barn too.

'I noticed your mum going in there one night. She looked really sick. She was clutching her stomach like she was going to throw up,' I said. I knew I had to tread carefully otherwise I might scare her off.

'Daddy gets her pregnant a lot, that's why she looks so sick half the time.' She rolled onto her back again, folding her arms tightly around her midsection. 'It looks like it hurts; having a baby inside you,' she said quietly, looking down at her stomach. The pieces began to come together in my head then fell apart again.

'But she only looks sick for a couple of days at a time. Aren't you supposed to be pregnant for months before you have a baby?' I said, trying – and failing – to hide the confusion in my voice.

'No, you idiot. It only takes a week or two before a baby is born. Where the hell did you get *months* from?' she said, also confused.

'But … what...? Wait... where do the babies go? What happens to them after they're born?' I demanded, flummoxed by what she was telling me; that hot little itch digging its way deeper into the back of my head with every second that passed.

'I've got to go,' she said suddenly, a nervous tremor in her voice.

'No wait I ... I didn't mean to...' I stumbled over my words as she quickly slid over the edge of the haystack and disappeared. I slumped back down onto the hay.

'Ah shit ...' I whispered under my breath.

CHAPTER FIFTEEN

lay in the dark, my body slowly melting into the mattress as I drifted in and out of consciousness. My eyes open, staring up at the black nothingness that hung all around me. My tiny room had become a sensory deprivation tank; a place for my mind to play tricks on me and to see things that weren't really there. All I wanted was for my racing mind to just turn off; to fall asleep like the rest of my body. To be swallowed up by that all-consuming black unconsciousness that I used to take for granted.

I closed my aching eyelids, then opened them again. I slowly curled my fingers around the sheets, gathering up two loose handfuls of soft bedding. I sat up in bed and scratched the top of my head with both hands, the sharp sensation of my fingernails scraping along my scalp waking me up just a little bit more. It was also reassuring in a way. Letting me know exactly where my body ended and the outside world began. I struggled up and slipped on my clothes in the dark – an action that had become second nature to me – and made my way outside.

Black clouds blotted out the moon and stars, casting an opaque darkness that seemed to stretch across the entire world. The cold night air cocooned my body as it blew around me; eating through my clothes and scraping its icy teeth across my skin. I looked across the way, widening my eyes until they were two perfectly round disks, peering into the vast black nothingness. I knew it was there, somewhere in the darkness, silent and waiting. A gust of wind slammed against my face, my greasy hair thrashed wildly around my eyes. The clouds parted and a single white beam of moonlight cascaded down from the sky like a stage light, shining directly onto the Forbidden Barn. It looked like a pale grey capsule, bathed in silver light; a spaceship drifting through the inconceivably vast, empty void of space; suspended in a vacuum. Silent and alone.

Something snapped inside me, maybe it was the sudden light or maybe it was the insatiable itch of curiosity, but whatever it was something broke and gave way. I began to walk towards the barn, breathing in slow, deep breaths. I broke into a brisk jog, then a half-crazed run, bounding over the fence, and tearing my way through the grass. Long strands of drool seeped out of the corners of my mouth and drizzled down my chin as I ran. Tears streamed from my eyes as the rushing wind stung and dried them out. I thought about Miles, running towards the barn, flaming shirt in hand, screaming the unhinged war cry of a man who had completely lost his mind. Lost his mind because of whatever insidious thing that lay just beyond those rotting grey weatherboards.

I slammed against the exterior wall of the barn, arresting

the momentum of my run with a sudden thud. I went to the padlocked door and threw myself against it, hammering it with my fists, kicking at it as hard as I could, but the door wouldn't budge. I felt my manic energy begin to wane as I rested my sweaty forehead against the little wooden door, gasping for air. I scrunched my swollen, burning eyes shut for a moment, trying to get a hold of myself. Then a single thought wafted calmly through my head, *What are you doing? What are you actually trying to achieve here?* But it was quickly drowned out by the answer that followed. *I'm trying to find out what the fuck they're hiding in this fucking barn!* My eyes flew open, and I found myself standing in front of the massive double doors that were barricaded shut – another microsleep. A small hatch above the doors caught my eye. It was no bigger than a manhole but it was open and uncovered: a tiny rectangular portal into whatever secret world that lay within. I grasped the horizontal wooden planks that were screwed tightly across the doors, using them like a ladder, and began to climb, slowly, carefully, feeling the strength of each plank of wood as I put my weight onto it. I got to the hatch and climbed inside. It opened up onto a small loft, holding several ancient bales of rotting hay, which had mostly composted down into slumping black blocks of dirt. I pushed past them, making my way over to the railing.

The first thing that struck me was a strange acidic sourness in the air. The kind of smell that creeps down your nostrils and stings the back of your throat. I peered over the edge of the loft, a galaxy of tiny pinpricks of moonlight blanketing the interior of the barn; shining through thousands of holes in the roof where old nails used to be. And one large square of pale white light shone through the tiny loft hatch onto the floor. I looked down at the dusty bones of this barn that had been tormenting my mind since the day I had arrived on the farm, only to feel my excitement diminish when I saw that it was mostly empty.

I carefully scanned the darkness. Empty, except for a strange cylindrical shape that lay in the centre of the room. My heart leaped in my chest as I squinted harder at the object. The shape was much larger than a car and covered with an old weather-beaten canvas tarp. I walked down the steep loft stairs – more like a ladder than a flight of stairs – carefully placing one foot in front of the other. Then I stepped in something wet. The sudden squelching noise made my blood freeze in my veins. Tightly gripping the banister, I looked down to see a thick, gelatinous mass, clinging to the side of the stairs. It was made of a tarry black substance that glistened in the dim moonlight; a cocoon of sorts, big enough to conceal a large dog or perhaps a small child. I felt my mouth drop open. Thick ropes of black ooze attached the mass to the floor and banister like the many thin threads of spider's silk holding an egg sac in place. I slowly lifted my foot, sticky strands of the stuff clinging to the sole of my boot like a quivering black honey. I shuddered, breathing out a long shaky breath as I stepped around it. It had several solid-looking football-sized lumps suspended in an otherwise viscid core. I wobbled the banister, too afraid to touch the slimy mass with my hands, but too curious to leave it alone. The vibrations rippled across its surface like ripples on a pond. I looked around again, my eyes now fully adjusted to the darkness.

There were more. They were everywhere. Clinging to support beams, slumped against walls, and laying on the floor in thick, messy piles. My skin felt cold and clammy as I curled my fingers into two tight fists. But I had come too far to turn back now. I had to know what was underneath that tarp. Whatever it was, it was important enough to cover up; more important than these odious black egg sacs.

I slowly approached the shape, leaving sticky black footprints on the dusty floor behind me. My hands were so cold I could barely feel them as I reached out and grasped the corner of the tarp, gritting my teeth as I yanked it as hard as I could. The tarp slid off to reveal a smooth, shiny surface, sending up a large plume of dust as it tumbled to the floor.

I stood back, in awe of what I had found.

It was an enormous bullet-shaped object with a reflective chrome surface. It didn't seem to have any joins or openings – just one continuous piece of solid silver metal, shined to a mirror-like finish. I walked around it, marvelling at its extraordinary appearance, soaking in its abrasive, unearthly presence. I could feel a strange warmth radiating from its surface, as if I were standing in front of a fire. Or perhaps, more accurately, as if I were standing in a hot ray of sunshine. But there was no light coming off the silver object or any tangible warmth thrown onto any of its surroundings. The floor was cold. The tarp was cold. It was more like a mental heat rather than a physical one. I could feel it inside my head and behind my eyes, but not on my skin or on my frozen hand that hovered just above its mirror-like surface.

'What are you?' I whispered, my own warped reflection staring back at me. A lightning bolt of pins-and-needles shot down my arm and through my entire body the instant my fingertips touched it. A sudden feeling of impending doom washed over me as the room seemed to wobble slightly. Every flat surface in the barn began to fizz and quiver as if everything were made of a liquid that had just begun to boil. My body felt weak and peculiar. I looked down to see that my fingers had begun to droop as if they had no bones. Instantly, I was drowning in an ocean of regret, wishing I had not touched the mysterious chrome object. The walls of the barn began to grow distant, floating away into an empty black void that first appeared in the corners of the room, then grew larger the further away the walls drifted apart. My breath was shaky, my lungs rattling around inside my ribcage as if my ribs had grown larger and my lungs smaller. *What is happening to me?* I thought to myself through the foggy haze that was beginning to cloud my mind. My fingers had too many joints and knuckles; growing long and spindly like tree roots the longer I examined them. My teeth felt strange and unfamiliar inside my mouth. I couldn't tell where exactly my body was inside my clothes, which seemed to pool loosely around me without any defining shapes or bends. I fell to my knees, curling up into a ball and covering my head with my shaking hands. My sense of up and down folded in on itself, and for a second it felt like I was falling, but then I planted both hands firmly on the floor to reassure myself that I was still on the ground. The floor rocked a little from side to side, bobbing up and down as if it were a raft floating on water. I felt like my torso was half-empty and my organs were sloshing around in the empty space left behind inside my ribcage and stomach cavity.

I raised my head, gaining some control over my senses again. I seemed to have a grasp on gravity and which way was up and down, but apart from that all the other bizarre bodily disorientation continued at full strength. I found myself sitting in a small rowboat, adrift in a vast, endless sea of inky black water. There were no islands or landmarks or even a horizon for that matter. The water just connected seamlessly with the featureless black sky that hung above me. It was impossible to tell where exactly one ended and the other began. I could see my little boat clear as day, but beyond that there was just a mysterious shadowy nothingness that seemed to stretch on forever. Small waves rippled across the water's surface, making my boat gently bob up and down. Two oars rested loosely in the rowlocks on either side of the boat, the flat ends dangling in the water and disappearing just below its dark, filmy surface. I grabbed hold of the oars, pausing for a moment to observe the curious way the hair on my arms seemed to retract back into my skin, growing shorter and shorter until it disappeared completely, leaving me smooth and naked for a moment before it grew right back again just as quickly as it had disappeared, pulsing back and forth in a continuous loop that matched the ominous thudding sound of my own heartbeat; labouring to force the thickened blood through my tight, winding veins.

I rowed aimlessly for a few metres before I realised that I had no idea which way I wanted to go. I scanned what I thought was the horizon, straining my eyes to see something, anything at all. But every direction seemed to lead to nowhere, and what was worse, I had the inescapable feeling that there might be huge ungodly creatures swarming and slithering underneath the inky black water. It pulsed like a sickness in the pit of my stomach. Creatures that probably wouldn't pass up the chance to snatch up a helpless sailor floating all alone in a little boat. And right as that thought crossed my mind an enormous snake-like creature burst out of the deep. Rising up and curving down, resting its head on the bow of the boat. The front half of its body – which protruded from the dark water – was about three times the length of a man's body, and about as wide as a man's shoulders. I pressed myself hard up against the back of the boat, paralysed with fear, nowhere to go. The snake didn't have scales like a reptile, but instead pale, human-like skin, hairless and white with small blue veins that twisted and throbbed beneath its almost translucent surface. It looked at me with wet, glassy eyes, its long thin nostrils flaring.

'W-w-what are you-u-u?' It said in a stretched out, raspy hiss, its voice vibrating deep within its throat. I said nothing, too scared to speak. Then, just as suddenly as it had appeared, it dived back into the water and vanished. Its long tail trailing behind it and slipping back into the water with not so much as a splash.

'What are you?' I whispered, repeating the question to myself. Then the water began to tremor; a low bass murmur vibrated through the air, making the hairs on the back of my neck stand up on end. Fast, tight little ripples cascaded across the ocean's opaque black surface, lapping against the side of the boat. I slowly turned my head, my eyes as wide as dinner plates. There was nothing there, nothing but the endless black void. But then a long horizontal sliver of milky-white light appeared in the distance. I thought for a moment that the sun might be rising over that strange phantasmic horizon. But it was coming up way too fast to be the sun. The darkness peeled away to reveal a colossal white eye, the eyelids the same shade of black as the sea and sky. Blending in so perfectly that I couldn't tell where that giant creature's skin ended and the empty space around it began. It was so massive that the top of the eye stretched well into the sky, and the bottom eyelid dipped just below the water's surface. The titan murmured again. The low vibrations of its voice causing my tiny boat to pitch and toss. I white-knuckled the oars, gritting my teeth as I frantically tried to turn the boat around. The eye looked down. Its monstrous wet pupil shrinking to half its size as it focused in on me. The complex patterns of its iris stretching and changing shape to fill the empty space left behind as the pupil halved, then quartered itself. Blues, greens, yellows and browns all mixing and swirling together like the storms of Jupiter. I rowed as hard as I could, the inky black water churning and foaming around me but it was no use. The water began to pull me in the opposite direction, a strong rushing current dragging my little boat backwards and towards that ungodly ocular horror.

'No! No! No! No! No!' I screamed, fighting the current with everything I had, But it was too strong. My warped and twisted body felt alien to me; my arms, clumsy and weak as I desperately tried to steer myself away. The eye grew larger and larger as I rushed towards it, the water violently crashing around me. The pupil following me along as I got closer and closer, constricting more and more as it focused more intensely on my movement. Both the oars suddenly slipped out of my hands and were swallowed up by the violent turning ocean.

'Oh God!' I screamed, tears streaming down my face, drool pouring out of my mouth as I felt my teeth drop out and turn inside-out inside their gums. The boat spun around in the swirling water and careened straight into the surface of the eye, the bow tearing into its soft milky-white jelly. The colossus shrieked, its long bass moan rattling my eardrums so violently that I had to clasp my hands over my ears, melding them to the sides of my head. Then its huge eyelids began to close, wrenching me and my boat out of the fleshy wall of the eye and sending me rocketing upwards. I flew into the sky, riding that colossal black bottom eyelid before the top one crashed down on top of me. The boat splintered into a million pieces and I was cast down into an unfathomable darkness.

CHAPTER SIXTEEN

My eyes flew open, as if I were waking up from one of my terrible dreams. And for a moment I dared to hope that might be the case. But it wasn't my bedroom I saw in front of me. I found myself standing on a long stretch of beach, with coarse, pale sand that hugged the soles of my damp feet. I was completely naked, and my body was warped and distorted. My limbs were too long, and my ribs jutted out harshly from my sides. I marvelled at the way the tiny hairs on my skin moved and danced in random swirling patterns, constantly changing in length and thickness. And I could feel my intestines writhe and squirm inside the fleshy prison that was my stomach.

That same black water lapped and foamed at the shoreline, the inky liquid washing over the sand in long, shallow waves. The sand itself seemed to swirl and move in strange geometric patterns, in the same way my body hair did. I spun around on the spot, short of breath, trying to get a sense of my surroundings. An impressive mountain range dominated the inland landscape, stretching upwards towards a stormy grey sky. The mountains seemed to be growing taller, their earthy features reduced to nothing more than a collection of amorphic smears; each one pushing and sliding its way to the top. Everything around me was twisting and swirling, all the way down to the microscopic level. I reached down and scooped up a handful of sand. The tiny grains seemed to pop in and out of existence, shrinking down to a microscopic size before growing back again.

'What are you?' A strangely familiar voice came from behind me. I turned my head, the wet handful of sand slipping from my fingers, but there was nobody there. Just a whisper carried by the wind. I scanned the water's dark glossy surface. My heartbeat thudding in my ears.

Some of the water began to curl upwards, becoming solid and morphing into the shape of a person. The inky liquid gradually changed colour, fading from a wet, glossy black into a pale, creamy skin tone.

Loreta stood, knee-deep in the water, the shallow black waves breaking against the back of her thighs. Her wet hair clung to her scalp and neck as the last few droplets of inky liquid trickled down her naked body, leaving not so much as a trace or stain on her skin. I marvelled at her – this phantom from the past – as she walked towards me, her legs effortlessly gliding through the water without resistance. She looked at me with relaxed, dilated eyes. The kind of eyes a girl gives you when she's in love. But as she got closer her belly began to swell, inflating with incredible speed, bringing her to what looked like a full term of pregnancy in under a minute. She reached the sandy shore and fell to her knees, clutching her bulging stomach.

I rushed over to catch her as she slumped onto the damp ground. She continued to look up at me with those soft, relaxed eyes. Our naked bodies pressed against each other. Then a puzzled expression washed over her face, as if she had just woken from a strange dream.

'How did you get here?' she asked, her large, round pupils shrinking down to the size of pinpricks. She examined my face as if she had never seen me before.

'What?' I whispered, tilting my head in confusion. Then she let out a sudden shriek of pain, clutching at my body and raking her fingernails across my skin. The baby was coming. We both stared down in awe and disbelief as its tiny body began to emerge from hers. I held my hands out and scooped up the infant before it could fall onto the cold wet sand. I held the baby as Loreta slumped down weakly onto the ground, the swell of a shallow black wave washing around her limp body. The little baby kicked her small legs and squirmed uncomfortably, her small body slick and shiny with little bits of blood and goo clinging to her skin. Loreta let out a sigh of relief and, as she breathed out that one last drawn-out breath, her body withered away and turned to dust. Her ashen skin flaking apart and blowing away in the wind before her dusty bones were dragged away and swallowed up by the lapping tide.

The baby suddenly began to grow in my hands. Her tiny body expanding and transforming into that of a little girl, and then quickly a young woman. I watched the face of a scrawny teenager with sharp jagged features and full pouty lips slowly morph – in the most bone-chilling way – into the middle-aged face of Nicole. I still held her naked body against mine. She looked up at me, swooning a little as her head lulled against my chest: the process of growing up in just a few seconds must have been a harrowing experience.

'I thought I was alone,' she said in an exhausted, breathy voice, looking up at me with confused eyes, with pupils the size of pinpricks. She tried to hold onto my shoulders with her thin, pale hands but they were still slippery with remnants of afterbirth. She let out a sudden cry as her stomach began to expand as well. Pushing out like a balloon filling with air. She shrieked again as a second baby began to emerge from her body; stretching open her vagina like a cosmic traveller passing through some kind of interdimensional portal. A small baby slid into my hands, curled up and pink, with tiny fingers that flexed and curled in the open air. I held the baby close, smearing another layer of blood and afterbirth against my naked chest. I looked down just in time to see Nicole's body turn grey and mummified. Becoming hollow and collapsing in on itself with one last eerie exhale that sounded like dry dusty air being squeezed out of a brown paper bag. She decomposed into a flaky dust that was both blown away by the wind and swallowed up by the shallow waves.

I held this second baby in my trembling hands. She was heavy and cumbersome, like a beanbag made of meat. I could feel the smallest parts of her body begin to stretch and expand underneath her skin. Morphing from a baby into a child, and then into an attractive young teenage girl with creamy white skin and long orange hair. I could feel my knees sinking deeper into the sand; its grainy wet texture gripping my skin with its cold damp fingers. My senses collided and melded into each other in a symphony of chaos and confusion. I could see sound, smell temperature and hear all the colours around me. I could taste her warm, smooth skin pressed against mine as if the surface of my tongue had been stretched out over my entire body. Soaking up not only the exquisite feminine flavour of her body, but also the putrid salty sting of the wet sand I was kneeling in. I breathed in the passage of time. I was actually breathing in time itself. Sucking it into my lungs and exhaling a thin blue smoke filled with glittering yellow stars. And through all the sensory chaos, my eyes focused in on the face of the adult Mrs Spicer, cradled naked and shivering in my arms; looking up at me as if she had never seen me before. Her pupils, two tiny black dots in the centre of a pair of bulging white orbs of jelly.

'What are you?' she hissed through her teeth, as if she had already asked me this question a thousand times before and the fact that I hadn't answered yet was beginning to enrage her. I tried to speak, but no words came out of my mouth. Her belly began to swell, and I winced as I wondered desperately when this cycle of death and rebirth would end. She clutched at my neck and shoulders, pure insanity burning in her eyes as she held my face close to hers.

'Tell me how you got here!' she demanded, her fingernails

digging into my skin, the tendons standing out in her neck. Her belly was completely swollen now and ready to burst. She shrieked, her head whipped back and forth as another infant began to emerge from between her legs. She let go of my neck and landed on her back in the sand with a wet thud. I instinctively held out my trembling hands but I didn't dare look this time. I scrunched my eyes shut, and felt two warm, salty tears gather between my swollen red eyelids. Trembling on the rims of my hollow, sunken eye sockets for a moment before squeezing free and running down either side of my gaunt face in two faint, glassy lines.

Please let it be over, I begged to myself as I felt something smooth and wet slide into my hands. I opened my eyes and saw what looked like some kind of hideous, infant-sized parasite leaving Mrs Spicer's body. It was some kind of enormous, pale worm, coiled limply around my shaking hands. I tried to scream, but no sound came out of my mouth, just more of that thin blue smoke filled with glittering yellow stars. Mrs Spicer gave one last exhausted exhalexhalation before lying motionless in the wet sand. Her eyes staring blankly up at the featureless grey sky. Her skin began to decompose around her bones, and in a matter of seconds she had vanished completely, her remains swallowed up by the beach and the lapping water.

I looked down at the twisted creature in my hands, my eyes still filled with tears. Tears of fear. Tears of confusion. Of despair and desperation. Then the worm began to engorge. Its white veiny skin becoming thin and translucent as it stretched. Its insides inflating with terrifying speed. I dropped it onto the sand and scrambled backwards away from it, a shallow wave of black water breaking against the lower half of my back as I blindly crawled towards the ocean. And once it had grown to its true monstrous size, I realised that it was the strange snake-like creature with the human skin I had seen right before my boat was destroyed.

'H-h-how did you get here-e-e?' the creature hissed, its spidery blue veins pulsing, its thin gill-like nostrils flaring. But I was so overcome by the psychedelic soup my mind had been marinading in that I could not find the words to answer. But I instantly recognised the pinprick pupils in the eyes of the snake and wondered if all three women were just this same creature taking on different forms. Losing its patience, it slithered around me, diving into the sand and disappearing, leaving behind a perfectly circular tunnel. Flustered and confused, I peered down the dark black hole and tried to yell, 'I don't know how I got here!' But all that came out of my mouth was a string of slurred gibberish. The vertical tunnel spiralled down into a darkness like the one the creature had emerged from. My fingers, which were curled around the edge of the hole, began to melt. With little drops of skin-coloured liquid dripping from my fingertips like hot candlewax falling down into the darkness. I could hear the drops hitting the bottom of the tunnel, like the sound of water dripping somewhere deep within a cave.

'What the...?' I panted, holding up one of my melting hands. Suddenly my entire body turned to liquid, sending me careening down into the hole, like water swirling down the drain of a sink.

I flopped jelly-like onto the ground below; a shapeless puddle of boneless, almost watery, human flesh. I gradually regained my shape and rigidity as I dragged myself to my feet; flexing my muscles and twisting my joints back into their original solid form. I scanned my new surroundings, picking wet rotten leaves off my arms and legs as I looked around. The leaves disintegrated into nothingness as I tossed them away one by one; folding in on themselves and vanishing before they could hit the ground.

I found myself lost in the centre of a dark misty forest. The crowded mass of tall, drooping trees that surrounded me had a blueish tinge to them that made them seem unnatural and threatening. They swayed and moaned in the non-existent breeze, creaking as their branches grew and twisted tightly together. The shadowy figures of tall, slender men and women loomed in and out of the darkness, all humming an unsettlingly deep, throaty chant in unison. I heard it more with my body than with my ears; the low bass vibrations rippling across my skin. I staggered, trying to keep control of my body as my limbs slumped loosely and uncooperatively around me. I combed my fingers nervously through my hair, dragging the loose skin on my face and scalp out of place like a rubber Halloween mask, as if it weren't properly attached to my body and I might be able to remove my skin if I simply stretched apart my lips and stepped out through my mouth. I rubbed my head with both hands, trying to pull my drooping face back into place.

'W-w-where did you come from-m-m?' The distant sound

of the creature's voice came from behind me. I whirled around but it was nowhere to be seen. I stared hard into the eerie, twisted shadows of the forest. Its constantly morphing shapes and dark swirling colours all seemed to dance to some kind of silent cosmic rhythm that was beyond my comprehension. But then a small white light appeared in the darkness. It was no bigger than the flame of a match, but it stood out in sharp contrast against the hellish black nightscape that surrounded it. Then it began to flicker, growing larger and brighter, becoming rectangular like a tightly folded piece of tinfoil that was unfurling itself. It slowly materialised into the shape of the mysterious bullet-shaped object. And I was struck with the sudden understanding that it was some kind of interdimensional craft, capable of travelling across the infinite plane of existence and into parallel realities that would be inconceivable to my tiny, primitive mind. The information felt as though it had been inserted – injected – directly into my brain.

I pulled my hand away from the craft; the dusty interior of the Forbidden Barn took shape around me as instantly as flicking on a light switch. I stumbled backwards, tripping on the tarp and falling onto the ground. I breathed out a shaky breath as I realised I had just had some kind of intense psychedelic experience. I could almost feel invisible smoke wafting off me as if I had just been struck by lightning.

The Interdimensional Craft loomed large in the dim light, my own confused face staring back at me from its reflective chrome surface. Questions bounced around inside my head, each one a weighty hailstone from a furious winter storm, born in the invisible black sky of phantasmagoria that existed somewhere between my own mind and the ominous silver capsule that lay before me. *Who or what was that snake creature? How did I get there? Where was 'there'? What was 'there'? Where did these egg sacs come from? What is inside them? Did they come from some other incomprehensible plane of existence? Where did this strange craft come from?* And, perhaps most importantly, *Who or what arrived in it and where are they now?* I scrambled to my feet and threw the tarp back over the craft, blocking out the mental heat radiating from it. I scanned the darkness around me. The black egg sacs seemed to writhe and bulge a little, but I didn't know if they were actually moving or if it was just a small trace of psychedelia still having its way with my brain. I squeezed my eyes shut, feeling them pound and throb behind my eyelids.

CHAPTER SEVENTEEN

sat bolt upright in my tiny bed, sweat pouring off my forehead, gripping the sheets as if I might suddenly float away. A small reassuring ray of dim sunlight pierced the thin gap in the curtains and landed on the foot of my bed.

'It was just a dream ... Just another fucking dream ...' I whispered to myself. My hair hung greasily in my eyes, and I combed it back with my fingers. A brief but potent disgust washing over me as I felt its oily texture. But overall, I felt an overwhelming sense of relief. Relief that the eggs sacs, the Interdimensional Craft, the psychedelic trip and the snake creature were all nothing more than just another one of my feverish nocturnal hallucinations. I sat on the edge of the bed and scratched away at my greasy scalp, hard, with both hands. Something I now did almost every single time I woke up, to prove to myself that I was awake and not dreaming anymore. I suddenly stopped, my fingernails resting in the jagged grooves I had carved under my hair, and looked down at my boots suspiciously. I picked one of them up and turned it over. The sole was covered with the usual layers of caked-on dirt and animal shit. I took one of the matches from my bedside table and began delicately scraping off the many layers of grime that were stuck to the bottom of my boot. The small wooden stick scraping smoothly through the dry soil, letting it drop to the floor in small powdery clumps. I scraped and scraped until the match met some resistance, becoming stuck in one of the layers of dirt. I gently pulled it out. A quivering strand of inky black ooze clung to the end of the match. I quickly dropped the boot onto the floor and kicked it into the corner of the room.

I needed answers, and right now there was only one person I might get them from. I stood beside the Hay Shed and looked across the land as the sun began to dip below the horizon, eclipsing the Forbidden Barn and all the horrors that were concealed inside.

Ever since I had touched the Interdimensional Craft I could feel a low, almost undetectable frequency calling out from across the field, calling out from that strange, unearthly vehicle. It came across in short bursts, in waves. Sometimes hours apart, sometimes only seconds. But never in any kind of predictable pattern which was driving me insane. It was like the Chinese water torture. It rippled across my skin and made all the tiny hairs on my body stand on end. It was like one of those high-pitched sounds only dogs can hear. Only it was turned all the way down, so low I couldn't actually hear it,

I could only feel it vibrating deep within my chest. Vibrating my bones and making my organs quiver like pale jelly. My own personal dog whistle.

I began to climb up the side of the haystack. Who would have thought tightly packed dead grass could be so solid? When I got to the top I saw Kelly sitting cross-legged on the other side, looking out at the sunset. She wore a washed-out black skirt with big orange flowers on it and a denim jacket that was way too big for her. It was the kind of jacket most of the farmhands wore around here as a sort of unofficial uniform.

'Returning to the scene of the crime?' I said. She whipped her head around in surprise, her two tightly weaved pigtails swinging around like heavy ropes.

'This is my hiding place,' she said, looking back at the sunset. I crawled over to her on my hands and knees, my head only just scraping underneath the corrugated iron ceiling. 'Is that Casey's jacket? I recognise the tear in the shoulder,' I said, sitting down next to her and letting my legs dangle over the edge.

'He put it around me the night I was attacked,' she said pulling it more tightly around her thin body.

'I miss him,' I said with a defeated sigh.

'Me too. It's funny, the night you stabbed that guy, I ran straight to Casey to tell him what happened,' she said, brushing a loose strand of hair away from her eyes with a small, thin finger. Poking it out of the oversized cuff of the jacket like the blade of a Stanley knife.

'I hid in his room the whole time until my mum came and

got me,' she said, looking down at her hands, pulling back the long sleeves to expose them.

'Why didn't you just go home?' I asked.

'I don't know ... I guess I don't feel safe at home,' she said, balling up her fists. 'You wouldn't understand. I have these dreams ... these really fucked up nightmares that feel so real ... and my dad ....' She trailled off, her words getting caught in her throat. Her eyes began to well up with tears and she turned her head away from me so I wouldn't see.

'Yeah I ... I have nightmares too ...' I said hesitantly, placing a reassuring hand on her back.

'I can't ... I'm not supposed to talk about it,' she choked out, batting my hand away with her arm. She quickly slid onto her stomach and climbed over the side of the haystack, pausing on the edge for a moment and looking up at me with large wet eyes.

'I'm sorry ... I'm just not supposed to talk about it,' she said in a shaky voice, then vanished over the side.

Something was definitely not right. And as I watched her hurry back to the Farmhouse – aggressively drying her tears with the back of her oversized sleeves – I got the inescapable feeling that she knew exactly what was going on around here. That she was involved in – or perhaps even an integral part of it. And that she was either trapped or bound to secrecy by whatever malevolent forces were at play.

CHAPTER EIGHTEEN

Once again it was night and once again I couldn't tell if I was awake or asleep, dreaming or lucid, here or there. I had once heard that when you fall asleep the part of your brain that controls eyesight begins to panic and hallucinate because your eyes have been closed for too long. Your ears can still hear, your skin can still feel and your nose can still smell, but your eyes have been completely shut off from the world. I thought about this as I lay on my back with the sheets pulled all the way up to my chin. Strange shapes and colours formed and twisted in the darkness. I watched, with wide-eyed fascination, as disembodied limbs and inhuman faces peeled in and out of the shadows, a thick line of drool escaping the corner of my mouth and running down the side of my face. I was experiencing another long episode of sleep paralysis, lying there, completely at the mercy of these half-dreamed apparitions that dipped in and out of the staticky black haze of my bedroom.

A thin, naked, female body slipped out of the darkness, peeling off the shadows like a woman slipping off her clothes.

I scrunched my throbbing eyes shut, trying to force myself to go to sleep. But my own masochistic, insomniac brain had turned against me and had decided that now was the perfect time – under the cover of darkness and far, far away from all those involved – to finally reflect on a dirty little secret I've kept hidden away in the back of my mind for months. Bottled up and festering, and almost forgotten about, until I saw that half-dreamed woman slipping off her clothes. It was so confronting, so unexpected, and so confusing that I had decided to simply push it as hard as I could into the dark recesses of my psyche, where I had hoped it would quietly dissolve and disappear.

I lay on my tiny stretcher bed on the oily garage floor. The radio clock read exactly twelve o'clock at night and I was wide awake, stroking my midnight erection underneath the itchy wool blanket; the half-formed image of a beautiful woman dancing behind my eyelids. Then I heard the back door of the garage slowly creak open and I instantly froze; trying to pretend I was asleep and not jerking-off. I heard the door close, and soft, almost silent footsteps making their way towards me across the oily concrete floor.

'Otis? Are you awake?' Nicole whispered in my ear. I kept my eyes closed, still pretending to be asleep, my hard cock flat against my stomach. I could feel her kneeling on the floor beside me. Her warm breath on the side of my face. My heart leaped out of my chest as I felt her gently press her lips against mine, her fat bottom lip filling up my mouth with a passionate intensity. I didn't kiss back, although I wanted to, but for some reason my immediate reaction was to continue pretending to be asleep. She drew back to see if she had woken me up but I continued to lay still and motionless. I peered through my eyelashes trying to get a look at her without letting her know I was awake. She slowly and delicately slid her hand underneath the blanket, dragging her long, manicured fingernails lightly across my skin as she reached lower and lower down my stomach. My breath snagged in my lungs as she curled her fingers around the hard shape of my penis, but she didn't seem to notice. Her eyes lit up as she squeezed it gently, biting that enormous bottom lip of hers. A lightning bolt of pleasure shot through my body. I tensed my pelvic floor, trying not to enjoy it, but it was no use. I was torn between two voices screaming inside my head. The first one was saying, *Holy shit, what are you doing?! This is Nicole for God's sake! Are you just going to let this happen?!* The second one was not so much a voice, but more like an instinct. An unyielding animal drive that had hijacked the rest of my mind, save for the first voice: an uncontrollable sexual fervour that coursed through my veins with a feverish, throbbing intensity. The sight of her walking around in her lacy panties, the way she would sometimes talk to me a little too flirtatiously, the less than plutonic way she would sometimes touch my hips, and the handful of times I had seen her naked, all flashed through my mind right at that very moment.

While I lay there, trapped in that strange cognitive limbo, the only reasonable response seemed to be to continue pretending to be asleep; after all, it couldn't be *my fault* if I was unconscious. I watched through my eyelashes as she stood up and unfastened her blue dressing gown, letting it slide off her thin, wiry body. Her pale, naked skin seemed to glow in the scant light. Her flat, almost non-existent breasts stretched tightly over her pronounced ribcage. The thin dividing line of her abdominal muscles plunged down towards the smooth mound of her vagina, topped only with a small patch of curly black hair.

I fought the urge to breathe heavily, forcing my lungs to take only small deliberate breaths as she gently peeled back the blanket, slowly bringing it down to my thighs and exposing my hard, twitching member. I was wearing a pair of boxer shorts, but my cock and balls hung shamelessly out of my unbuttoned fly – I didn't have time to put them away before I was caught masturbating. She stepped over the stretcher bed, one foot on either side of my supposedly unconscious body. Her eyes twinkled with predatory delight, like two white stars shining inside a pair of dark, shadowy sockets. She gently scooped up my penis and slowly lowered herself down on top of me.

*   *   *

My cock slumped limply against my thigh, slathered in cum and vaginal fluids. I watched through my eyelashes as Nicole draped her dressing gown over her arm and strutted triumphantly out of the garage door naked, a small trickle of semen running down her inner thigh. The second she gently closed the door behind her I reached down and squeezed my genitals, a pleasant empty feeling throbbing inside my balls.

Oh my god, I thought as I sat up and rubbed my face. I got to my feet and walked over to the door, my body still wobbly from the sexual encounter, my legs weak and uncooperative from the orgasm. I turned the doorknob and pushed the door open, stepping out onto the Farm compound, packing my cock and balls back into my shorts as a pleasant breeze blew through my hair. I looked around at the deserted scene, everything was bathed in a pale blue twilight. Not a soul around. Then my eyes zeroed in on Nicole, walking naked up the verandah stairs and disappearing in through the front door of the Farmhouse, hypnotically swaying her hips from side to side as she walked. I decided to follow her, making my way towards the Farmhouse. But I stopped in my tracks when I suddenly heard a loud cracking sound, like a tree falling over. But the sound was coming from all around me. Every single building on the Farm suddenly sprouted short, spider-like legs and lifted themselves up off their foundations. I watched with a mixture of terror and bewildered amazement as they all slowly walked away, scattering in every direction. The loud sound of cracking and twisting timbers ringing out into the still evening air. They all reached the edge of the Farm and vanished into the woods that bordered the property. Enormous flocks of birds took flight and fled from the hulking monstrosities that came their way.

Only the Farmhouse remained, stretching tall into the sky, challenging me to enter and see what was inside. As I walked onto the verandah, all the outdoor furniture suddenly sprouted legs and scatted off in every direction. Wicker armchairs and varnished coffee tables scrambling over the railing and disappearing over the side of the deck. Even the small glass ashtray Mrs Spicer kept beside her chair fled the scene, like a mouse running away from a cat. As it ran it dropped several cigarette butts behind it, which also sprouted small, insect-like legs and walked off in single file like a trail of ants. I stood in stunned silence at the top of the stairs, slowly passing my eyes over the now empty verandah, making sure nothing else was going to suddenly come to life and frantically scramble away. I placed my hand on the heavy brass doorknob, hesitating for a moment before twisting it and shoving the door open. It hit the wall inside with a loud bang that echoed through the dark, empty house.

There was a long hallway and a flight of stairs right next to the front door. They were both adorned with a pair of long, threadbare Moroccan rugs, their faded red and green patterns each beckoning me to choose the path they presented. The house was completely silent, except for the sound of running water coming from upstairs. I gripped the banister as I looked up the staircase, an ominous feeling washing over me as the sound of the water grew louder. I slowly made my way up, my heart beating in my throat, my veins throbbing in my temples. Everything was dark except for one door which was cracked open slightly, a wedge of yellow light pooling out into the stark, empty hallway. There was a blue shape in a small, crumpled heap on the floor, and I quickly realised it was Nicole's dressing gown which she must have tossed onto the ground. I reached down to pick it up but before my fingertips could touch it, all the strands and fibres separated and disintegrated into a mass of writhing blue worms, which hastily slithered away, some down the stairs, some down the dark hallway and some underneath the door and disappearing into the mysterious room. I slid my fingers through the small crack in the door and opened it, bracing myself for what I might see inside.

Two taps were open full blast over an overflowing bathtub, the water was spilling over the side and trickling down onto the floor in a long, unbroken film that stopped just short of the doorway. At first I thought there was nobody there, but then a long, smooth hand with manicured red nails rose out of the water and turned off the taps. I felt an invisible force shove me into the room, my bare feet splashing in the water as the door slammed shut behind me. A woman materialised in the tub, fully clothed, with her long, wet hair clinging to her head, neck and shoulders.

'Hello Otis,' Mrs Spicer said, delicately brushing aside the long strands of orange hair that hung in her face.

'You ... You wanted to see me?' I stammered.

'Yes, it has come to my attention that you have been poking around inside the Forbidden Barn, where you have absolutely no business of being,' she said, sitting up in the bath and looking at me with blank, deadpan eyes. There was something about her voice; some eerie dream-like quality I could not quite put my finger on.

'No, I ... You see ... I ...' I stumbled over my words, a cold sweat breaking out across my forehead.

'My husband would like to have a very serious word with you about this,' she scowled, standing up in the tub, the bathwater dripping heavily off her drenched clothes. She was wearing the floral sundress she wore the day we met, which was plastered against her body, the tiny pictures of fruits and flowers washed-out and waterlogged.

'No, you've made a mistake!' I pleaded, holding up my hands defensively. She stepped out of the bath and walked towards me with her signature confident stride, forcefully grabbing me by the ear and yanking me towards the door.

'Right this way,' she spat through her teeth, wet flecks of bathwater dripping off her lips. The bathroom door swung open behind me, and she shoved me through it with a violent push. I tumbled backwards into an empty black void, watching the tiny rectangle of the open doorway grow smaller and smaller as I fell deeper and deeper into the nothingness. My sense of gravity suddenly turned sideways, and I landed on an old brown leather couch with a thud. A well-kept office with tall bookshelves and a large desk fell into view as the darkness slowly dissolved around me. A small fire crackled in the fireplace, casting an ominous orange light that flickered over every surface in the dimly lit room. A huge, high-backed leather armchair faced the fire, obscuring my view of whoever might be sitting in it.

'My wife tells me you've been causing trouble, boy. That you've got a problem with rules and boundaries,' a deep voice drawled from behind the chair. I gripped the seat of the couch with white-knuckled terror. I tried to speak but no words came out.

'You should know that what I keep in that barn is none of

your business,' he went on, the sound of the crackling fire filling the uncomfortable silence between his words.

'Mr Spicer?' I managed to force out.

'You know … ever since I had my stroke, I've had trouble getting things to run smoothly around here,' he said. A quiet creaking, splintering sound coming from underneath him. I watched, speechless, as thousands of insectile legs of wildly varying sizes sprouted from the legs and base of his enormous armchair. Some were almost as big as my arm; others were as small as the tiny hair-like legs on a millipede. But they all lifted the chair off the ground in perfect harmony with each other, slowly turning it around to face me. I pressed myself hard up against the back of the couch, my hands slipping off the seat and curling into two tight fists. The mummified corpse of a man in striped pyjamas and a red silk dressing gown sat slightly slumped in the armchair. His thin, greying hair combed tightly back, his beard long and bushy. His head slumped lifelessly against his shoulder, looking at me with open, hollow eye sockets; the eyes long since devoured by time. His skin was a dull, leathery grey, and hugged his withered skull like a deflated balloon.

'Now, I'm sure whatever you think you saw in there was just a figment of an overactive imagination,' the corpse drawled. But he didn't speak with his mouth. Instead, his voice seemed to resonate from his dead, motionless skull; speaking to me telepathically. 'But I must ask you to cease your childish trespassing immediately. I can't have my employees poking around my private property,' he continued, his chair slowly walking sideways across the room like some kind of demented crab, riding the orgy of movement beneath him.

'I'm sorry sir, it won't happen again, I promise. Please, I would like to get back to work if I could,' I said, each word coming out slowly and thoughtfully as I watched the corpse of Mr Spicer with large, unnerved eyes.

'I accept your apology young man. But I can't have you back in the fields just yet, seeing how first I must punish you for your transgressions,' he said, menacingly stretching out each word. The room began to tremor, as if some kind of invisible force were vibrating the walls and floorboards, causing small objects to jitter across surfaces and fall off the edges of the desk and bookshelves. The corpse of Mr Spicer rose up out of his chair with is arms stretched out like the crucified Jesus. The bottom half of his body stayed fused to the chair, causing him to tear in half at the waist as his upper body levitated in the air. Everything in the room began to float, defying gravity and swirling around Mr Spicer's disembodied torso in a violent maelstrom of books, papers, and furniture.

Only myself and the couch I was sitting on stayed firmly planted on the ground.

'Don't you fret now, I'm sure your mind will be delicious. A clever young man like yourself will take months to digest ...' His voice had become more distorted and unearthly. A mass of writhing, insect-like legs emerged from the bottom of his torso, kicking and squirming in the air. A large bloodshot eye appeared in the palm of each of his outstretched hands, gazing down at me with feverish intensity.

'And when I'm done with you, your empty mindless body will be able to work on my farm forever,' he drawled as he slowly floated towards me. A cluster of human-like fingers emerged from beneath his dressing gown and yanked it open, the buttons flying off his pyjama shirt to reveal a huge gaping mouth that ran sideways down the entire length of his naked chest and stomach. A lipless mouth with human fingers for teeth. Inside was a space as vast as the known universe, with millions of distant white stars shining and twinkling inside that foreboding black abyss.

'You'll be in good company, boy. Patrick and Luther are in here too, dissolving away inside my extradimensional guts,' he said, his menacing voice melting away into an unintelligible bass slur.

CHAPTER NINETEEN

fell out of bed and onto the floor, my whole body shaking uncontrollably.

I grabbed a fistful of sheets and jammed it into my mouth, using the sweaty fabric to muffle my own screams of terror. My bedroom materialised around me. I could feel the close, almost suffocating presence of the walls in the darkness. I lay on the floor in a sweaty, hyperventilating mess, with the overwhelming feeling that my nightmare was somehow real and that I had only just narrowly escaped being lobotomised by that floating, disembodied torso. A mixture of relief and terror washing over me in bleak, bitter waves. I ran my fingers slowly over the edge of the mattress to reassure myself that I was back in my room, only to discover that I had ripped two gaping holes in the top of it while I was thrashing about in my sleep, probably from when I was gripping the leather couch in my nightmare.

The low siren call of the Interdimensional Craft rippled across my skin, and for a moment I thought I might still be dreaming. I scratched my head as hard as I could, carving deep, bloody gashes into my scalp. I even slapped myself in the face a few times just to make sure I was truly awake before yanking on some jeans and boots and stepping outside. I still couldn't find any particular pattern to the vibrations. If I only knew when the next wave was coming then it might not be so unbearable, but they seemed to be more intense and frequent at night.

I looked over at the Forbidden Barn with a glaze-eyed, catatonic stare. With red-rimmed, bloodshot eyes and loose hanging jaw I stood there, shoulders slumped, incapable of doing anything else. Another wave of vibrations washed over me, my skin becoming raised and bumpy as all the tiny hairs on my body erected in unison.

What does it want?

Suddenly, I heard a door open and close, and I instinctively pressed myself into the deep, black shadows that surrounded the Bunkhouse. The silhouette of Mrs Spicer appeared on the Farmhouse verandah, in her gaunt nocturnal form. She was wrapped neck to ankle in that brown herringbone coat that completely obscured the shape of her body. She descended the stairs, slowly and carefully before quickly walking across the compound, slightly hunched over, her arms folded loosely around her stomach. Her face looked hollow and skull-like in the moonlight, with deep sunken eye sockets and concaved cheeks. She looked around suspiciously with a pair of white, pinhole eyes; looking for anyone that might be watching. I submerged myself deeper into the shadows, crouching low to the ground and against the wall as she passed her gaze obliviously over me.

That red-hot itch burned in the back of my skull as I watched her stagger in the direction of the Forbidden Barn; taking the long way around through the gate rather than climbing over the barbed wire fence. She stumbled through the grass, walking with a desperate, stilted lurch.

As soon as she closed the small barn door behind her I exploded out of the shadows like a tiger. Like a wild animal giving chase to its prey. I leaped over the fence and tore across the field, sprinting with incredible speed. I reached the edge of the long black shadow cast by the barn and knelt there in the dirt, gasping for air. I was sweating bullets, but I didn't care, I woke up sweating. I walked up to the large double doors and began to climb up the side of the building, carefully, silently, like a thief in the night. I climbed in through the open loft hatch and slid down onto the floor head first, crawling on my stomach through the rotting hay, spreading my weight out evenly over the creaking floorboards so they wouldn't make a sound.

I could hear a stifled moan of pain coming from below as I pulled myself over to the edge of the loft, peering down from my hiding place. The inside of the barn was exactly how I remembered it: several glistening, gelatinous egg sacs fused to the walls and supports. The pale moonlight giving them a wet, sickly shine. The weathered green tarp still covered the Interdimensional Craft, showing only the strange outline of its huge cylindrical shape and conical tip. My eyes zeroed in on Mrs Spicer, lying on the floor, partially slumped against one of the support beams. She had propped herself up against a collapsed hay bale, with her coat spread out across it like a picnic blanket. I pressed myself harder into the floor, curling my fingers tightly around the edge of the loft.

That is when I noticed the round bulge of her stomach. It had swollen, not all the way to the size of a fully pregnant belly, but most of the way there. She wore a thin dress with big yellow sunflowers on it, which stretched tightly over her round abdomen, augmenting the shape of the flowers. She pressed her fist into her mouth to silence a sudden cry of pain, grinding her knuckles against her teeth as tears oozed out of her hollow, sunken eyes.

What the fuck? I thought feverishly as I looked down with a mixture of wide-eyed fascination and disgust. She fished around in one of the coat pockets and pulled out a wooden spoon, its long, thin handle gnarled into a shapeless mess. She put the handle into her mouth and bit down hard, clamping onto it. Her jaw flexed, the tendons in her neck standing out like cables. She pulled up her dress to expose her naked hips and vagina; spreading her legs as wide as they would go. Another wave of vibrations called out from the craft, rippling across my skin, and leaving behind an electric feeling in my hair. She breathed fast and heavily, alternating between looking down at her stomach with intense concentration and letting her head loll backwards, exhausted and frustrated. Her pallid face glistened in the pale light, drenched with sweat and anguish.

An inky black fluid began to trickle out of her vagina, forming a small wet puddle on the floor between her legs. I felt my eyes stretch wider and my jaw hung open in disbelief.

She let out another muffled wail as the liquid began to grow thicker, as if she were squeezing a thick black molasses out of her body. Her teeth dug even harder into the wooden spoon as a dark, tumorous lump the size of a man's fist stretched its way out of her body and landed on the floor in a gooey mess between her thighs. She grabbed two fistfuls of the coat and white-knuckled them as she squeezed out five more slimy egg-like lumps, each one heavily lubricated by the sticky black ooze.

Her body went limp as she rested her hands on her now flat stomach. The wooden spoon slid out of her mouth and landed on the floor as her chest heaved up and down, gasping for air. Her vagina continued to ooze with the shiny black liquid, which stood out in sharp contrast against her smooth white skin. But no more eggs came out. Exhausted, she curled into a ball, biting her index finger gently with her eyes closed. I stayed perfectly still, although my muscles ached from trying not to move and my eyes burned from not blinking. I lay on my stomach with my arms and legs splayed out like a spider for what felt like an eternity. Too sane to stay, too crazy to leave.

She eventually stirred, pressing her palm against her crotch and trying to wipe away as much of the glossy black substance as she could. She crawled onto her hands and knees and began to scoop the eggs and the gooey discharge into a messy pile, moulding it into the same recognisable shape as the other egg sacs before fastening it to the floor with several quivering strands of the stuff in a crosshatched, net-like fashion. Her hands and forearms were painted an inky black, appearing slick and glossy as she delicately smoothed out the surface of the new cocoon-like structure she had just given birth to. It was only a third the size of the other egg sacs, but if I had to hazard a guess, I would say that in time it would grow to be just as large.

Then I watched, shocked and revolted, as she began to lick her hands clean. Closing her eyes thoughtfully as she sucked on her fingers, savouring the flavour of the sticky black goo that had leaked out of her vagina only moments ago. A spike of hot acidy vomit shot up my throat and into my mouth. I scrunched up my face as I swallowed it back down again, desperately trying to remain silent. My eyes watered as I watched her lazily tongue her forearms, like some kind of woman-sized cat. When she was finished she smoothed out her dress, running her hands over her now very flat stomach and down her thighs. She put her coat back on and made her way towards the door, her body slumped and loose as she walked, her muscles relaxed and exhausted. She paused for a moment and looked back at the Interdimensional Craft. She turned around and approached it; even going so far as to reach out to touch it. But her fingertips stopped only centimetres from the surface of the tarp before she thought better of it and drew her hand away, quickly walking out of the barn and locking the door behind her.

I rolled onto my back, my aching muscles all groaning in unison. I pressed my hands against my swollen eye sockets, forcing my thin, papery eyelids closed just for one exquisite moment. When I opened them again I was standing on the stony ground floor, crouched beside the wobbly newborn mass, staring into its wet, shiny surface. I scratched my scalp hard, relishing the sting of my nails, and shredding the skin underneath my hair even more. I was trying to punish my brain, in some indirect way, for all the microsleeps it had been inflicting on me. And for this reason, there was almost always blood underneath my fingernails now. This new egg sac looked different to the others. Despite its obvious smaller size, it also looked more watery and wet, with a pungent acidy smell that burned the back of my throat and made my eyes water. The older ones appeared more rubbery and solidified, but still just as sticky. I reached down to touch it, but some powerful mental block stopped me, as if my fingertips had hit some kind of invisible wall that surrounded it.

'What are you?' I whispered.

sat at the mostly empty table, drooling into my bowl of soggy cornflakes. The spoon dangled from my lifeless fingers as I stared at the Farmhouse with red, unblinking eyes. The missing piece of the puzzle – it had been right there under my nose this entire time. The hot itch of obsessive curiosity burned in the back of my head, but I didn't dare scratch it. My scalp was so carved up and pulpy from my incessant clawing that people had started to notice the mass of bloody red fingernail marks beginning to creep over the edge of my hairline. Dark red marks on top of tattered flesh, encroaching onto my forehead and temples. That coupled with the fact that I had literally – and brutally – castrated one of their co-workers in a homicidal rage, had made people somewhat weary of me. The other farmhands kept their distance whenever I slipped into one of my many catatonic states, fearing that I might jump to my feet at any moment and begin stabbing people left and right, screaming gibberish as hot ropes of foamy spit oozed out of my mouth.

I scrunched my eyes shut. A pleasant pulse of pain washing

over me as my moist eyelids slid down over my dried-out eyeballs. And inside that exquisite, restful darkness the image of a disembodied vagina materialised out of the void and hung luminously in the air in front of me. The pleasant flesh tones and lovely pink colours coming together to form something more beautiful to me than any artwork any human being could ever produce. I couldn't move, or speak, or reach out and touch it. I was just there, observing it in this tiny little universe that contained nothing but the two of us; its singular physical form and my disembodied sense of sight. I watched as a tiny drop of dark fluid appeared at its opening and slowly rolled downwards, leaving behind a thin black trail. It reached the bottom, gathered some weight, and trembled for a moment before dripping off and disappearing into the dark, shapeless void that surrounded us. Then more of that watery liquid began to trickle out, running down in a thin line before dripping off the bottom. Its surface appeared slick and glossy, but not see-through in any way. Just a thick, solid black, like a stream of wet paint. The liquid became more and more thick and viscose, oozing out and spilling down in rich, sticky strands. Then the vagina's soft elastic opening began to stretch and widen as a twisted shape the size of a man's fist began to push its way out. A mass of hard, jagged crustation-like legs emerged, writhing and wet, dripping with the repugnant black ooze. Then a pointed nose with hundreds of tiny tentacles that ran down the underside of the creature's face. It heaved the rest of its long, twisted body out of the opening; its bulbous tail-end slipping out with a sickening *pop*.

The woman's orifice snapped back to its original size as one last gush of liquid spilled out after the creature. Its scorpion-like tail was tipped with a large, toothy mouth that screamed with an eerily human scream.

'Ghhaaaa!' I shrieked, my eyes flying open. All heads turned to look at me as I raked my fingernails across the table, knocking the bowl of cornflakes onto the ground. I was foaming at the mouth like a rabid animal, thick strands of spit spilling down my lip and dangling from my chin. 'Ffffuck!' I managed to spit out through my clenched teeth, my body shaking uncontrollably. I covered my trembling mouth to silence myself; everyone looked back down at their breakfast and murmured to each other. I breathed heavily through my fingers, trying to get a grip on myself. *Just a little micro nightmare to go with your microsleep,* I reasoned to myself. *That's all it is, just another pain in the arse. It's not real,* I thought as two fat, salty tears rolled down my hollow cheeks. I let out a shaky sigh, using the sleeve of my jacket to mop up the spit that covered my jaw. *Everyone thinks I'm crazy, but they're all too stupid to see that something rotten is going on here. Or maybe they're all in on it?* said a paranoid voice in the back of my mind. I looked around with narrowed, suspicious eyes as a dozen grown men avoided eye contact with me. The only one with his head still up was Patrick, staring straight through me with a vacant, comatose stare. He had grown thin through his inability to eat, and his skin was oily, washed-out and devoid of colour. I watched as a long, glistening strand of drool escaped his open mouth and dripped down his chin. His face reflected my face: a deflated husk of a human being, brought to – or perhaps past – his breaking point. I looked around for signs that I might still be dreaming, like people growing extra limbs or anthropomorphic objects, buildings turning inside out or the sky changing colour. Everything looked normal, but God-help-me I was fast forgetting what normal was supposed to look like. I felt there was some kind of puzzle I had to solve. Some kind of huge conspiracy I had to uncover to prove to myself and everyone around me that I wasn't losing my mind, and that something was seriously wrong here on Spicer Farm. *You could just leave. Run away*, a voice prompted inside my head. But no, I was in too deep. The entire universe seemed to orbit around this one, dark little spot; swirling round and around in an all-consuming cosmic vortex. And if I ran now, the inescapable forces of gravity and destiny would pull me right back to where I was. What was my other option? Travel straight to the centre. Plunge myself headlong into the dark little singularity that concealed all the secrets, all the answers, and perhaps even the way out.

CHAPTER TWENTY-ONE

walked in a crooked, lurching stupor towards the back of the group. I was returning from a long day of fence maintenance with people I no longer recognised. Somehow, I still managed to do my farm work during the day while at the same time being trapped inside my own decaying mind. My body running on autopilot while my brain slowly rots from the inside-out. The sun dipped low over the horizon, transforming the clouds into cascading shades of pink, orange and gold. But it all felt unreal to me, as if I were imagining it. Or as if it were all just an enormous painted backdrop someone had hung up in the sky to fool me. The men trudged brutishly across the compound like a pack of lumbering Neanderthals, their backs slumped, their arms swaying loosely from their sockets. A flash of flickering white caught my eye and I quietly peeled away from the group, discreetly making my way around to the back of the Farmhouse.

Two large bedsheets flapped in the wind, as well as several colourful items of clothing that hung from the two long wire clotheslines. Kelly jumped when she saw me; dropping the large wicker basket she was carrying. I marched right up to her and grabbed her by her thin shoulders, pushing her behind one of the hanging sheets to obscure us from the view of the house and its many windows.

'What's going on here? What's going on *in there*?' I demanded in a forceful whisper, pointing an aggressive finger towards the Farmhouse – her home. She looked up at me with large, frightened eyes.

'Otis, get out of here,' she pleaded.

'What happens to your mum? Why does that stuff come out of her?' A line of deranged spit ran down my chin and dripped onto the dirt. 'You said your dad gets her pregnant, what's wrong with him? Is he still your dad? I mean, is he still the original Mr Spicer, or did something happen to him?' I said, gripping her shoulders even tighter.

'Are you insane? What the fuck are you talking about? Get out of here right now,' she hissed, grabbing hold of my collar with both hands to drive her point home. But there was no anger in her eyes, there was only fear, fear coated with an intense sense of urgency. I fell silent, my eyes slowly turning towards a dress with big yellow sunflowers on it, hanging on the clothesline next to a long herringbone coat.

'If my mum sees you here we're both in big trouble, you more than me, so get the fuck out of here right now.' Her face was deadly serious; the sound of her tense, nasal breaths filling the awkward silence that followed.

'I'm going to find out what's going on, whether you tell me

or not,' I spat, jamming my index finger harshly under her chin. I could see my own reflection in her watery, pleading eyes, my skeletal face, my putrid bloodshot eyes and trembling cracked lips. She shoved me away, hard, and walked quickly back into the Farmhouse, leaving the wicker basket on the ground where it fell. I braced myself for the sound of the backdoor slamming, but she must have closed it gently because there was only silence. I walked out from behind the sheet and looked up at the Farmhouse. The windows were dark and empty, but it felt as though each one were filled with clusters of tiny little eyes, peering down at me from the darkness. Thousands of them, tightly packed together; scrutinising my presence with their insidious gaze.

CHAPTER TWENTY-TWO

t was time. Time to let myself be sucked into the centre of the vortex. To plunge myself deep into the singularity of this unending nightmare in search of that one last missing piece of the puzzle. I lay on my bed with my eyes closed, trying to get what little rest I could. The darkness seemed to drip off the walls, with an intangible wet quality that was difficult to describe. I stared up at the thin membrane of my own closed eyelids; those tight clusters of tiny little inhuman eyes appearing all around me, all staring down at me with a ferocious intensity. They were all shiny and black, without a single rim of white to be seen around the glistening jelly that made up their pupils. I watched as they slowly sank backwards into their sockets, leaving behind thousands of tiny holes that looked like a dark, fleshy honeycomb.

My eyes flew open, and were met with only more darkness. I hadn't even bothered getting undressed. Denim jeans, denim jacket, work shirt, undershirt, second-hand brown leather boots and my own greasy human skin pulled tightly over my withered frame. I sat up in bed, suddenly snapping wide awake with the kind of nocturnal awareness only wild animals have. It was a strange feeling. An unnatural cocktail of heavy, fatigued eyes, an enormous adrenaline spike and the sensation of thousands of microscopic insects with long spidery legs crawling and burrowing underneath the surface of my skin.

I walked silently down the hallway and out the back door and was greeted by the distorted image of the farm compound at night. Some buildings seemed too far away; others seemed too close. And I wondered if I had seen them more in my dreams or more in reality. The low, bass hum of the Interdimensional Craft rippled silently through the air, vibrating all the tiny hairs on my body and making the acid in my stomach ripple and murmur. I walked quickly towards the Farmhouse, keeping to the deep shadows that stretched across my path, passing only briefly through the dim slithers of moonlight between them like a ghost in the night.

I pressed myself hard up against the exterior of the Farmhouse, sliding flatly across it as I climbed over the verandah railing. There were no lights on outside, just the many subtle shades of darkness that folded over everything I could see. I tiptoed around the verandah furniture, holding my breath.

Nothing moved. Or squealed. Or sprouted legs and suddenly came to life.

I breathed out a shaky sigh of relief as I placed my hand on the heavy brass doorknob. Then I suddenly yanked it away as if I had just touched a red-hot stove. It felt as though the doorknob were covered with a mass of writhing, twitching legs, as if a swarm of frenzied insects were squirming all over it. But there was nothing there. The smooth, clean surface of the brass glinted at me as I cautiously reached out to the doorknob again. It felt smooth and hard and a little cold underneath my hand. *You just imagined it,* I scolded myself as I gripped it more firmly. I tried pushing the door open, but it was locked from the inside. I walked around and peered through the ground floor windows but it was too dark inside to make out anything beyond the odd piece of furniture. And what was worse, all the windows were tightly bolted shut. The backdoor was also locked, and I didn't have a hope of reaching any of the second storey windows. I walked back out into the compound to get a wider view of the house. There had to be a way to sneak in. That was when I noticed a small flicker of light in one of the upstairs windows. It was so dim I could barely see it, but it was unmistakably there, in the righthand corner above the verandah roof. I studied the exterior of the building like a cat burglar; looking for a way to climb up and investigate that single lit window.

I climbed up the side of the verandah, standing with my feet on the railing as I looked for a handhold on the edge of the skillion roof. I tried to grab a hold of the gutter, but it twisted as I tried to pull myself up, the tin warping underneath my weight. I quickly shifted myself onto a steel pipe that ran down the side of the house and used that to haul myself up onto the verandah roof. It was a delicate balancing act, equal parts trying not to fall off or through the roof while also trying to remain as silent as a ghost.

I crept along on all fours as slowly as a sloth. Placing each limb, one in front of the other, with delicate precision onto the slanting corrugated iron. If it felt like it was going to creak or bend I would gently lift it up again and look for a new place to rest my hand or knee. I crawled for what felt like an eternity, all the while being sharply aware that I wouldn't be able to make a fast escape if I was suddenly caught. But the window was so close now and the light got a little brighter as I got a little closer. Despite it being a cold night, sweat poured down my forehead and dripped into my eyes. I rubbed them with the back of my hand, trying to stop the salty sting from blurring my vision. I finally reached the edge of the window, the light flickering slightly as I approached. *Probably candlelight ... or perhaps a small fireplace,* I thought to myself as I slowly – so slowly I was barely moving at all – slid one solitary eye into view of the windowpane.

What I saw inside was so shocking, so vile, and so unspeakably nightmarish that I was sure I had finally gone completely mad. Plunged fully into that final, all-encompassing hallucination. That one you don't come back from. That final permanent night terror from which you will never escape.

I slowly slumped down, face first, onto the verandah roof. Blood spontaneously gushed from my nose as if my brain had suddenly liquefied. I pressed my forehead against the cool metal of the corrugated iron as the blood mixed with the foamy spit that drizzled out of my trembling lips and down the slope of the roof in a washed-out pink trickle. I clamped my hand against my face to stop the flow of bodily fluids that were oozing out of me and slowly made my way down off the roof.

I landed on my feet, tumbling sideways onto the dirt, my hand still tightly clamped over my mouth and nose. A burst of hot, acidic vomit shot up my throat and sprayed out between my fingers. I raked myself across the ground, gagging on the bile as I slowly staggered to my feet. *What had I seen exactly? What was it that had defied my comprehension? What was this walking nightmare that had finally severed my already tenuous grasp on reality?*

My ability to think and reason had been completely stupefied. I had definitely found that final piece of the puzzle I was looking for. But somehow it answered nothing. As if the completed image were only a smaller piece of a much larger puzzle. And what was worse, there was no way out of the madness. No convenient door marked 'EXIT'. Only a door that opened up into an endless labyrinth of other doors, leading to even more doors beyond that. Each one taking me deeper into insanity.

The whole world seemed to swirl around me; all the familiar shapes and images becoming twisted and distorted in a jarring, panicked blur. I ran back to my room, closed the door behind me, and pushed my small bed hard up against it. I sat slumped against the other end of the bed, sitting on the floor, and staring at the wall with vacant eyes.

What had I seen exactly? It was alive. It had movement. Oh God, so much movement. Such an overwhelming assault on the senses that I can scarcely describe what it looked like.

When I peered through that upstairs window a spacious

bedroom materialised before me. The room was a picture of pure carnage: the walls were painted a deep gory red. Hard up against the right-hand wall was a large bed with its stylish wood-turned legs snapped off and lying discarded on the floor beside it. There were deep, peeling claw marks on the floor and walls, and even some on the ceiling, as if a grizzly bear had torn the room apart. There was a small vanity table with a smashed mirror and a red and brown Moroccan rug that lay crumpled in the corner like a wounded animal. My heart had skipped a beat as I saw Mrs Spicer, completely naked, reclining on the bed. I ducked down a little more, an electric feeling buzzing through my skin as I gazed at the sight of her naked body. But then I saw something else: a collection of disembodied, black, leathery fingers curled around her wrists. And then the hands they were attached to appeared as well, materialising out of thin air. I moved myself slowly across the bottom of the window. More of the floating pair of hands revealed themselves as I adjusted the angle I was looking from. A pair of enormous forearms slid into existence; completely covered with thick, shaggy black hair. It was like some kind of magician's mirror trick. All you can see is a floating pair of hands while the rest of the magician is hidden behind a well-placed invisible wall. But it wasn't just the end of the arms that were the cut-off point. The fingers – which I originally counted to be eight on each hand – seemed to also slide in and out of existence. Going from eight, to five, to ten, and everything in between. But once I had completely shifted myself to the other side of the window, I found an angle from which I could see the creature in its entirety. A hulking beast the size of a horse, loomed over Mrs Spicer. It appeared to be quadrupedal in the same way an ape would be, with human-like arms and legs but an overall body shape that suggested it walked on all-fours. It was completely covered with that same thick black hair that seemed to disappear depending on what angle I saw it from; exposing the creature's smooth grey skin for a moment – complete with throbbing veins and bulging muscles – before the hair reappeared as I shifted my perspective again. The hair also had a second, unearthly quality. It seemed to defy gravity; floating and swaying in the air as if it were underwater.

The creature held down Mrs Spicer's wrists – its enormous hands encompassing the entirety of her forearms – pinning her to the bed as she lay on her back, with her smooth, hairless legs spread wide open; inviting the creature to enter her. She looked as though she were in a trance. Even though her eyes were open, they stared vacantly into empty space. Or perhaps she could see something I could not. The ghost of a smile crept across the corners of her slightly parted lips as her fingers curled into two tight little fists.

The creature straightened its wide muscular back, letting go of her arms and instead grabbing hold of her ankles, holding her legs up as a writhing mass of short, thin, tentacle-like appendages sprouted out of the creature's spine, running down the length of its back like a horse's mane. Each one tipped with a vicious little circular mouth filled with tiny, pointed teeth, flailing around blindly like a tightly packed mass of carnivorous worms. These appendages were hairless;

despite the shaggy fur that sprouted around them. But they weren't a pale grey like the rest of the creature's skin, but rather a slick, leathery black colour that matched the creature's hair and fingers. As it straightened its heaving body – holding Mrs Spicer's ankles and spreading her legs as wide as they would go – I could see exactly what it was doing to her. A mass of thick, waving tentacles spilled out of the creature's groin and lower abdomen. Each one was as long as a man's arm and seemed to move independently of each other; sliding over her white gossamer skin, curling around her thighs, and snaking their way over her stomach; blindly searching her body for her reproductive organs. Some had a pointed end, others had a rounded one with a urethra-like slit on the tip. And all at once I understood the origin of her strange pregnancies, those sickly black egg sacks, and the thing that had been responsible for all of it.

The creature suddenly turned its grotesque head towards the window and my blood ran cold. It looked straight at me. But it couldn't have seen me because it had no eyes. Just a thick mass of squirming trunks tipped with savage, gnashing mouths, exactly like the ones that ran down its spine. They all clustered around its head forming a sort of lion's main, with one enormous central mouth in the middle of the lower half of its face. It wasn't on the end of a tentacle or a stalk; but imbedded in the actual head itself, right where an animal's mouth should be. With a functioning jaw and a pair of thinly stretched black lips, it looked like a shark's mouth with the same general shape and several rows of razor-sharp teeth lining its blackened gums and throat. The image was instantly burned into my eyes. I could still see it in my mind as I sat there on my bedroom floor in complete silence. I scratched my head as hard as I could, hoping the sensation of my nails scraping across my scalp might wake me up from this terrible, terrible nightmare. One of my nails hooked underneath a little piece of tattered skin and peeled it away from my skull, exposing the raw, throbbing nerve endings underneath. 'Fffuck …' I hissed, spit dribbling through my clenched teeth as I tried to swallow the shriek of pain that was rising in my throat. The tiny flap of skin was no bigger than a fingernail, and I managed to mash it back into place with the tip of my finger.

I got off the floor and looked out of the tiny window. The Farmhouse was dark and silent. Nothing going in, nothing coming out. Not a light turning on or a single speck of movement in any way. *What was that thing?* Clearly it was the father of whatever would eventually emerge from those cocoons: those grotesque, viscid egg sacs. Or perhaps it was a mother, forcefully depositing her young inside the body of another living creature, like a wasp laying its eggs inside live caterpillars and spiders. I suddenly remembered what Casey had told me about Miles. About how he had screamed, 'Burn them before they hatch!' *And the Interdimensional Craft?* It was probably safe to say that the creature had arrived in it. *But from where? And to do what? Kill a random farmer in the middle of nowhere and assume his identity? Just to hide out in his house and impregnate his wife?*

My eyes focused in on my own reflection in the darkened

window. The Farmhouse becoming blurry as my eyes readjusted. I no longer recognised myself. It was as if I were seeing a stranger for the first time. I stood there, confronted with the jarring image of my own ghoulish face, smeared with blood and vomit. I scratched at my scalp again, peeling another piece of skin off the top of my head, this time from the back of my skull. My fingernails curling underneath the shredded flesh. 'Ghhaaaaaa!' I shrieked, forcing my knuckles against my mouth to muffle my cries of pain. Maybe Miles was right. Maybe I do need to burn the egg sacs before they can hatch. God only knows what putrid monsters might emerge from those fleshy cocoons.

I dragged my tiny bed away from the door and marched outside to the shed where we kept the tractors. I grabbed two full jerry cans of fuel and an axe before marching back towards the compound, strategically leaving one of the cans in the shadows beside the Farmhouse before carrying the other one towards the Forbidden Barn.

The call of the Craft vibrated through my body, as if it were sensing my imminent arrival.

'Oh, I'm coming for you,' I muttered as I marched towards the barn. A strong gust of wind lifted some of the other tabs of peeling flesh off the top of my head, making them flap loosely as the air blew against my raw, exposed nerve endings. The burning sensation made my eyes water, but that wasn't going to stop me now. I reached the tiny door and began breaking it down with the axe. Long, sharp pieces of splintered timber shooting out in every direction as I slammed into it again and again. The door finally ripped in half, the side with the hinges swinging open as the side with the lock hung loosely from the doorframe, dangling there for a moment before the sliding bolt fell out and it all came crashing down onto the floor.

I squeezed my way in, pushing past the jagged remains of the door and charging inside, wielding the axe like a crazed berserker, and slamming it down on top of the first egg sac I saw. It sliced through the quivering jelly, becoming lodged in one of the hard lumps about a third of the way in. I wrenched it out and attacked it again with the unrestrained fury of a deranged axe murderer. The egg sac deteriorating more and more into a chunky mess with each swing of the axe; separating black viscus curds from hard tumorous lumps.

The axe scraped across the cobblestone floor as I dropped to my knees, gasping for air. One of the exposed football-sized lumps lay directly in front of me. It appeared to be some kind of twisted, infantile creature, curled up unconsciously in the foetal position. It had the head and torso of a human baby with sickly grey skin but the limbs, genitals and spinal appendages of the creature I had seen in Mrs Spicer's bedroom.

I shrieked in disgust, smashing it apart with the blunt side of the axe. It split open with a revolting crunch. A combination of bright red blood and pale malformed organs spilt out and slid across the floor, some of them suddenly shrinking down and disappearing into thin air, others inexplicably growing larger. Its small limbs twitched as I bludgeoned its tiny head in.

The Craft let out another wave of low vibrations, and I swung around and threw the axe at it. It bounced off the tarp covered surface with a loud clang. It sounded hollow, as if it had thick walls but was largely empty on the inside. I yanked off the tarp and gazed into the shiny, reflective chrome, that harsh mental heat radiating off it with a feverish intensity. Another wave, more powerful than the last, washed over me.

'No!' I shrieked, picking up the axe and smashing it against the cylindrical metal wall with everything I had, again and again, leaving behind not so much as a scratch on its smooth, seamless surface.

I unscrewed the jerry can and poured the petrol all over everything nightmarish and revolting I could see. Then I struck a match and held it up to my face.

'Here's the way out,' I whispered to myself as I looked into the little orange flame. The Craft sent out another wave of vibrations as if trying to blow the match out. I turned to face it. To face my own augmented reflection. And let the match slip from my fingers. It landed on the floor, a gargantuan fireball exploding all around me. The inferno engulfed me for a moment, before rising up and away from my body, burning off all my hair and charring the outer layer of my clothes.

I walked towards the door, the rubber soles of my boots beginning to melt and leave behind sticky footprints on the cobblestone floor. I paused in the doorway and looked back, the fire cascading upwards like an upside-down waterfall, crashing and curling against the corrugated iron ceiling of the barn. The egg sacs bubbled and burned, melting into a runny crackling liquid before being completely consumed by the flames. The Craft shone bright orange, reflecting

 Chapter Twenty-two

the fire that raged all around it. It let out one last wave of vibrations before I turned away and walked back towards the Farmhouse.

CHAPTER TWENTY-THREE

leaned against the darkened exterior of the Farmhouse, pressing myself hard up against the wooden weather boards. The Forbidden Barn was now completely consumed by the flames, appearing as a gargantuan fireball in the night. Men poured out of the Bunkhouse, shouting, 'Fire! Fire!' and ran towards the blaze, scrambling to set up some kind of rudimentary firefighting system with pump-powered hoses and water tanks. I flattened myself against the shadows as I heard rushed footsteps approach the front door of the house. The door flew open and Mrs Spicer ran out onto the verandah, hastily doing up a chocolate coloured dressing gown, her wide, shiny eyes reflecting the bright dancing orange of the flames.

'No! No! No! No!' She shrieked, with a kind of helpless, unhinged panic I never thought I would hear coming from those matriarchal lips. She rushed barefoot down the verandah stairs and ran towards the burning barn. Everyone was down at the fire now, everyone except Kelly. 'Where are you, Kelly?' I whispered as I watched Mrs Spicer tearing across the field.

I had to get her out of the house before I set it on fire. The front door had been left wide open, the long darkened interior stretching back deep into the hallway like an unexplored cave.

I put the jerry can down so I could scratch the top of my head again, my fingernails peeling more skin away from my skull. Almost every single hair on my head had been incinerated, exposing the tattered pulp of my shredded scalp; the long bloody grooves and flaking patches of missing skin and exposed bone. I could feel the sensation of tiny little creatures with long insect-like legs crawling all over my skin as I groped around blindly underneath my clothes in a vague, panicky haze. I clenched my teeth in a combination of pain, terror, and discomfort; a large foamy glob of spit rolling down my chin as I felt for the insects.

I could still hear the fire raging outside as I clutched the axe close to my chest, placing one foot in front of the other as I mounted the stairs. My thoughts were like shards of broken glass whizzing around inside my head.

Just go now! Escape while you can or the creature will kill you!

What about Kelly?!

Just leave her!

You can't leave the creature alive! It will come after you!

Burn down the house!

With Kelly inside?!

My mind fell silent as I reached the top of the stairs. A short, dark hallway with two doors on either side stretched out in front of me.

Oh God, which one is hers? I scrunched my eyes shut and

tried to remember the time I caught her spying on me from her bedroom window. When I opened them I found myself standing in front of one of the doors with my hand on the knob.

It's got to be this one. The door creaked open and stopped against the wall revealing a deep, gaping darkness inside. 'Kelly?' I whispered then flinched. I hardly dared to breathe, let alone speak. My whispered words shattering the delicate silence like a hammer smashing apart fine china. As my eyes slowly adjusted to the darkness she materialised before me. I found her asleep in a small bed in the corner of the room with the covers pulled all the way up to her chin. I could only make out the faintest outline of her face, but it was definitely her. Her eyes were closed with her lips slightly parted, breathing softly.

I crouched beside her and put my hand firmly over her mouth. Her eyes opened and she tried to scream. I clamped my hand down even harder over her face to blot out her cries of terror.

'Shhhhh, shhhh, it's me,' I whispered. She stopped screaming but she still looked at me as if I had come to murder her in the night. 'If I take my hand away, do you promise not to scream?' I said, suddenly painfully aware that I was looming over her with an axe in my hand and all my hair scorched off. 'You're not gonna scream?' I asked again. She shook her head, her dinner plate eyes reflecting my own gruesome face back at me.

Did the fire burn off my eyebrows as well?

'We've got to go right now,' I whispered taking my hand away from her face and grabbing her by the wrist.

'What are you talking about? Let go of me!' She slapped my hand away.

'There's no time to explain, we've got to go *right now*,' I ordered, still trying to keep my voice to a hushed whisper.

'*You* have to get out of here right now. If my mum catches you in here she'll kill us both.'

I grabbed her by her shoulders and stared straight into her eyes.

'How much do you know?' I whispered.

'Know about wha—?'

'Where's your Dad?' I cut her off.

'Maybe he's in his office, I don't know,' she said, a confused glaze washing over her eyes.

'No ... no ... no he's not.' I shook my head, my words spilling out of my mouth like a stubborn child having a disagreement with his mother.

'He's too sick to come out during the day so he works at night.' Her eyes welled up with tears.

'You've seen it haven't you? The creature with black snakes for a face?' I whispered.

'Oh my god ... it's real?' she said, her words getting caught in her throat as two glistening tears rolled down either side of her pale face.

CHAPTER TWENTY-FOUR

crept out of the bedroom, holding up the axe, ready to cut down any cosmic horrors that stood between me and the front door. Kelly stood behind me with her hands on my shoulders, shielding herself from whatever it was that we might encounter there in that dark upstairs hallway. The walls felt closer than they did before, as if they were closing in around us. Moving too slowly to see, but still moving nonetheless. I turned my head, holding my finger up to my lips to make the 'shh' gesture. She nodded, her wide, frightened eyes bulging from their sockets. I paused as we reached the top of the staircase, a sharp breath snagging in my throat. It was too dark to see what it was exactly, but I thought I saw a large shape lumber past the foot of the stairs. An icy spike of fear pierced my heart like a knife as I stood there, paralysed with my knuckles turning white as my fingers curled tighter around the handle of the axe. Kelly peered around my shoulder and looked down the staircase.

Back, back, back, I mouthed, turning around, and pushing her back the way we came. I opened a different door and stepped unknowingly into that same fateful bedroom where I had first seen the creature. An ungodly rank smell hung heavy in the air. It smelt like sulphur and acid and was baked into every surface in the room: the threadbare Moroccan rug on the floor, the heavy dusty curtains and especially the bedsheets, some of which had long claw marks and dark crusty stains of preternatural size and texture. Kelly stood in the doorway, staring into the mangled room as if she had never seen it before.

'Come on,' I whispered, waving her over to the window.

'I'm not supposed to be in here,' she whispered back, still standing frozen in the doorway. I grabbed her by the wrist and yanked her over to the window, sliding it open and poking my head outside. The fire was still raging in the field. I watched as the roof of the barn collapsed in on itself, spewing a torrent of orange flames into the night sky.

'Come on,' I whispered, helping Kelly through the open window. She looked at me as if I were feeding her into the gaping jaws of a hungry monster. She slid silently onto the verandah roof, pressing her body flatly against the corrugated iron so she wouldn't fall off.

'What now?' she demanded, with a tremor in her voice.

'You have to go that way and climb down the pipe,' I whispered back, pointing in the direction of the steel pipe that ran down the side of the house. Suddenly I heard a low growl coming from behind me and my skin turned cold. It sounded like the low, throaty growl of a lion, winding itself up before pouncing and tearing apart its prey. My heartbeat pounded in my ears. I felt my lungs shrivel up and my blood turn to ice in my veins. I slowly turned my head.

A disjointed black and grey mass clung to the top of the open doorway like an enormous hairy lizard, with its back end still in the hallway and its front lying flat against the wall. Its elbows and lower back seemed to dip into that invisible space my eyes could not see, leaving its disembodied hands and shoulders rising up out of empty space, independent of the rest of its body. The creature's tentacle-clad spinal column peeled into view, growing long and angry as it slowly shifted its body; turning its head towards me, claws sunk into the wall, muscles hard and tight. I was still holding the axe, but it suddenly felt useless in my hands, as if I were holding a rubber mallet.

I slowly backed up against the window, feeling the opening on the back of my thighs and shoulders, not taking my eyes off the nightmarish monster that stared me down with its hideous, eyeless face.

Could it see me? Can it see? Does it know I'm there? I watched with terror and amazement as the creature turned its head and all the thick writhing tentacles on its face folded up and out of existence – or perhaps just out of my field of vision – to reveal four, glistening, milky-white eyes that lay beneath. Two large ones, proportionate to the size of the creature's head, and two smaller ones that rested just above them on its forehead.

And, in that crucial moment, just before the panic could seize me completely, I dropped the axe and threw myself out the window. The creature exploded off the wall and came after me with terrifying speed. As I cleared the windowsill it lashed out at me with one of its wicked forelimbs, the tips of its claws just grazing my forearm as I fell.

Then suddenly everything seemed to be frozen in time. I was suspended in a freefall with the creature's fingertips still touching my arm. Then there was a sound. A sort of sharp *pop* sound, as if every soundwave in the world had suddenly been sucked out of the air by some invisible implosion, leaving behind nothing but the most profound silence I had ever heard. Then the entire Farm – including the barn-shaped fireball and all the people standing around it – folded in on itself. As if each individual building were nothing more than a two dimensional sheet of paper that was being folded over and over again, becoming smaller and smaller until they all disappeared completely. All the trees in the distance shrunk and vanished one by one. And the window, which contained the creature and its outstretched arm, also folded in on itself and disappeared. The remaining empty world and what little was left inside it swirled around me in a vortex of blurred colours, like water swirling down the drain of a sink. Draining away and leaving me suspended in a vast, black nothingness. Even the moonlight turned to liquid. The moon itself falling from the sky and diluting into the inky black darkness below, like a drop of white paint being whisked and blended into a bucket of black. Becoming stretched out and spaghettified before fading away somewhere just below the surface.

All that was left was an all-consuming darkness that felt as though it were physically pressing against my body, as if I were encased in some kind of mould. I pushed against it, suddenly realising that I was submerged in a pool of thick, viscous liquid, like honey or molasses. I opened my mouth and gasped for air, thick strands of goo clinging to my lips as I pulled them apart. I wasn't submerged in a liquid; I *was* the liquid. I opened my eyes just in time to see the back of Mrs Spicer walking away in her brown herringbone coat, the heels of her boots sinking slightly into the muddy ground with each step.

I had become a puddle of that shapeless black ooze I had come to fear and loath. I tried to raise my arm off the ground, only to be met with the sight of a drooping, boneless limb made of the gooey substance. I watched with morbid fascination as it slowly took the shape of my arm again, growing fingers and fading from a slick, glossy black into my own familiar skin tone. I raised my other arm which morphed out of the ooze in the same way, feeling a strong sensation of pins-and-needles as it slowly took shape. I pulled the rest of my body off the ground, transforming it from the soupy horror that was probably birthed only moments ago, into my original human form.

I found myself in a cold, dark forest, with an icy wind that howled through the trees and stung my naked skin. My eyes strained to see through the darkness. All the trees seemed to be adorned with human faces made of twisted bark and knotted holes. Their eyes were closed but the faces themselves seemed to follow me as I walked, rotating around the tree trunks so that they were always facing me. I soon realised that it wasn't just the howling wind I could hear, but also a deep, throaty hum that came from the gaping mouths of the tree faces, all vibrating in unison; identical to the sound made by the slender forest people in my previous vision. But then there was a third sound. A low, drawn-out screech in the distance. It came from the sky and as I tried to look up I tripped over some twisted roots and fell onto the muddy forest floor which was covered with damp leaves and shallow puddles of freezing water.

It was from there, lying on my back with the world swirling around me, I saw it. A horrifying entity with huge, outstretched, bat-like wings circling around a dark ultraviolet sky. It dived like a hawk and landed in front of me with a powerful gust of wind that shook the trees. As if it had sensed that I was vulnerable and now was the time to attack.

'You! You murdered my offspring!' the monster shrieked in a deep, booming voice. It had a head like a dog, only without ears, just a small hole covered with a thin membrane of skin on either side of its skull like a lizard, and a pair of solid black eyes. It was completely hairless, with thin translucent skin through which I could clearly see the creature's branching blue veins, and – much more faintly – the texture of its bones, muscles and organs. It was twelve feet tall and had the body and legs of a man, and a pair of leathery, translucent bat wings instead of arms – which were huge compared to the rest of its body – with a twisted human hand attached to the bend of each wing.

'You gave birth to the fire that consumed them!' it hissed, its long lizard-like tongue flickering between its pointed teeth. 'And now, I will consume you!' It straightened up its body, revealing a wide, sideways mouth that ran from its collarbones down to its stomach; identical to the vertical mouth Mr Spicer had in my dream. It yawned open, with interlocking fingers for teeth, revealing a vast black space that lay beyond, littered with a galaxy of glittering white stars that shone in the endless darkness. I scrambled to my feet, skidding clumsily over the mud as the creature advanced on me. I broke into a run through the forest, narrowly avoiding the creature's gaping jaws that snapped shut behind me.

My body lurched and drooped as I ran, struggling to maintain its shape, as if I had no bones or as if I was slowly melting back into that shapeless, liquid form. All the hairs on my body morphed and swirled in strange patterns and my hands and feet appeared large and apish as I ran. I crouched beside a tree as I tried to catch my breath, looking up at the quasi-human faces that hummed their throaty hum above me.

'I will consume your mind!' The creature's voice shrieked in the distance, echoing through the trees and bleeding through the darkness. I scanned the shadows behind me until I spotted the pale spectre chasing me. The creature pushed trees aside as it scrambled after me – its body awkward and clumsy on the ground – cracking their trunks and toppling them over with the push of its enormous, folded forelimbs. It was closing in, and with a single beat of its ghostly, translucent wings, launched itself high into the air, gliding over the trees and landing in front of me with a monstrous crash. The gust of wind from the creature's landing knocked me to the ground. I felt my organs shift and squirm underneath my skin as I toppled onto the knotted mass of twisted roots that dominated the forest floor. That's when I saw that some of the roots spiralled around a narrow hollow at the base of a tree and I scrambled towards it, diving down the muddy opening as the phantom lunged after me, trying to grab a hold of my ankles with its webbed hands and dog-like snout; unable to squeeze its grotesque bulk into the tunnel.

I clawed my way deeper and deeper into the rabbit hole until a larger space opened up underneath the tree. The space concealed a door. Just an ordinary door with a brass doorknob and a dark varnished surface, only it was lying horizontally in the dirt, embedded in the ground. But before I could wonder how it got there and where it might lead to, I felt the creature's vile lizard tongue slide across the soles of my feet and curl around my toes. I turned the doorknob and tumbled downwards into the dark space beyond it.

I felt gravity abruptly turn sideways as I fell onto a hardwood floor. The door – now standing upright – slammed shut behind me, shutting out the sounds of the forest and the snarling mouth of the beast, leaving me completely alone in an abrupt and eerie silence. I found myself standing in a long, twisting hallway, with doors lining the walls on either side. My heart slowly ceased its pounding and my breath slowed from giant panicked gasps into small calm breaths. But then the silence was suddenly broken by a violent explosion of shattered plaster and splintered wood behind me. The creature tore through the door, ripping it apart and destroying the walls around it. The forest was now gone, and only an empty black abyss lay beyond the hole where the door used to be.

'I will consume your mind!' it shrieked. Terror coursed

through my veins as I turned and began to run down the hallway. The creature clawed its way after me. Its enormous body didn't quite fit inside the long, narrow room, forcing it to rip apart the walls, making the hallway shorter and shorter; the debris floating away into the black void behind it. I grasped one of the doorknobs and wrenched the door open. But there was no exit, only a wall of wet, clammy flesh taking up the space behind the door. A leathery barrier made of moaning mouths, flaring nostrils, deaf ears, groping fingers and harsh, angry eyes, all knitted together on one seamless sheet of veiny human skin.

'You have nowhere to go!' the creature taunted, clawing its way towards me, destroying the hallway inch by inch, metre by metre.

I ran further down the hall, watching as the creature reached the open door and tore down the wall of flesh as easily as it tore down the rest of the hallway. Ripping it out of the doorframe like a huge sheet of paper, revealing nothing behind it except more of that same black void. I flung open another door, then another. Nothing but the same repulsive dead end made of living human skin, again and again.

I was almost at the end of the hallway – the last of the dead ends – with the creature closing in on me, when I suddenly felt a hand on my shoulder and somebody spun me around. I didn't have time to see who it was before what felt like several pairs of human hands all reached into my mouth and stretched it apart, lifting my skull, spreading apart my cheeks and wrenching my jaw downwards. I felt my entire body turn inside out. And for a moment, all my senses were plunged into darkness before I suddenly regained my human form.

I dropped onto all fours, my head spinning, and vomited up a puddle of sickly orange liquid. The vomit pooled around my hands and I realised that I was on some kind of soft, spongy surface.

'Where am I?' I whispered to myself.

'We are in the space between your mind and ours.' A collection of voices replied in unison. I looked up – vomit still dripping from my trembling chin – to see what looked like a slim, wiry girl with an androgynous face and a boyish body, with only the slightest hint of a feminine shape to her bones. There was not a single hair on her entire body, even on her head. Strange psychedelic patterns rhythmically morphed and flowed across her naked skin that seemed somehow both monotone and technicoloured at the same time.

'Who are you?' I asked in a shaky voice, still shivering, with my hands submerged in the warm puddle of vomit.

'We are Yar'zee,' she replied. She didn't open her mouth, but instead spoke telepathically, with a thousand identical voices appearing inside my head all at once, all speaking in unison.

'We?' I asked, as a wave of confusion washed over me.

'We call ourselves 'we' because we are the many that make up the mind of the being.' As Yar'zee spoke, I could see soundwaves rippling out from their collective forehead, like ripples on a pond, spreading out vertically through the air. 'There is so much to explain, and so little time,' they said, taking my hand and pulling me to my feet. It felt like nothing, like an invisible force curled around my fingers. As Yar'zee moved they left behind a series of fading copies of their body; a trail of overlapping still images that faded away after a few seconds. Every time they turned, walked or moved in any way they left behind a thousand eyes, a thousand faces, and a thousand arms and legs. I wobbled a little, trying to find my balance. That was when I noticed that we were standing on top of an enormous jellyfish, lazily floating across an ultraviolet sky, surrounded by other, equally huge, jellyfish with smooth, glassy bodies, all bobbing along through the air like living clouds.

'My kind have evolved to communicate telepathically. That is how we are speaking right now. But our two minds are so vastly different that the telepathic link is causing us both to hallucinate,' Yar'zee explained.

'So, this is all in my head?' I asked, marvelling at the gargantuan creatures drifting across the purple sky.

'It is in *both* our heads. You are also experiencing extreme time dilation. Which is normal for those of us with telepathic minds but will appear very confusing to you in just a few moments. The truth is you are still falling out of the window and we are still reaching out to grab you, with our fingers touching your arm. But the moment you slip away from us, the telepathic link will be broken, and this conversation will end,' Yar'zee said with a restrained sense of urgency.

'Wait ... if that's *you* out there, then why are you trying to kill me?' I asked, cautiously taking a step back, my knees buckling on top of the wobbly surface of the jelly fish.

'No, that is not us. We have lost control of our body. We

are the first of our kind to travel across parallel dimensional planes. We came here in the craft we built, not knowing exactly where it would take us. But the process of transporting a living organism in this way had unforeseen consequences. It shattered our psyche into a near-infinite number of smaller fragments, left to drift apart in the empty void left behind in our mental landscape. We are the collection of most of those fragments that have managed to find each other again in the darkness. And in time we will be whole again and take back control of our physical form from Thorz'akk,' Yar'zee said, their many voices feeding directly into my consciousness, their thoughts rippling out of their forehead in tight, visible waves.

'Who is Thorz'akk?' I asked, fearing that I might already know the answer.

'Thorz'akk is the one in control of our physical body – the entity you first encountered –who established the telepathic link. Be careful Traveller, for he will consume your mind if he can, feeding on your consciousness until there's nothing left but an empty, lobotomised husk. He formed in the empty space left behind after we were fragmented. With no conscious mind left to ensure the body's survival, it created a new one to take over. A simple proto-consciousness with only a fraction of our intelligence and driven only by the basic animal instincts of self-preservation and procreation. But now that we have resolidified enough to take back control, Thorz'akk will not relinquish his power. His will to stay and replace us is too strong.' As Yar'zee spoke the patterns that danced across their body intensified, making their overall shape distorted and difficult to look at.

'Why hasn't he eaten Mrs Spicer's mind then?' I asked, aching to know the answer.

'We don't know Traveller ... perhaps he has somehow hijacked her mind, controlling her like a puppet and using her body to gestate his young. Or perhaps she was able to convince him that she was somehow vital to his survival. They have communed telepathically many times and she has appeared here many times in this psychic space. But she will not help us, she has sided with Thorz'akk. *You* must help us, Traveller. If not for us, then for yourself. If Thorz'akk cannot kill you in here then he will kill you out there, in the physical world.' As Yar'zee spoke, the jellyfish heaved its enormous body upwards, making me lose my balance and fall back down onto my hands and knees.

'What can I do?' I asked, with equal parts adrenaline and fear mixing together in the pit of my swirling guts.

'There is one vital part of our mind that we cannot find. The missing fragment that will allow us to reconnect to our physical body and disconnect Thorz'akk from it. But we have searched the darkest reassesses of our mental landscape and have found nothing, as if it had somehow been removed and taken away. But we believe *you* have encountered it, somewhere, outside of this space,' Yar'zee said, spreading out their arms and leaving behind a cascading trail of identical, fanning limbs.

A missing fragment? Where could I have seen it? How would I recognise it? I have seen so much, hallucinated, dreamed, and imagined so many terrible things and unearthly oddities that

I didn't have a hope of remembering an encounter with just one specific thing. I saw a flash of movement in the corner of my eye and turned my head just in time to see one of the distant jellyfish in the sky folding in on itself and warping out of existence. Then another, and another.

'You are slipping away from us, Traveller. Do not be shocked when the link is broken, you have to be ready to run. There is one more thing you need to know. We are a four-dimensional being. We are not bound by the same three-dimensional constraints you are. From your perspective it would appear that we can see through objects and pass through many of them in ways you cannot. And most importantly, our body can be obscured by this fourth dimension. Making us appear invisible to you and your limited perception of the world. But make no mistake, we are still there, hiding where your eyes cannot see. Thorz'akk will know this and use it to his advantage! Now go! Run!' And at that very moment even Yar'zee folded up and disappeared, leaving me behind in a swirling vortex of ultraviolet colours; quickly draining away into an inky black darkness. Even my body turned to liquid and drained away along with everything else. Leaving behind only my disembodied sense of sight and awareness, to watch the rest of my being be sucked down into the shrinking vortex, sucked down into the psychedelic drainpipe of non-existence.

CHAPTER TWENTY-FIVE

The world fell back into sharp focus as the creature's claws slid off my arm, tearing seven deep gashes across my skin. I hit the corrugated iron and slid down the slope of the roof, desperately trying to grab a hold of something. I tumbled over the edge, snagging my fingers around the flimsy tin gutter. It bent and snapped off under my weight, but it was enough to arrest my fall before I hit the ground too hard. I landed on my back, with the long piece of gutter slamming down on top of me and knocking the air out of my lungs. Kelly grabbed me by the back of my shirt and yanked me to my feet.

'Run! Run! Run!' she screamed. I broke into a sprint, still gasping for air after being winded by the fall, my mind still reeling from the jarring psychedelic trip. A trip that took place in less than a nanosecond.

'This way!' she yelled, yanking me by the sleeve and swinging me around.

I slammed against the side of a dark red ute. I threw the door open and jumped behind the wheel, jamming my hand instinctively against the ignition.

'Where the fuck is the key?!' I screamed. She fished around in the glove box and tossed it to me with shaking hands. The car roared to life and I looked back just in time to see the creature explode from the second storey wall, its enormous body passing straight through the weatherboards like a ghost and landing on the ground on all fours like a savage black panther.

'Go! Go! Go! Go!' Kelly screamed. I hit the accelerator and tore off down the long driveway, leaving behind a jet of dust in the shadowy night. I looked hard into the rear-view mirror, but all I could see was darkness.

'Look out!' she shrieked, right before we ploughed straight through one of the long farm gates, ripping it off its hinges and sending it barrelling over the bonnet of the car. 'Hold on!' I yelled, tightening my grip on the steering wheel. The engine revved as I hit the accelerator even harder, ramming straight through a second gate and then a third, flinching each time a mass of twisted wire and jagged metal was sent tumbling over the windshield. We peeled out onto the deserted highway, careening around the corner with only one of our headlights still casting a solitary beacon of light in front of us. The other was obliterated by the gantlet of carnage that had been the long farm driveway. Tall, looming trees leaped up at us from out of the darkness; the road taking us away from the vast, empty fields into the dense forest that surrounded them.

'Where are we going?! What about my mum?!' Kelly cried.

'The creature won't hurt her,' I said ominously.

'How do you know that?!' she wailed.

'Because it told me so!' I yelled back. The road twisted and turned around the edge of a rocky slope.

'Where are we going?! What do you mean *it told you*?!' she asked, looking at me with large, frightened eyes. I turned my head, trying to think of how I could explain it all to her.

'We just need to—' I was cut short when the passenger side of the car suddenly caved in, violently throwing the car sideways off the side of the road as if we had just been T-boned by another vehicle. The creature had lunged out of the darkness and spear tackled the ute, sending all three of us rolling down the steep, rocky embankment beside the highway. And although the windows weren't open, the creature's wicked claws still managed to pass through the exterior of the ute and swing past my face, only missing it by millimetres. It lost its grip on the outside of the car and tumbled away as we continued to violently spiral down the hill.

The car slammed upside down into a tree with a savage crunch, our ribs bruising against our seatbelts. The one remaining headlight flickered on and off, like a dying animal taking its last few panicked breaths. All was silent except for the whistling sound of the tyres still spinning in the air.

'Kelly? Kelly?' My words came out in a dusty, choked whisper, a combination of spit and blood pooling on the roof of my mouth. She hung upside down with her long hair resting on the ceiling and her arms dangling limply. I undid my seatbelt and slumped sideways onto the ceiling of the car, trying to turn myself upright in the tight space.

I emerged from the wreckage, dragging Kelly's unconscious body behind me through the dirt and glass. I looked around, hyperventilating through my teeth, every muscle in my body hard and tight with adrenaline. We were on the edge of the forest now, looking up at the long slope we had just crashed down. The moonlight shone from behind the hill, blotting out the embankment with a plunging black shadow. There was no telling where the creature might be. I strained my eyes but all I could see was darkness. I scooped up Kelly and ran into the woods. I ran down another steep slope and pressed myself into a thick tangle of exposed roots underneath a tree, trying to catch my breath. I sunk down onto the ground, Kelly slumped loosely in my arms, her head lulling backwards as a white ribbon of frozen breath escaped her lips. My arm was haemorrhaging blood from the claw marks and I had to fight the urge to slip backwards into unconsciousness. I hastily ripped some makeshift bandages from the bottom of her nightdress; clumsily tearing off strips of the silky pink fabric in a desperate attempt to stop the bleeding before I passed out.

I wrapped up my forearm and tied it off, tight. I looked back at her, her exposed skin was paper white, her eye sockets grey and sunken. I was suddenly sharply aware that she was barefoot, with her arms and legs exposed to the icy night air.

'Oh fuck …' I whispered, a shaky plume of frozen breath wafting around my face. I peeled off my jacket – all the while listening for the faint sound of an eight-toed foot treading on the damp leaf litter – and gently fed her arms into the sleeves, buttoning up the jacket all the way to her throat. I picked her up again and began to run deeper into the woods.

I was a scrawny guy, with thin, gangly arms and legs, but my veins coursed with that special cocktail of 'fight or flight' chemicals that nature had specifically tailored for this exact situation. And in this case it was most definitely 'flight'. I tore through the forest in a feverish haze, with my unconscious companion slung over my shoulder as if she weighed nothing at all. Her bare shins and feet flopping loosely against my stomach, her arms slapping against my back. I panted, huge gasps of frozen breath billowing out of my mouth and hot threads of thin, translucent drool running down my grinding jaws. I dropped to my knees and looked over my shoulder in a flustered panic. I lowered Kelly's body down onto the rotten leaf litter. There was no sign of the creature. My heart thudded against my ribcage.

'What do I do? I don't know what to do,' I cried to myself in between short, panicked breaths. The overwhelming pressure of this impossible situation had finally begun to crush me. I squeezed my eyes shut as two tears rolled down either side of my face in thin glassy streams. I slapped at my forehead with both hands.

'A missing piece ... A missing piece ... What the fuck is it? What the fuck am I supposed to be looking for?' And in my mind an image began to form. A distant white spiral that curled and weaved its way through the nothingness. It looked like a tiny, faraway worm, travelling towards me through black, empty space. That's when I noticed that I could feel grass in between my toes. I opened my eyes and saw that I was standing in a swaying field, the morning twilight slicing across the horizon with a thin blade of pale blue light. I looked down and saw that I was still wearing shoes, but somehow I could feel the sensation of the soft grass on the soles of my feet as if they were naked. The Forbidden Barn stood in front of me intact and unburned. Its timbers seemed to heave and ebb as if they concealed an enormous pair of lungs, taking in large, laboured breaths. I rolled my tongue around the inside of my mouth. My own heartbeat thudded in my ears.

'Y-y-you're so clos-s-se.' A faint voice came from behind me, carried by the wind. I turned my head to see that same distant winding worm, spiralling through the air like a pale corkscrew. As it got closer, it landed on the ground and slithered up to me like an enormous snake. The strange snake-like entity from my original vision. It coiled its long body loosely around mine, its spidery blue veins bulging and pulsing underneath its eerily human-like skin.

'Th-h-his way-y-y …' It whispered, its forked tongue flickering between its teeth before slithering away towards the barn. Leaving me behind in a stunned silence.

It plunged its long body straight into the huge double doors, passing through them like a ghost passing through a wall. The surface of the barn rippled as if it were made of water.

'This way …' I repeated in a low whisper. I ran towards the barn. There were no barricades sealing the enormous doors shut this time and I threw them open with a violent push. Beyond them lay another identical field with the same barn resting halfway across it. I had thrown open the doors just in time to see the end of the entity's tail vanishing through the surface of the next pair of double doors. Confused, I looked behind me, only to discover that the doorway I had come through and the barn around it had vanished. I rushed towards the next barn and flung the doors open again and was met with the same sight. I did it again and again, running as fast as I could. Each time the doorway was a little closer to the next, until finally the space between them had become so small they had become the same door. I burst through them one more time and was finally met with the interior of the Forbidden Barn. Panting and sweating, I dropped to my knees as I tried to catch my breath.

The barn was empty. No ungodly horrors, no dust, no hay, no cocoons, just the uncovered Interdimensional Craft laying in the centre, its sleek chrome body throwing my own twisted reflection back at me. The snake entity silently slid in through the doorway behind me – somehow I had got there first – its enormous bulk twisting and bending in the most unearthly ways. It slithered up to the Craft, pausing for a moment to look back at me with its dark, fleshy eyes.

A sudden moment of exquisite clarity washed over me. A realisation: *the* realisation. And as if sensing my epiphany, the snake entity – the final missing fragment of Yar'zee's mind – plunged headlong directly into the side of the Craft, slipping through its smooth chrome surface like a ghost, leaving behind a metallic ripple.

My eyes shot open, I found myself standing on the edge of the forest, with only a barbed wire fence separating me from the long stretch of field that led back to Spicer Farm. Exhaustion had gotten the better of me, and with one foot in and one foot out of consciousness I had somehow managed to sleepwalk all the way back to the edge of the farm. Kelly's unconscious body was still cradled in my arms, a glistening layer of congealed blood clinging to the side of her face. My thin biceps straining to hold her, my shoulders aching. The adrenaline had worn off hours ago and she slipped from my exhausted hands, tumbling limply onto the ground. I fumbled, unable to grab a hold of her before she slammed down into the cold wet dirt. I rolled her onto her back and gently slapped her thin pale cheeks.

'Kelly? Come on Kelly, wake up. I know what we have to do now,' I whispered. She didn't move. Her lips were parted but her chest remained still.

'Come on, we don't have time for this, you have to wake up,' I said with muted panic, slapping her cheeks a little harder. Her skin was cold and white as chalk, except for a couple of huge purple bruises on her neck and arms from the crash.

'Come on get up. You need to get up,' I pleaded, my words getting caught in my throat. 'Kelly, get the fuck up right now!' I demanded, forcing my words through my teeth. My eyes welled up with tears, blurring my vision. I forced her eyelids open with my fingers, reaching into those dark, grey hollows to find them. She stared straight through me, as if I wasn't even there. Her large, frightened eyes had been replaced with a glassy, washed-out stare. Emotionless. Vacant. Dead.

'You've got to get up … got to get up … got to get up,' I repeated, more to myself now than to her. Spit oozed through my clenched teeth and ran down my trembling chin. 'Got to get up... got to get up... got to get up.'

A deep, bass vibration rippled across my skin. The Craft. It was still there, buried beneath the smouldering rubble. I climbed over the barbed wire fence, dragging Kelly underneath it before slinging her over my shoulder again. Mud and damp leaves clung to her cold body, mixing with the dried blood to make a sickly brown paste that rubbed off on my arms and chest. I could see the smoking wreckage of the Forbidden Barn – now a twisted black mass, like an enormous dead fly, or a giant, overflowing ashtray. Everyone had left. Probably all gone back to bed as soon as the fire was out. Or perhaps they were out combing the woods, looking for the missing girl who was now slung over my shoulder. The first few thin rays of early morning sunlight pierced the horizon, casting an eerie, pale blue light across the field.

I ran as fast as I could towards the blackened, smoking heap. The muscles in my legs threatening to collapse any second as Kelly's weight pressed down on my spine.

'We're almost there. We're almost there!' I panted. Her head lulled against my back, her limbs dangling loosely around me. I was about three quarters of the way there when a sudden sense of impending doom washed over me. I turned my head to see a hulking black shape peel out of the aether, appearing at the fence line we had just come through. The creature had found us. It leapt over the barbed wire fence and ran towards us with the speed and ferocity of a crazed racehorse, slipping in and out of visibility as it ran. I broke into a sprint, bolting as fast as I could towards the Craft. I got to the mound of smouldering rubble and scorched corrugated iron and – dumping Kelly onto the muddy ground – began frantically digging through the debris, throwing aside charred beams and blackened pieces of roofing tin. I yanked aside a large piece of collapsed frame. And there it was: an exposed part of the Interdimensional Craft. The mental heat hit me as if I had just opened a scolding hot oven, accompanied by a powerful blast of its low, bass vibrations.

I stretched out my hand and held it just above its reflective chrome surface, looking back for the creature that was charging towards me. But it had vanished into thin air.

It's still there, you just can't see it. I held my breath, my heartbeat throbbing behind my eyes. Then the creature suddenly materialised in front of me, peeling into my three-dimensional field of view in that unnatural, fragmented way, its tenacles flailing, mouths foaming, teeth gnashing. I pressed my hand against the side of the Craft making contact with its psychoactive surface the second the creature's dagger-like fingers touched my skin.

CHAPTER TWENTY-SIX

There was that sound again – the sound of all the air in the world suddenly imploding all at once. Every soundwave, every ripple or murmur travelling through Earth's atmosphere suddenly silenced by the vacuum left behind. And in that instant my physical body melted away, like tissue paper dissolving in a pool of water. The world began to evanesce; transforming into a shapeless, soupy mess before draining away into nothingness. Even my thoughts and emotions fizzed and dissolved into the aether like an aspirin in a glass of water. Only my self-awareness and a handful of physical senses remained, but even those were churned up and blended together. I could see sound, smell colours and taste the flavour of blurred images that were quickly receding away from me. Everything was turned up, turned down, augmented, stretched out, blurred, mixed together and transplanted. What was left of my conscious mind transcended to the psychedelic plane to witness the cosmic ballet that unfolded before me: a visual symphony of deep plunging fractals that grew more and more complex by the second.

Thousands of identical human-like entities materialised all around me, appearing in countless rows, standing side by side and one in front of the other in a perfect grid formation that stretched off into the horizon. Each one had a multitude of overlapping female faces that encircled their heads and a large colourful crown that fanned upwards like a peacock's tail. The tops of their crowns and the bottoms of their thighs, just above the knee, curved and melded into that of their sisters beside them, forming a psychedelic canopy of incomprehensible complexity, and an undulating floor to match. They occupied this vast four dimensional space in its entirety; containing it within themselves because they *were* the space in its entirety. It was as if I had just been transported into a sentient pocket universe.

The base of their crowns came halfway down their faces and covered their eyes like a blindfold. But as they stretched up and away from their heads they began to display an incalculable number of other human eyes that cascaded upwards into infinity, all shifting and blinking in irregular patterns. They had shapely hourglass bodies that stretched out beneath them, with a multitude of psychedelic shapes and colours that danced across their naked skin. Starting at their navels and travelling outwards like ever expanding mandalas, alive with movement. They each had four sets of arms, eight in total, that encircled their bodies the same way their faces did. Every side of them was the front, and they cupped their four pairs of breasts with thin, slender hands, their fingernails adorned with even more watchful blinking eyes. They all parted their lips in unison and began to hum a single, drawn-out note; harmonising into a cosmic vibration.

They then collapsed into a cascade of pulsing colours and swirling textures. I could hear my own heartbeat throbbing in my ears and I became suddenly aware of the sensation of my own eyelids covering my eyes. I opened them slowly. They felt crusty and heavy, as if they had been closed for a thousand years. I found myself kneeling on all fours in a field of soft ankle-deep grass. The grass was an eerie pale blue, almost grey, and swayed violently as if a strong wind were blowing across it. But the air was dead still; not so much as a light breeze or breath of wind blew in any direction. I looked up at the sky; a vast, deep ultraviolet sky with long swirling clouds that careened across it with incredible speed. But still no wind, or at least none that I could feel.

I could feel my body slowly morphing and twisting beneath my clothes. My skinny arms appeared alarmingly vascular and seemed to be gradually growing longer, but at the same time remaining the same length. I sat back on my heels and let my head roll backwards towards the sky, taking in enormous lungfuls of air.

'Okay ... okay ... on a mission... we're on a mission ...' I panted to myself in a breathy voice that sounded both distant and unfamiliar to me. I knew I had come here for a reason – to find something – but for the life of me I couldn't remember what it was. I felt so mixed up and scrambled, as if all the usual pathways in my brain had been rearranged and turned upside down. Trying to maintain a coherent string of thoughts was near impossible.

'What am I meant to be doing?' I whispered to myself, crouching on my haunches as I scanned the undulating horizon.

'You can start by walking.' A voice came from beneath me. It sounded slow, drawn-out, and dopey, like a recording of someone's voice that had been slowed down to make it sound deeper. The voice made me jolt and I toppled over onto my arse, my legs stretched out in front of me.

'Who said that?' I whispered, an unsettling feeling crawling up the back of my spine. 'I did,' the voice said, but this time it seemed to be coming from in front of me.

'He's right, we need to get moving. Time dilation doesn't last forever.' A second voice interjected. The two voices seemed to be coming from the ends of my legs. 'Where are you?' I whispered, my eyes darting from side to side. 'We're in your shoes, Otis,' one replied in its slow, dopey voice. Slowly, with long drooping hands that were difficult to control – as if they belonged to someone else – I undid my shoelaces and slid off my boots. I peered inside one, tapping it upside down to see if anything would fall out.

'We're still inside your socks, Otis,' the second voice said coyly.

'What ...?'

'We're your feet Otis,' the first voice drawled, and both voices laughed with an eerie slow chuckle. The boot slipped from my fingers, falling to the ground and sinking into it. The blades of grass wrapping around it and dragging it down, like a sea monster consuming a ship. I pinched the end of one of my socks and cautiously slid it off, and then the other. I stared down at my bare feet with disbelief as my socks and other shoe sank into the grass and disappeared. The shape of two faces appeared on the tops of my feet, as if they were trapped beneath my skin, like human faces pressed against a flesh-coloured clingwrap. My toes fanned out on top of them making it look as though each one was wearing a five-pointed crown.

'We better get moving if we're going to find that entity in time,' my left foot said.

'Yeah before we all get eaten – inside and out,' my right foot added, the mouth moving up and down like a puppet. Even the hair and veins on my feet seemed to move and bend in a way that added to the overall shape and texture of my two unexpected new friends beneath my skin.

'W-what are you t-t-talking about?' I stuttered. I had continued to draw a total blank as to what I was supposed to be doing, as if there was some kind of obstructive black smudge on the inside of my brain that was blotting out what I needed to know.

'Don't you remember? We're here to find that missing entity for Yar'zee,' my right foot said.

'I don't think he remembers,' my left foot added in a sceptical tone. I tried to comb my fingers through my hair, forgetting that most of it had been scorched off in the barn fire and my scalp had been ripped to shreds from weeks of incessant scratching. Instead, my fingers traced along the angry red grooves and fingernail marks that roped across my exposed scalp.

'Yes … yes, I remember now … Shit, we've got to go! I don't know how much time we have left!' I exclaimed to my feet. I stood up and scanned the horizon. 'Every direction looks the same … where are we supposed to go?' I jabbered in a confused tone as I struggled to find my balance. My bones felt rubbery and it took a moment to right myself as my body twisted and drooped uncontrollably.

'Don't worry, we know the way,' my right foot said.

'Trust us, we're your feet,' my left foot added confidently. I began to walk mindlessly over the ridge of a hill. The soil was loose and powdery underfoot but the grass was soft and comfortable to walk on. I gradually quickened my pace, eventually breaking into a run.

I came over the top of another hill and saw a field on the other side, full of strange creatures that seemed to be grazing on the blue-grey grass. The field itself was lined with tall, thin trees that stretched into the sky, expanding upwards in wide, veining patterns, constantly growing but not getting any taller. One of the strange animals was laying on its side, taking large, laboured breaths, its engorged midsection heaving up and down. My eyes widened when I noticed an old man, clad in wobbling brown denim and a crumpled old hat, approaching the animal.

'Maybe he can help us,' I said, looking down at my feet. But the faces had vanished. They were just normal feet again. My scrambled brain was finally beginning to untangle. I could feel my thoughts becoming more and more coherent and organised with each passing second. I wasted no time running down the hill, the strange animals all jolting into a short-lived stampede over to the other side of the field as they saw me coming. They looked like cows, with dark brown hair and bovine bodies, but they had no heads. Instead, each one had a long, worm-like neck tipped with a circular mouth that they dragged along the ground to eat the grass. Several large glassy eyes appeared in random places across their bodies. And when an eye blinked, it closed and disappeared before reappearing on a different part of the cow. It was quite disorientating to look at.

The old man stood in front of the sick animal with his hands on his hips, his clothes folding and bending around his body in bizarre, distorted patterns.

Perhaps he is Yar'zee's missing entity and he's just assumed a human form for some reason, I wondered to myself.

'Excuse me!' I called to him, my voice still sounding distant and unfamiliar to me. He turned his head, his leathery skin wrinkling up with a warm smile.

'You're just in time,' he said in a gentle voice. He had a long white beard and a wispy head of hair that poked out from beneath the brim of his hat that seemed to shift between long and short, combed and tangled, white and grey, depending on what angle you looked from.

'Just in time for what?' I asked, giving another confused look down at my feet, which remained smooth and silent. He held a long, gnarled finger up to his heavily moustached lips before crouching down beside the worm-cow. I crouched down beside him, the creature's eyes frantically blinking in and out of existence, its swollen midsection heaving up and down. A slippery purple liquid began to ooze out of the creature's rear end; the same shade of purple as the ultraviolet sky that stretched out above us. And, without warning, the old man grabbed my wrist and gently pushed my hand inside the cow, plunging both his own hands in after it.

'Gently now,' he said softly. I felt around the slimy insides of the cow – vaguely remembering doing something similar with a pig once – until I found something that felt like a small leg. I grabbed a hold of it and we both gently pulled out a newborn calf; sliding it out of its mother and letting it plop onto the ground beside her.

'How wonderful,' the old man whispered, as the calf began to enthusiastically drink its mother's milk.

'I'm looking for an entity ... a big snake with human skin. That wouldn't be *you* by any chance would it?' I asked, looking at him sideways, choosing my words carefully.

'Oh, no ... that wouldn't be me ... You'll have to go a little deeper if you want to find what you're looking for,' he said matter-of-factly, as if he had already had this conversation with me a thousand times before and knew everything I was going to say before I said it. Not quite to the point of tedium, but just before it, when it stopped being amusing.

As the calf fed on the milk, it quickly grew to the size of an adult – its tiny body engorging as the mother's withered away – becoming a hollow, desiccated husk before collapsing into a pile of dirt. The dirt broke down and flattened into the ground as new grass sprouted up on top of it, erasing the mother cow without a trace as if she had never existed.

'Fortunately ...' the old man continued, '... a "little deeper" is never too far away.' He reached into the air, and a stool and bucket materialised in his wrinkled old hands. He sat down and began to milk the new cow, squeezing its strange drooping udders as his fingers bent and multiplied in a way that was both fascinating and grotesque to watch.

'There we are,' he declared, triumphantly showing me a bucket filled with a glossy silver liquid. The cow briskly walked away as the old man stood up, knocking the stool over in the process. Without missing a beat, the grass absorbed the little stool and swallowed it up the same way it had swallowed my shoes. I peered into the bucket. It seemed deeper on the inside than it did on the outside and the milk looked slimy and unappealing.

The sky suddenly turned dark, as if something had swallowed up the sun, and a powerful wind began to roar. Or perhaps I was finally hearing the phantom wind that had been roaring all along.

'You better drink up now if you want to find that entity,' the old man prompted. I heard a familiar dragon-like screech slice through the air, accompanied by an even more all-too-familiar feeling of impending doom. 'Looks like I better be going,' the old man said. He tipped his hat and began to sink down into the grass just like everything else, and vanished beneath the swaying blades. I looked up at the sky with wide-eyed panic as the terrified cows fled in a stampede.

Thorz'akk had found me and he wasn't going to let me slip through his twisted fingers again. He swooped towards me like a bird of prey, missing me by a hair's breadth as I dived out of the way, still clutching the bucket, the milk sloshing around inside. Quickly, and without hesitation, I gulped down the warm, filmy liquid as Thorz'akk bore down on me again. His previously humanoid feet had transformed into that of a hawk's, with a collection of long, curved talons on the ends of his scaly avian toes. He snatched me off the ground; the empty bucket falling out of my hands as I was violently dragged into the sky. We were only in the air for a moment before he lost his grip and I tumbled down onto the ground again, sliding down a grassy hill and slamming onto the flat surface below. Thorz'akk landed beside me with a thunderous crash. Clumsily folding his wings into the shape of rudimentary arms and seizing me by the throat with one of his enormous hands. He lifted me off the ground, snarling at me with his ghostly dog-like face. I clawed at his wrist, desperately trying to keep my windpipe open as my feet dangled helplessly in the air.

'You will meet your doom!' he growled as he peeled open the long horizontal mouth that ran down the front of his body. That infinite void with distant shining stars and galaxies opened up before me. I tried to gasp as an icy spike of fear skewered the pit of my stomach, but Thorz'akk tightened his grip and clamped my windpipe shut. A combination of spit, tears and silvery milk squeezed out of my face as I tried in vain to wrench myself free. But it was no use. He lowered my helpless body – kicking and punching – towards the portal of oblivion that was his gaping mouth. Then suddenly my body began to melt. Turning into a waxy liquid and losing its shape. I melted right through his fingers and drizzled onto the ground in a puddle of amorphic ooze. He shrieked with rage, but those shrieks gradually grew quieter as my ears dissolved into my head. All my senses faded away as I slipped into a warm soupy darkness.

TWENTY-SEVEN

At first I was only aware of my own heavy breathing. Then a colour … a pale rusty brown. An ocean of pine needles blanketed the ground, forming sharp intricate patterns like the ones found in a kaleidoscope. I found myself in a vast, dark, pine forest, with huge looming trees that stretched upwards and twisted together, blotting out the sky and casting a long, unbroken shade across the forest floor. I felt my stomach heave as I keeled over and vomited up the silvery milk. It swirled around in front of me in a slick, glossy puddle before soaking into the ground and disappearing below the pine needles. I looked up, wiping the last few strands of spit and bile off my chin with a trembling hand. Even the green pine needles on the trees seemed to be made up of geometric shapes and patterns of overwhelming depth and complexity. Everything around me seemed to move, wobble and drip. I tried to stagger to my feet but the constant melting sensation that gripped my body made it impossible to stand.

What now? I thought. Even the sound of my own thoughts

inside my head seemed strange and unfamiliar to me. As if I were overhearing someone else's thoughts.

'The entity ... I have to find the missing entity ...' I said aloud to myself, scanning the darkness with wide disc-like eyes.

I crawled along on my hands and knees, my head lolling sideways, my fingers and toes curling in the cool, damp pine needles.

'I have to find ... I have to find ...' My own words echoed through the forest, bouncing off the trees and coming back to me from all directions. The hair on my skin swirled and pulsed as my fingers began to grow long and spidery.

'*Find* something ... *Look for* something ...' My voice seemed to drizzle out of my mouth as if it were made of a dense, heavy liquid. A deep confusion had begun to take hold of me. I was fast forgetting where, or *who* I was. And I was struck with the sudden realisation that I could no longer remember what my own face looked like. I slumped onto my back and began probing my face with my fingertips. A mouth, a nose, eyes, teeth. I stretched and pulled at my lips, becoming fixated on my teeth and gums, running my fingers along them, exploring their shape and slippery texture.

'Something ... Someone ...?' I rolled onto my side and saw a spread of large caramel-coloured mushrooms peeling out of the ground, their rubbery bell-shaped caps opening up like little umbrellas. 'S-s-s-something ... S-s-s-someone ...'

My arms and legs had grown so long and lanky that I could no longer control them properly. So, I crawled along on my elbows and knees, letting my hands and feet flop limply on the ends of my elongated limbs. My spine had become stretched and curved, arched like an angry cat.

'S-s-s-s-s-o-m-thing … S-s-s-some-one …' I could feel the features of my face drooping like a Dalí painting. 'Oh g-g-g-god … what am I doing h-h-h-here …?' I sobbed, burying my face inside my large, twisted hands. Huge salty tears streamed from my eyes as I felt a dark, crushing wave of hopelessness crash down on top of me.

I cried so much my tears formed a large puddle in front of me, flowing silently into a shallow dip in the ground, like water filling up a bathtub. I looked up from my wet, quivering fingers to see what I had made. The puddle's glassy surface stood out in sharp contrast against the overlapping patterns of the forest floor. I peered down at my reflection and all the awful, twisted sensations in my body suddenly fell away the instant I saw my own face. It was exactly how I remembered it: my slashed and peeling scalp and scorched-off eyebrows were a jarring sight, but I was relieved to see it given that I expected to see my own liquefied skin sliding off my skull. I suddenly felt a powerful sense lucidity, along with the disturbing realisation that I may have already remembered and forgotten who I was and why I was there several times already. Maybe even countless times. *Oh god, how long have I been here? How much time do I have left?*

The world seemed to spiral around me, the forest becoming a blur of dull shaded colours as a new kind of fear gripped me. I now remembered what I had to do. But how was I going to find the missing entity if I remained stuck in this loop of confusion? How was I supposed to navigate this nightmarish landscape?

The forest stopped spinning and my eyes zeroed in on the circle of trees that surrounded me. A ring of seven pines with grotesquely thick trunks and long, spidery branches loomed over me. The forest beyond them too dark to see. There was a hole in the canopy directly above me which exposed the full moon and painted the tree trunks with an eerie pale glow. I watched with horror as each trunk transformed into a collection of colossal conjoined faces. They wrapped around the tree trunks, each one six feet tall and each one sharing an eye with its neighbour. With faint, translucent fractals and other patterns snaking and dancing around them, following some kind of cosmic geometry I could not understand. Then they spoke in unison, with voices so deep and bass that it vibrated the blood in my veins.

'You have committed crimes against the Interdimensional Being, the Great Traveller, the Apex one, Thorz'akk, the Eater of Minds and of Physical Beings! You have slaughtered his unborn offspring and sort to destroy him! For this we find you guilty!' they declared. I white-knuckled two fistfuls of pine needles, hyperventilating through my teeth.

'Guilty! Guilty! Guilty!' they all chanted in unison. Their mouths moved up and down mechanically like puppets, out of sync with the words they were saying.

'Guilty! Guilty! Guilty!' I clamped my jaw shut, grinding my teeth hard against each other. Then I felt a painful crunch and a lightning bolt of pain shot through my mouth. Stunned, I spat out a tooth into my cupped hands: a little white stone nestled in a crimson pool of blood. Then the tooth began to shake, vibrating into a blur for a moment before transforming into a little grey moth. It stretched out its wings, the little brown and grey eye patterns blinking and looking at me for a moment before flying away, disappearing into the darkness between two of the chanting tree-heads.

'Guilty! Guilty! Guilty!' I probed my remaining teeth with the tip of my tongue. They wobbled loosely in my gums before dropping out one by one into my cupped hands. The little pile of teeth all rustled and vibrated together, transforming into a cloud of grey moths that all flew away in the same direction the first one had. I scrambled to my feet and ran after them. One of the heads yelling,

'Stop him!' as I ran past it. But it was too late. I had vanished into the darkness.

I chased after the cloud of moths. The forest becoming more and more twisted and mysterious the further I ran. The cold, damp leaf litter stuck to my naked feet as the pine needles that blanketed the ground were slowly replaced by a layer of grey rotting leaves. I leapt over decomposing logs and swerved to avoid exposed tree roots and swirling puddles of purple water. I crashed to a stop against a tree, gasping for air as I leaned against its thick, scaly trunk. The moths had gotten away from me, leaving me once again directionless and alone. All the trees seemed to grow and curl at the finest tips of their twigs. And darkness clung to everything, obscuring even the simplest shapes, making them appear distorted and monstrous. I stared at my fingers with amazement as large flesh-coloured drops of liquid formed at their drooping tips, growing heavy and dripping off onto the ground.

'Y-y-you have return-n-ed?' A low, serpentine voice whispered from above me. I looked up and wrapped around a large branch of a looming tree was the missing entity, hanging there like a gigantic white boa constrictor. 'W-w-why are you here-e-e?' it said slowly, its thin nostrils flaring, its voice hissing from somewhere deep within its throat.

'I was looking for *you* ...' I whispered. 'A creature called Yar'zee is looking for you ... You are a part of their collective mind ... and they need you to return to them ...' I said slowly, hoping the entity would know what I was talking about.

'I t-t-thought I was once part of a *collectiv-v-ve*... be-e-efore I was *s-s-split* from them-m-m ... I have been here-e-e, alone in the darkness for so long, it s-s-seems only like the ghost of a memory now-w-w ...' it said, descending from the tree and sliding down onto the ground.

'They sent me to find you,' I said as I watched it coil and uncoil its long, thin body, tracking its movements with bulging eyes, my pupils dilated all the way.

'Th-h-hey sent *you-u-u*, an *alien* creature, to f-f-find *me-e-e*?' the entity hissed in a suspicious tone.

'Yes ...' I replied in a breathless whisper. The air around us suddenly turned cold as a distant screech echoed through the forest. The entity widened its eyes, then narrowed them again.

'Th-h-here are *others-s-s* in here with *us-s-s*?' it asked, slithering closer to me. Its paperwhite skin gliding over the leaf litter like a ghost.

'Yes ... that's why we need to go *right now*. Otherwise, a creature called Thorz'akk will kill us both,' I pleaded. The entity coiled its body like a python.

'L-l-lead the way Traveller-r-r,' it breathed.

Before I could say that I didn't know the way, I heard a low hum coming from behind me – a sort of distant metallic grinding sound – and I turned my head to see that a door had materialised there. It stood alone, like a wooden monolith in between two swirling puddles of ultraviolet water. No house, no walls, just a door standing there by itself. I could see rectangular soundwaves radiating off it. Thin and translucent, like rainwater on a windowpane. Expanding and disappearing into the air around it as the hum vibrated through the closed door. I placed my melting hand on the heavy brass doorknob, my fingers still drooping and dripping as I pushed it open.

As I passed through the doorway the humming suddenly stopped. Even the ambient sounds of the forest dropped off the moment I crossed the threshold. Then a room slowly faded into view as the darkness melted away. We were standing inside my father's garage. With only one car in the middle – the one that was there the day I left – and the greasy, cluttered workbenches and stacks of dusty paperwork lining the exposed brick walls. And for one exquisite moment I dared to let myself believe that it all – the Farm, the creature, the nightmares and all the psychological torment I had suffered – had been just one long bad dream that I had suddenly woken from, and everything was going to be okay. Then the entity slithered in beside me and the spell was broken. My stomach lurched as the familiar place I once called home grew distorted and unrecognisable – the same as everything else in this nightmarish dreamscape.

The walls warped, the furniture drooped and twisted, and the proportions and colours of everything shifted ever so slightly. Dismayed, I turned back to look at the door I had just come through, still open and leading back to the forest.

The door swung closed with a sharp slam that echoed through the small brick garage. The silence that followed was quickly broken by the sound of a socket wrench coming from underneath the car. *Zzzzzt, zzzzzt, zzzzzt.* I tilted my head. Puzzled, I bent down to look under the car. My dad slid out on his back, the tiny wheels of the creeper he was laying on scraping against the concrete floor. I marvelled at the oil stains on his brown coveralls. Each one looked like a Rorschach ink blot. The spidery black stains constantly morphing and twisting into different shapes and patterns like a lava lamp.

'I thought I told you never to come back here, boy,' he hissed through his teeth, a cigarette dangling loosely between his thin, peeling lips. His eye sockets were like ashtrays, with two smouldering cigarette butts for eyes. He lunged to his feet and seized me, twisting the fabric of my shirt tightly around his scabby, callused knuckles.

'You little fucking rat! Living under my roof! Eating my food! First you murder your mother, then you fuck my woman! What more can you possibly take away from me?!' he spat through his needle-like teeth, bending in their gums under the force of his words. He stumbled forwards and we both fell against one of the cluttered work benches, a flurry of dusty papers and greasy engine parts falling to the floor.

'Wwwhat morrrre?!' he shrieked, his words slurring in

the most ungodly way. I watched with horror as his nose and mouth stretched forward, becoming a rumpled, upturned muzzle. His clenched fists slowly transformed into trotters, losing their grip on my shirt as his fingers melded into each other and disappeared. He slid down onto the floor still looking up at me with those furious cigarette butt eyes which shrank down into two dark little beads, sinking deep into the fleshy pink pockets that had formed around them. The back door suddenly flung open and a stampede of filth-streaked swine rushed into the room, with the pig that used to be my father disappearing amongst them. They all screamed and squealed as they shouldered their way into the garage, forcing me to climb up onto the bonnet of the car as they all ran in a big circle around the room, taking up every inch of empty space on the floor.

As they ran the room began to mould into a circular shape; the square walls slowly bending into a cylinder. As I watched, my eyes fixed on the crazed frenzy of pigs, I noticed that each one was coming apart at the seams. A gorish red line appeared around each of their necks as their heads began to move faster than their bodies, tearing off and floating independently around the room as their headless bodies continued to run after them. And although I could not see from above, it looked like their bellies had fallen open as well, because suddenly the floor was flooded with a pool of rank, swirling entrails and churned-up, watery blood.

The smell was unbearable, rising up from the floor and forcing its way into my nostrils. Eventually all the fixtures of the room were pulled sideways as the whirlpool of blood and gore turned into a spiralling vortex, sucking up the car, the furniture, and even the snake entity, which careened helplessly down the centre of the vortex.

Suddenly, the ceiling was violently peeled away to reveal a vast black sky and the large translucent wings of Thorz'akk circling above me. I fought the pull of the vortex, desperately trying to swim against the current and hold onto the brick wall. But the pull was too strong, and the gore was too thick. The last thing I saw before I was sucked down, as I was taking my last gasp of air, was Thorz'akk diving towards me.

Everything went black; all my senses blotted out by the liquid carnage I was drowning in. Then, I could hear myself gasping for air. I resurfaced, frantically wiping the blood from my eyes as I tried to stay afloat in the heinous fluids. I was adrift in an endless ocean of bowels, guts, and gore, all bobbing up and down in the blood. With an acid orange sky filled with swirling grey clouds stretched out above me. Even the disembodied pig heads and gutted carcases floated half-submerged in the viscera, their blood-streaked hair clinging tightly to their thick, rubbery hides. My eyes watered as I gagged, trying to paddle my way through the blood.

This is it, I thought to myself in a panicky haze.

This is how I die. An ear-splitting shriek came from behind me as Thorz'akk burst out of the vile sludge, trying to claw his way towards me. His enormous body was drenched in blood, which weighed him down and made it impossible for him to fly. But he still scrambled towards me, flattening his enormous wings over the surface of the gore, and trying to claw his way across it with unrestrained fury. I paddled away as fast as I could, my hands and feet sliding over soft, rubbery organs and through thick, congealing blood. Gasping for air as my mouth and nose dipped above and below the surface of the bile. But there was nowhere to go, and Thorz'akk was closing the distance.

Then I heard it; that sound; that low cosmic hum, getting louder and louder. I pivoted on the spot, trying to find where it was coming from. I wiped my face with the back of my hand, thick lines of blood rolling down my forehead and stinging my eyes. There it was. Another door sitting pristinely atop the ocean of blood, radiating strange rectangular soundwaves: the song of the Infinite Beings.

'You have already failed!' Thorz'akk's voice pierced my heart, letting true fear gush into my body. I flew into a panicked frenzy, flailing my arms and legs through the stinking viscera; the most pure desperation a human being could ever feel – even in this place – coursing through my veins. I felt a serge underneath me, as if the gore were rising up and pushing me out. The missing entity exploded from the ooze, sliding up in-between my arms and legs so that I straddled it like a horse.

'Th-h-he door, Traveller-r-r!' It hissed as I clutched its smooth, veiny skin; riding it towards the portal. I grabbed the knob as we both slammed into its cold wooden surface, flinging it open and tumbling inside as Thorz'akk's gaping cosmic jaws bore down on us. I tried to slam it shut, but he managed to get the fingers of one of his grotesque hands in the opening before it could close properly; sliding his other hand in as he tried to push it open. I pressed my full weight against the door, desperately trying to force it shut.

'You think you can escape me?' Thorz'akk hissed, pushing the end of his snout through the gap in the door. I could see his serrated teeth through his thin, translucent lips.

'Fear makes you weak... and I can *taste* your fear ...' he taunted, as his long, thin lizard tongue slid out of his mouth, feeling its way along the inside of the door. I could actually *feel* the soundwaves of his voice; each one taking away just a little more of my strength as it rippled across my skin. His tongue curled around my wrist. It was smooth and wet, with pulsing veins that made the bile rise in my throat. His tongue slid back into his mouth, leaving behind a layer of spit and mucus on my forearm. He chuckled, with a low throaty growl.

'Delicious ...' he hissed smugly, sliding his tongue back out and lapping at my chin. He pressed it against my face, flicking the tip against my cheek and forcing one of my eyes closed with a thick film of saliva. Then he forced it in between my lips and into my mouth. The taste was so revolting that hot, watery vomit shot up my throat and spilled down my chin. Thorz'akk laughed again, exploring the roof of my mouth as my hold on the door weakened. Then I shrieked, biting down as hard as I could on the tip of his vile tongue. Thorz'akk screamed, pulling his snout out of the crack in the door, with his long, bleeding tongue trailing behind it.

I gave one last big shove, with all the strength I had left, and the door slammed shut behind him.

CHAPTER TWENTY-EIGHT

'W-w-where are we Traveller-r-r?' the entity whispered in the darkness.

'You are in the space between minds,' a thousand voices replied in unison. There was a sound like a thunderclap and a flash like lightning as an infinite number of multi-faced, multi-armed goddess-like beings appeared all around us. Shifting, morphing, and transforming in the ever-moving dance of celestial harmony; of a self-containing cosmic entity. Once again my body had been stripped away, leaving behind only my awareness and a cocktail of altered senses. And even though I could no longer see the missing entity, I could feel its presence somewhere near me.

'We have regained much of our mind since we last met, Traveller. Growing from a small spec in the darkness, to occupying most of the psychic plane.' Their lips parted, but they only used their mouths to produce a quieter, much more ambient version of their cosmic hum. They spoke telepathically; their words travelling through the air in faint, visible ripples from the centre of their foreheads.

'Yar'zee?' I asked, communicating telepathically as well, since I lacked a mouth with which to speak.

'We are Yar'zee,' the infinite goddesses replied in unison, their incomprehensible colours flaring brighter as they spoke. In their presence I felt both holy insignificant, like a speck of dust floating through the vastness of space, but also as if I were the centre of the universe, with their trillions of eyes all focused on me; or rather, the invisible space my awareness occupied.

'We have waited eons for you to return to us with the missing fragment of our mind. And in that time, we have chased Thorz'akk to the deepest recesses of our psyche. All the while he remained in control of our physical form; his rage and short-sightedness endangering us all. But not anymore, thanks to you Traveller.' There was another thunderclap and I sensed that the missing entity had vanished; absorbed back into the infinite collective all around me.

'What will happen to Thorz'akk?' I asked.

'He will be destroyed. Now that we are whole again there is no room left for him within our mind,' they replied. 'We want to thank you for your help, Traveller. But now we must return to our own world. We have been here far too long and have come far too close to causing irreversible damage to your dimensional plane.'

'But what are you? Where did you come from?' I pleaded, begging for answers.

'We are scientists of a most sophisticated kind. We come from a race of telepathic beings that evolved in a dimensional plane parallel to your own. For you see, the fabric of reality is far more dense and multi-sided then you could ever possibly imagine. It bends in on itself, creating parallel physical worlds wildly different from the thin slice of reality you and your kind call home.' As they spoke the entire world began to fold in around us. Each one of Yar'zee's many bodies disappeared row by row in a complex flash of bending white light.

'Goodbye, our friend.'

*   *   *

The physical world suddenly materialised around me. I had never seen things so sharply before. Colours were brighter and more vivid than I ever thought possible. The grass was greener, the sky was an exquisite blue-grey and I felt a profound sense of peace and harmony with all things. I slid sideways down onto the pile of smouldering rubble, the creature's claws gently pulled away from my side as I fell. It looked down at me with its eyeless face. Its mane of tentacle-like appendages swaying from side to side. Its thick, shaggy hair floating weightlessly in the air. I wasn't scared, knowing what lay within. I felt as though I had lived a thousand lifetimes with this strange four-dimensional being. I stood up, my face only inches away from its serrated, shark-like mouth and watched as the mass of writhing appendages that covered its face peeled away to reveal the four milky-white eyes that lay beneath, concealed only by a separate dimension of its being. There were no pupils, no irises, or colour of any kind. Just a solid white jelly nestled inside four pairs of dark, wet eyelids. But behind those eyes I could see the internal world of Yar'zee from which I had just emerged: powerful and eerily beautiful. Like the swirling storms of Jupiter.

After lingering for a moment, Yar'zee turned away and began dragging the rest of the debris from the Craft, unearthing its seamless chrome surface which gleamed in the dim twilight that had just now begun to pierce the horizon.

As Yar'zee approached the pointed end of the Craft, it began to warp into a strange, distorted shape before they slipped through its silvery shell like a ghost passing through a wall. Then Yar'zee turned, their head and shoulders protruding from the Craft as it gently rippled and vibrated around them. We exchanged one more solemn look before the emerging mass of tentacles recovered their face and the Craft morphed back into its original shape, concealing my strange new friend inside.

I felt a sense of awe. Awe mixed with relief. But relief for what? Not that I had escaped death but that I no longer feared it. I no longer feared anything. It was as if the anxiety, hatred and paranoia had all been bled from my mind. And all that was left behind was a quiet peacefulness that was so welcome I almost burst into tears. I was still so exhausted I thought I might die, but sleep no longer scared me. I now welcomed the oblivion that lay just behind my eyelids. I knew that there would be no more nightmares, no more horrors emerging from my subconscious to torment me while I slept. Nothing, except a sweet restful darkness.

The Craft began to warp, twisting into some kind of

incomprehensible four-dimensional shape before folding in on itself and disappearing in a flash of blinding light.

I felt lightheaded, lost my balance and dropped to my knees. My arm was still bleeding – my bandage must have fallen off at some point – with heavy crimson drops that ran down my hand and dripped from my fingertips onto the ground. The world looked so beautiful. And I soaked in those colours. Those colours that were brighter and more vibrant than ever before. I slumped down onto my side.

Have you ever seen grass so green? I thought to myself, as I gazed at the symphony of shades and textures that dance before me. I looked over at Kelly, her lifeless eyes staring up at the huge swollen clouds that slowly drifted across the sky.

'Grass so green ...' I whispered to myself as my vision began to grow blurry, and I felt myself slowly falling backwards into a peaceful black sleep.